Black Wall Street New Dream Publishing Presents...

NEVER GIVE UP ON YOUR DREAMS!

RONALD GRAY

Also by Ronald Gray

RONALD GRAY

Also by Ronald Gray

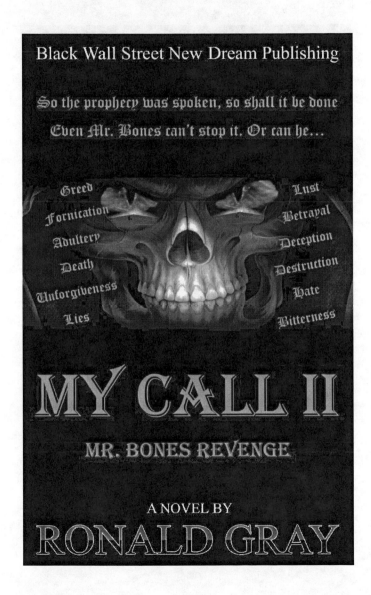

Black Wall Street New Dream Publishing

So the prophecy was spoken, so shall it be done

Even Mr. Bones can't stop it. Or can he...

Greed   Lust
Fornication   Betrayal
Adultery   Deception
Death   Destruction
Unforgiveness   Hate
Lies   Bitterness

MY CALL II

MR. BONES REVENGE

A NOVEL BY

RONALD GRAY

RONALD GRAY

Also by Ronald Gray

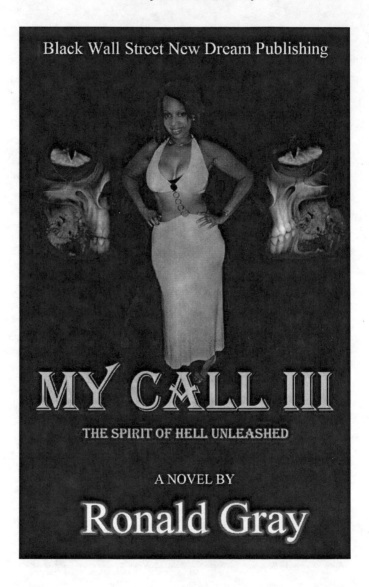

RONALD GRAY

Also by Ronald Gray

Black Wall Street New Dream Publishing

My Call IV
The Origin of Mr. Bones

You
ask
you
get…

Ronald Gray

RONALD GRAY

𝕿𝖍𝖊 𝕸𝖆𝖘𝖙𝖊𝖗 𝕯𝖊𝖈𝖊𝖎𝖛𝖊𝖗
𝔅𝔢 𝔈𝔞𝔯𝔢𝔣𝔲𝔩 𝔚𝔥𝔞𝔱 𝔜𝔬𝔲 𝔄𝔰𝔨 𝔉𝔬𝔯

Also by Ronald Gray

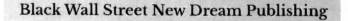

Black Wall Street New Dream Publishing

I don't have much money but I will love you for the rest of your life.

Or

Money for a Lifetime

HAVING THE BEST

IF YOU HAD TO CHOOSE MONEY OR LOVE

A SHORT STORY BY

RONALD GRAY

RONALD GRAY

Black Wall Street New Dream Publishing Presents... **The Master Deceiver**
Be Careful What You Ask For

The Master Deceiver
Be Careful What You Ask For

Ronald H. Gray

BLACK WALL STREET NEW DREAM PUBLISHING
Owned by
MY PROVIDER PRODUCTIONS LLC
www.myproviderproductions.com
myproviderproductions@yahoo.com

RONALD GRAY

My Provider Productions LLC
The Master Deceiver Be Careful What You Ask For
Copyright © 2016 By Ronald H. Gray
Revised Edition: 6/30/2017

Library of Congress Control Number: 2016915302
ISBN-13: 978-0-692-78238-5
ISBN-10: 0-692-78238-9

Author: Ronald H. Gray
Cover Design/Graphics: Ronald H. Gray
Printed in the United States of America

Distributed by Black Wall Street New Dream Publishing
My Provider Productions LLC
www.myproviderproductions.com
blackwallstreetnewdream@yahoo.com

RONALD GRAY

Dedication

This book is dedicated to family and friends who constantly believe in me and the vision and tell me the same thing, "Never stop, never give up!" And I want to thank Mr. Sid Burston who I had the pleasure of connecting with a few years ago, thus, establishing a great business and personal friendship. He is a good business mentor for me which I have learned a lot from and thank him for allowing me to add him in this book concerning his much-needed assistance for a song I wrote titled, "Am I Ready". Sid has more than 30 years of experience in the field of communications; has performed in more than 40 stage plays including 14 national tours; has played lead and/or supporting roles in 50+ films and/or television productions; has written, directed, and produced 4 made for video release films; has written, directed, and produced 10 nationally touring musical stage plays; has co-produced nationally touring stage plays; has performed in more than 120 industrial, commercials and/or voice-overs; has written, directed and produced two independent television shows; and has owned and managed a highly successful communications consulting firm for nearly two decades. He is blessed with a very lovely wife Mrs. Betty Burston who has always been very supportive of his many endeavors. I am very thankful that God allowed our paths to cross. Thanks Sid for everything.

RONALD GRAY

Chapter 1
The Richardson House

James and Sherry Richardson are a wealthy married African American couple with six children. They met in junior high school and married when James was twenty-three and Sherry was twenty-two. James is a clean cut handsome forty-six years old six feet three, two hundred forty muscular pounds from years of swimming and working out. James has a great voice and sang R& B music professionally at sixteen but stopped singing R & B music when he was twenty-four because he gave his life to the Lord and felt conflicted. He sold over thirty million records in his career and made millions but he has also seen the very ugly side of the music business. He knows how ruthless some people in the business can really be and now he is a pastor. James is playful and often flirts with his wife whom he is very sexually attracted to and loves deeply.

Sherry is an attractive forty-five year old, five-feet-four two- hundred pounds. She has a very attractive face but is self-conscious about her weight and has been trying to lose seventy pounds for years but has not been successful. Sherry dresses very fashionably but conservative. They have four sons and two daughters. Jimmy is twenty-one, John is nineteen, Raymond is eighteen, Jacob is fifteen, Katrina is seventeen and Crystal is sixteen.

The Richardson's are not what would be called a typical family in this day and age because they all live in the same house. A four million dollar, three level, thirty thousand square feet, six car garage, eight-bedroom mansion in north Raleigh that sits on six acres. The house has a seven-feet fence around it and the back yard has a full basketball court, a large swimming pool with indoor pool house, cook out area, and a tennis court. Each bedroom has its own bathroom. The basement is huge with a private entrance, separate kitchen, large fitness room, movie theater room, game room, sauna, whirlpool tub and two full baths with showers. The main seating area in the basement is twenty-four feet wide by forty feet long.

It's a warm summer evening and the family still tries to eat together when they can which is difficult with everyone's busy schedule. Everyone except Jimmy is sitting at the table in the large dining room. Food is spread out on the table and James who is sitting close to Sherry is about to bless the food.

"Lord, I thank you for blessing us to eat together once again as a family especially in the times we live in and I pray that you bless this food that we are about to eat and make it nourishing for our bodies. In Jesus name, amen."

Everyone say.

"Amen." And starts eating.

Jimmy drives up in his corvette with his music playing very loudly. Jimmy is handsome six feet two, two hundred, thirty pounds with a muscular physique. He owns the best body shop in all North Carolina. He steps out of his car with his work coveralls on and walks in the house and then stops at the dining room table holding his arms out.

"My wonderful blessed family. Act like you love me and save me some food and slow down on the chewing baby." He starts laughing.

James looks at Jimmy with a serious expression on his face.

"You are late Jimmy. You know what time we eat around here and we heard you before we saw you son. I told you about that loud music around here so save that for the streets."

Jacob is a five feet eight one hundred fifty-pound mild mannered clean cut handsome young man.

"The sound system in that corvette is nice and I know you pull a lot of ladies in that ride setting them up to put some work in." He spoke with confidence while smiling at Jimmy.

"Jacob don't talk like that at the table." Sherry said.

"Don't even think like that son. The bible says; *out of the abundance of the heart, the mouth speaketh.* Women are to be respected not treated like they are a piece of meat." James points at Jimmy. "Take those coveralls off, wash your hands, and come sit down and eat. And keep that music down son. This is not the park."

"Yes sir." He nods at James and walks to his bedroom.

"Katrina, don't forget we have choir practice tonight at church and don't be late." Sherry said.

Katrina is five feet five, one hundred, twenty-five pounds and very attractive with hips and butt that she uses well to have her way with guys. More than anything in life she desires to sing R& B music and travel.

"Mom I am really tired of just singing in the choir at church. I want the world to hear my voice and know my name even though my voice is not what it should be. And I want to sing in night clubs where the money is and tour the country. Singing in the church choir is nice but so boring."

James stops eating and looks over at Katrina with care and love in his eyes as a loving Dad.

"Katrina if you put the Lord first you never know where or how God will use you. I put God first in my life and he has blessed me with a wonderful family that I would not trade for anything. Yes, you can make a lot of money singing R& B music but it's not all glitter and fun like so many people think."

Katrina has heard this story so many times from James she could quote him word for word and each time she hears it, more irritation builds up in her.

"Dad you sang R& B music for years before you did gospel and you made a lot of money and it did not corrupt you. God still blessed you. Dad, you know a lot of people so you could help me if you wanted to but you won't." She stares at James with serious attitude.

"Baby, please listen to your Dad he is just trying to protect you because he knows how cold blooded and ruthless the music business can be. Yes, he did make a lot of money but he was almost destroyed in the process and he could never get his life in order and he had no peace until he put God first." Sherry smiles at Katrina with love.

Jimmy walked in the room while his mom was talking and sits down.

"Tell her again mom. Put the Lord first Katrina." He raises his arms. "Hallelujah, praise him." He starts laughing.

Crystal is five feet four one hundred twenty pounds and attractive with too much body for her age that brings her the wrong kind of attention.

"Don't play with God like that Jimmy and it's not funny." She said with attitude.

"That's right, shut up boy. I don't need you telling me what to do." Katrina said with much hostility in her voice while staring at Jimmy.

"Alright that is enough of that. Katrina, don't talk to your older brother like that." James points his finger at Jimmy. "Jimmy I told you about playing with the Lord and don't let your mouth get your soul and body in trouble son. Believer or not you are the oldest and need to set the example of respect." James said with sternness.

"Dad I was just having a little fun I didn't mean any harm." He looks at his Dad thinking... *man, pops is uptight, mom must not have given him any this week.*

"Dad I am writing a song and I need to go to the studio. Yes, it's an R& B song but will you help me please and before you say no, remember how you helped Jimmy get his business started." Katrina said and rolled her eyes.

"I knew that one was coming." Jimmy said looking at Katrina.

"Two things Katrina. One, you can save all that eye rolling you do for your friends and don't forget who I am. And two, yes I did help Jimmy get his business started and if you wanted help with something that I knew would not lead you on a path of destruction then I would help you as well."

"Okay Dad. No matter what I say or do it will be wrong. Well, I will be eighteen soon and will step out on my own but remember your daughter asked you for your help but you turned me down." Katrina said staring at James with a nasty attitude.

James stopped eating and looked at Katrina.

"Katrina, you will never know how much it does bother me not to help you with this because I know you are very determined and you will go out on your own. But at what price will you pay to get what you want." Shaking his head.

"Fine Dad, you made your point. I will not ask you any more for your help." She can feel the anger rising within and starts thinking... *I can't wait to turn eighteen and get out of this house and do me. And I am still a virgin, damn that. I want it all and I am going to get it all, believe that.*

Jacob taps his fingers on the table.

"Dad, my grades were excellent this year and I will be sixteen very soon so can mom buy me a new Lexus, please." Smiling looking at James.

Sherry starts laughing.

"I like the way you put that. Can I buy you a car? Very good son, very good." She winks at Jacob.

"If he gets one then I want one." Katrina said shaking her head.

"My grades were good and I want one to." Crystal said looking very serious.

James leans his head back and laughs.

"Oh, the joys of being a parent. No, you can't have a new Lexus but yes at that time all three of you can have a car because you have earned it." He looks up. "Lord, what am I getting myself into."

Sherry reaches under the table and rubs James on his leg while smiling at him then looks at Jimmy.

"Jimmy how are you, John, and Raymond getting along at the shop?"

"Things are great mom and business is wonderful but if I could keep Raymond off the basketball court and John out of the mirror then we could probably expand and open another shop."

Raymond is six-feet-seven, two-hundred forty-pounds bald head and clean cut. His life goal is to become the shooting guard for the Charlotte Hornets.

"This is part time for me so I have no desire to work in some dusty body shop all of my life and I will become a player for the Charlotte Hornets. So, I have to practice all I can and when I can to work on my jumper and dribbling."

John is five feet eleven two-hundred twenty pounds. He dresses very nicely but has always had very bad acne on his face and no matter what he has tried, nothing works for him.

"Well, I would not have to stay in the mirror so much if I did not have to keep washing my face so often and keep putting this cream on my face that is not working. I hate my skin, its ugly and I would do anything to have smooth nice looking skin."

"Everyone has things about themselves that they do not like. I don't like being this fat and I have tried everything to lose weight but nothing has worked, it's depressing. But life goes on and God still loves us." Sherry said.

James leans closer to Sherry and rubs her leg under the table speaking softly to her.

"Baby you know I love you, morning, noon and night and I am just as attracted to you now as I was twenty years ago. Yes Lord, aint no shame in my loving game." James is looking and smiling at Sherry as he slides his hand under her dress.

Sherry pushes his hand away.

"James behave yourself in front of the children." She smiles at him and licks her lips.

"Oh God, not again, you two are being disgusting, and at the table of all places." Crystal said shaking her head.

"That's what I am talking about pops, keep on macking mom." Jimmy said while smiling and looking at James.

James points his finger at Jimmy.

"Watch your mouth boy." He stares at Jimmy. "Anyway, I am aware that all of you have dreams and desires but if you just put God first you never know what he will do for you. Please, just wait on the Lord children."

"I hate my skin and I am tired of waiting on God, there has to be another way. I am sick of this." John said with pure disgust and frustration.

"Son don't even talk like that because the devil will deceive you and open a door that looks like it's from God but it's not. He will spiritually corrupt your mind and heart. Now everyone just relax and enjoy this great dinner."

The family continues to talk and eat until they are finished. They all get up and leave the table taking their dishes with them putting them in the kitchen except for James and Sherry who sit for a while and talk. Then they get up and start clearing the table. Working together doing the dishes is a routine for James and Sherry because they use this as quality time where they talk, play and flirt with one another. They finish the dishes and go into their bedroom. Sherry takes a shower and walks out with a towel wrapped around her and James is on the floor in his boxer briefs doing pushups. She stands next to him looking at his body becoming turned on by his great physique wondering how can a man this fine be attracted to her because she is so heavy.

"James get up and stop showing off because you know your body looks good." She walks over and sit on the bed and starts putting lotion on her body. "James, you are a pastor and I know you love Jesus but how can you still be attracted to me; I am so fat. I am pretty but very fat and I see all these skinny women with tight sexy bodies in church lusting over you." Looking at him while still putting on lotion.

James stands up and walks over to the bed standing in front of her.

"Baby I love you just as much now as I ever did and I'm still very attracted to you. Anyway, I'm not a vegetarian; I like meat with my meal." He smiles and rubs Sherry's leg.

Sherry pushes his hand away.

"Stop, go take your shower." Smiling looking at his tight muscular body and noticing his growing erection.

James knows his wife well and he can feel her sexual excitement building so he decides to tease her before going into the shower. He rubs himself to become fully erect and steps closer to Sherry with his hand in his underwear.

"You know you turn me on with all that big round butt you are working with and I got something for you baby." He leans down and kisses her on the lips and reaches inside his underwear rubbing himself.

Sherry playfully smacks his hand and quickly stands up facing him.

"James Richardson stop being so nasty and go take your shower please." She kisses him.

He quickly grabs Sherry's waist pulling her into him pressing his erection against her body and starts caressing her hips and butt then slides his hand underneath the towel. He stares into her eyes.

"Don't fight the feeling baby. I don't just love you but I'm in love with you and no matter who else I see it's you that I want every single day." He kisses her and smacks her on the butt then walks towards the shower and stops and turns around looking at her. "You can play hard to get if you want but when I come out of the shower you know what it is." He laughs and walks into the bathroom.

Sherry stares at him walking away thinking how blessed she is to have a man that really values and loves her. She removes her towel and sits on the bed and puts lotion on the rest of her body, then lays down and falls asleep.

James comes out of the bathroom wearing a towel and sees Sherry lying on her stomach naked and asleep. He immediately becomes aroused and drops his towel while walking towards the bed and slowly gently slides on the bed trying not to wake Sherry. He starts kissing and licking her legs working his way up. Sherry wakes up feeling her husbands' mouth on her body and it feels so good, she desires more. She slowly spreads her legs apart giving James easier access to what she wants and what she knows he is about to do. James hands are on her hips pulling her butt up while kissing and licking her butt cheeks and sliding his tongue between her legs tasting her juices. Sherry grips the sheets because James is making her feel so good she raises up her butt to feel more of her husbands' incredible mouth. James stops, moves his body up over Sherry's and slowly slides inside her.

The moment Sherry feels James sliding inside her she tightens her grip on the sheets and pushes her butt up into him.

"Oh James, baby you feel so good inside me. Don't stop baby, make love to me."

James raises his body up and begins sliding in and out of her, increasing his pace and then leans forward whispering in her ear.

"You got some good loving now throw that ass back on me." He leans down and kisses her neck while thrusting himself in her feeling how close he is to exploding inside her.

"Oh James, that's it baby, just like that, give it to me. Harder James, harder baby."

James bites her neck thrusting faster and harder into Sherry until he explodes in her and she is pushing up into James faster and harder until she climaxes so hard, making her body shake and tremble.

"Yes James, I can feel your dick getting even harder. Ahhhhhh I am cumming. Ohhhhhh James, ahhhhhh." She screams because it feels so good and grips the sheets so hard her hands hurt. Sherry continues to climax calling her husbands' name over and over thinking there is no place she would rather be right now.

RONALD GRAY

10

Chapter 2
The Body Shop

Early in the morning Jimmy, Raymond, John, and Shawn Black are working in the shop. It's a large three bay body shop in north Raleigh and the sign on the front of the building reads, *"Richardson & Black Body Shop"*. All three bay doors are open. Shawn is Jimmy's best friend and business partner. He is Caucasian, twenty-three years old, six one, two-hundred twenty-pounds, cocky and arrogant. Jimmy and Raymond are doing body work on one car while Shawn and John are working on another.

A white 2015 Porsche 911 Carrera S Cabriolet drives up in front of the shop playing loud music. A very attractive Caucasian lady steps out of the car wearing heels, mini skirt and a low-cut top. All four guys stop working and stare at her.

"Relax fellows and put your tongues back in your mouth, she is mine." Shawn said and walks towards her smiling.

Alexandria Brown is a twenty-two year old, five feet five, one hundred thirty-pounds brunette with a nice tight body and curves in all the right places. She eats healthy, runs often and works out daily; her favorite exercise is squats. She is standing close to the car with that, *I know I am sexy look.*

"Hi Shawn, I know you are working but I wanted to see you since you have been so very busy."

"But never too busy for you. Damn you look fine Alex. The many hours that you spend in the gym is worth it." He hugs and kisses her and caress her butt.

"Don't start something that you have no time to finish." She kisses him and pushes his hands off her.

"I think I need to make time for you but while you are here let me introduce you to my business partner and best friend, his two brothers work with us as well." He turns towards them and wave. "Jimmy, Raymond, and John come here for a second."

All three walk towards him.

"This is my business partner Jimmy." He points toward him.

"Hello." Jimmy said.

"His brother John."

"Hello." John said.

"And this tall guy here is Raymond. The best player the Charlotte Hornets will ever have."

"Hi, well I have not made the team yet but it's only a matter of time and I will give it my best like I do everything." Raymond said, while staring at Alexandria thinking, *"How did Shawn get a girl this fine? Damn the things I would like to do to her"*.

"Mr. Raymond, tall good looking and ambitious. What more could a lady ask for. Too bad I did not meet you first." She looks at him up and down licking her lips. "Very nice." Thinking, *"Damn he is fine and the things I would let him do to me"*.

Shawn looks at Raymond and Alex with attitude.

"So much for that. I just wanted you to meet the guys that I work with, not for you to flirt. Anyway, we need to talk."

The brothers walk back into the shop.

"That girl is fine." John said.

"Shawn can't handle that he needs to step aside and let a pro work that body and show him how it's really done." Raymond said.

They are in the garage now standing by the cars when Jimmy turns to look at Raymond.

"Don't even think about it Raymond and I am only going to tell you this one time, leave her alone. Don't mess with Shawn's head and don't do anything to put my business in jeopardy. You know how hard I have worked to get this business started and build the elite clientele that we have."

"Whatever you say my brother, for today." Raymond said looking at Jimmy smiling and watching Shawn and Alexandria.

Shawn is standing closer to Alex pointing his finger in her face.

"Was all that really necessary? I really wish you wouldn't do that; your flirting ways are going to get you in trouble one day."

Alexandria pushes his finger out of her face.

"Do not put your finger in my face like I am some child. And if you give me the attention that I want and deserve, then maybe I wouldn't flirt so much. Every lady likes to be treated special Shawn, you remember that."

Shawn steps closer putting his hands on her hips pulling her into him kissing her neck.

"I have no problem making you feel very special Alexandria." He slides his hands underneath her skirt caressing her butt.

She pushes him away.

"Stop! I am not talking about sex and I am tired of that attitude. We don't spend a lot of time together and when we do, it's just sex. I want romance Shawn, romance. Damn, when will you men learn we want more than just sex. When was the last time we went for a walk together?" You can hear the frustration and attitude in here voice.

"Look, I adore you and you know I love you but I have a business to run and do not have time for all of this romance that you want. No woman wants a broke man so get real and let me do my thing and make this money."

"Fine, I love you also but do you Shawn? I don't want to lose you but I want romance so you better make time and start paying more attention to me because I deserve it and you know it." She sees Raymond looking at her and Shawn and decides to really give him something to think about. She kisses Shawn. "Baby I am thirsty; can you get me some water please." Looking into his eyes.

"Sure, no problem. We have some bottled water in the office. I will be right back." He kisses her and quickly runs towards the office.

Alexandria sees Raymond is still looking at her while talking to his brothers so as soon as Shawn runs off she turns around and bends over leaning into her car so her mini skirt can raise up knowing Raymond has a clear view of her butt since she is wearing thong panties. She purposely leans in further to make sure he gets a very good look.

Raymond sees her bending over and his mouth drops open and he quickly hits Jimmy and John to get their attention.

"Look at that, she is bending over on purpose. Look at that ass in those thong panties, damn."

Jimmy and John turn to look at Alexandria and say at the same time.

"Damn."

"That doesn't make any sense." Jimmy said.

"Yes, it does. Nice round tight booty on that girl. Look like she has been hanging out with the brothers." John said shaking his head and walks back over to the car and begins working on it.

"She can hang out with this brother all day long. Damn she got hips and a fat ass for a white girl." Raymond said while grabbing his crotch.

Alexandria grabs a towel off the seat and turns around wiping her face looking directly at them lusting over her. Shawn comes out of the shop with a bottle of water in his hand and gives it to

Alexandria. She drinks a little of it so he will not get suspicious of her actions. Displaying herself like she did has made her horny and she has made up her mind to find out more about Raymond and keep up with him and his life. Smiling she kisses Shawn with passion but her thoughts are elsewhere.

"Thanks Shawn. I was thirsty. Now if I could only get more of your time, all would be well."

Shawn steps closer grabbing her hips.

"You can get more of my time tonight." He put his hands under her mini skirt caressing her hips and kissing her.

She pushes him away and gets in her car starting it and staring at Shawn.

"You know Shawn, sometimes I wonder why I am with you."

"Because you love me and I make love to you long time." He smiles and starts laughing.

"You better stop taking me for granted and by the way Shawn, fifteen minutes is not a long time." She rolls her eyes and quickly drives away.

Shawn walks back into the shop seeing Jimmy, John, and Raymond standing close together knowing they have been watching him and Alex. He approaches Jimmy.

"Females, they change their minds about what they want like the wind changes direction and Alex is something else. She is always talking about romance. Who has time for all of that? Making money that's what's happening, make money, get booty later."

"Ladies want romance Shawn and just laying pipe won't get it." Jimmy said.

"Is there trouble in paradise Shawn? A player like you should know that women want romance." Raymond said and starts laughing.

"Nothing I can't handle and anyway you just focus on your basketball career and keep working on that dribbling and jump shot of yours and I will take care of Alex. In more ways than one."

"Romance Shawn, romance." Jimmy said."

John stops working and walks toward the bathroom.

"John, where are you going? We need that car finished today." He stops walking and turns to look at Jimmy.

"I have to go and put this stupid acne cream on my face. I will be in the bathroom so don't call me." He walks to the bathroom mumbling.

"He has been putting different creams on his face for years and it has not done any good. He can't get no loving looking like Freddy Kruger." Raymond said laughing.

Jimmy gives Raymond a serious look letting him know he does not like him talking about John like that.

"Leave him alone, he already has very low self-esteem."

"Yeah but he is a great body man. The guy can make any car look brand new and he is one of the main reasons this body shop has the reputation of being the best in the state. Customers come from all over North Carolina to us and request that John work on their very expensive cars." He looks at Raymond. "So, cut the guy some slack, besides customers don't care about what his face looks like, just his results for great body work. Now, we all need to get back to work and finish these cars."

They continue working on the cars. John comes out of the bathroom and joins them but Raymond is distracted by his mental image of Alexandria. He has made up his mind to find out just how devoted she is to Shawn devoted she is to Shawn. He smiles and keeps working.

RONALD GRAY   16

Chapter 3
The Lexus Dealership

Sherry is walking around on one of her Lexus car lots in north Raleigh wearing a long form fitting dress. Rick Preston one of her sales managers is walking with her as they do inventory on the lot.

"Rick, make sure all of the cars on the lot are kept clean and that they are not parked too close together. Every one that comes to this dealership is a potential customer and all of our customers are treated like royalty."

Rick is walking behind Sherry carring a note pad taking notes trying not to look at her like he secretly always does. He thinks Sherry is truly gorgeous and would love to have her for just one night because her size is such a turn on for him and her face is beautiful.

"No problem Sherry, I will take care of it but we did have one of our cars broken into last night and another car had all four tires removed." He is looking at her butt while talking.

Sherry looks back at Rick and notices him looking at her butt. She loves all the attention she can get so she shakes her butt a little extra just for his pleasure then stops walking and turns around to face him. Sherry notices a bulge in his pants and smiles within but she must maintain a professional face and attitude.

"I am sick of all this stealing and vandalizing. We have police patrolling the area along with our own private security and yet, this mess keeps happening. Why? Money just wasted."

"Would you like for me to check into another security company."

"As a matter of fact, yes I would and check their references very thoroughly."

RONALD GRAY

17

They keep walking looking at the cars when James drives on the lot in his 2016 Lexus LS 460 and drives up next to them, stops and rolls down his window and sticks out his head.

"Excuse me Miss but I am looking for someone very special and gifted to go to lunch with me. I will pay for lunch, so how about you Miss, will you go with me?" Smiling at his wife because he loves the flirtation games they play.

"James what are you doing here bothering me and stop looking at me like that, husband."

"Miss, I am trying to get a lunch date. I am lonely and hungry so will you come with me please." He steps out of his car and gets on one knee holding his arms out. "Miss, I beg you come to lunch with me. I promise to treat you right, yes Lord." He laughs.

"James Richardson get up from there you are embarrassing me. I can't believe this; you are too much." Smiling at him loving all his attention.

"The man knows what he wants." Rick said with a fake smile because he desires to be the one to have her.

James stands up and steps toward Sherry.

"Does this mean you will go to lunch with me?"

"Sherry I will talk with you later." Rick walks away wishing to hit the lottery.

"James, you really are something else and yes I will go to lunch with you since you embarrassed me. You need help."

James steps closer and kisses her.

"All that begging I just did you better go to lunch with me." He leans closer and whispers in her ear. "And I will give you some more of all that good loving you had last night, and yes I do need help. So, help me with some lovin." He bites her ear and kisses it.

Sherry looks around and grabs his butt.

"Keep working out baby because I love your tight ass and all the muscles in it that you were using last night making me scream. Now, how much time do you really have?" She squeezes his butt smiling.

"I see that look in your eyes so what do you have in mind dear? Are you trying to get your freak on? You know I am down."

"Well, none of the children are home so after we eat, let's go home and consummate this marriage some more." She kisses him slow and passionately.

"Baby we have been consummating this marriage for over twenty years which is why we have six children now. But I understand. You want some afternoon dick." He laughs.

She playfully smacks his face.

"James don't talk so dirty and nasty and that word sounds so bad."

"Oh okay. So, you want me to say, dear do you want some penis? Yeah right. You know you want some more of this good, hard stiff dick. Say it. Say, baby dick me down, good." He starts laughing and caresses her hips.

Sherry tried to hold it in but she could not keep herself from laughing.

"No I am not saying that but take me to lunch sweetheart and I will let you do whatever you want to with me in bed." She leans closer to him. "Including the kinky stuff." She kisses him.

James opens the car door for her and Sherry gets in and he smiles and drives away.

"I knew you wanted some good loving, good dick down. Don't fake. Just ask for what you want, wife." Rubbing her leg.

Chapter 4

The recording studio

Katrina is in the sound room at *Washington's' Recording Studio,* wearing heels, tight spandex pants and a shirt that stops just below her breast to show off her flat tight stomach. The studio is owned and managed by Terrence Washington who has a hands-on approach concerning all artists that he produces. He has a reputation for being a little rough with his artists and how he gets things done. His concept is, anything can be done, it just depends on how badly you want it and what you are willing to do to get it. Terrence is considered nice looking by many women. Thirty years old five feet ten, two hundred ten solid muscular pounds. There is a stool in the sound room where Katrina is singing but she is standing up singing into the mic. Terrence is working the sound board along with his two assistants. Katrina has been working on the song for three hours so far today and Terrence is still not completely satisfied. He pushes the speaker button to get her attention.

"Katrina stop and start from the beginning but put a little more heart and feeling into the song. This is taking far too long."

"I am singing with feeling I always do, that is why I am good at what I do." Speaking in a flirtatious manner, looking directly at Terrence determined to get what she wants for her music career.

"Yeah that sounds good but always remember this, it's the people that decide how good you are. Record sales dear, record sales. Now start from the beginning please, thank you."

"No problem but can we take a break. I am thirsty and a little tired." She sits down on the stool.

One of the assistants looks at Terrence while leaning back in his chair.

"We have been going none stop for a while, I could use a break myself. That girl can sing and she is sexy. Young but a tight banging body and she got ass. Good combination if you don't mind me saying."

The other assistant stands up.

"Well, I have to go to the bathroom and I need a break myself. The girl can sing and she got it going on in the looks department which makes her more marketable. Yeah she got a nice ass too." He walks out laughing.

Terrence looks at the other assistant and nods his head at him signaling for him to leave as well. The assistant gets up to leave but Terrence touches his arm.

"You are both right she can sing and is young but she is hungry to succeed which I like and I have plans for her. Professional and personal." He smiles.

The assistant nods at him.

"I am sure you do Terrence. Later." He walks out.

Terrence pushes the speaker button for the recording room.

"Katrina, can you come in here please." He walks over to a small refrigerator in the room and get two bottles of water and sits back down in front of the sound board. He opens one and takes a drink sitting both bottles on the table close to him.

"Yes, I will be right there." Katrina walks out of the room making sure to shake her hips and butt to get Terrence attention.

Terrence watches Katrina's every move as she walks and he likes what he sees. Young, attractive, hungry and dumb to the industry, just the way he likes them.

Katrina walks in and stands very close to Terrence.

"Hi, thanks I really needed this break." She reaches in front of Terrence for the bottle of water, purposely brushing her breast lightly against him and takes a drink holding the bottle in her hand. "That was good nice and cold. So, what do you think about the song, is it ready for the radio stations and the stores?"

He is staring at Katrina thinking; *She is sexy and does have a little heart. Playing these, brush up against the body games. Yeah, I got plans for her, for sure.*

"The song is nice and your voice is good but it needs a little polishing. At times, I can hear it crack when you hit the high notes."

"I know it does that and I hate it. I would give anything to have a smooth flowing voice, I am sick of this." She backs up from him putting her hands on her hips.

Terrence stands up and steps closer to her looking into her eyes feeling Katrina's frustration. He knows he must get her to relax because a frustrated artist cannot focus.

"Relax, I know you want this to happen and it will. Sometimes we push ourselves too hard so this is my suggestion. You have been pushing yourself very hard so take a short break and get your voice right and when you come back, it will be show time."

Katrina is looking at Terrence like he is crazy thinking he is trying to get rid of her. No way am I leaving here knowing he can just replace me like some old shoes, no way. She put the bottle water down on the table and steps closer to Terrence putting her hand on his shoulder staring into his eyes.

"Terrence, I am young and new to the business but my Dad has been doing this for many years and has taught me a lot about the inside workings of the business. Right now, I feel like you are telling me what I want to hear but really interested in getting rid of me. Don't do this. No one will work as hard as me or want this as much as I do, no one." She moves closer brushing her breast against his chest staring at him.

Terrence is looking at her thinking how easy it would be to take shorty right now but he has bigger plans for her. But he is curious to see how far she will allow him to go right now. So, he puts his hand on her hip slowly caressing it.

"Let me tell you something about me. I am not like anyone else and I do not waste time; life is far too short to waste. If I did not think you had what it takes to succeed you would not be standing here now, believe that. So just relax and stay focused." He moves his hand on her butt rubbing it.

Katrina smiles looking at him thinking, "*Yeah, I know you want this nice tight young body*". She moves closer pressing her body into him feeling his growing erection.

"Thank you for being direct with me. So many people lie so damn much. You are sweet." She leans forward and kisses him on the cheek making sure to press her body harder against him.

Terrence likes her aggressiveness and boldness but dislikes any female trying to play him for a sucker like he is new to this business and life which is what she is doing now. He decides to teach her a grown man lesson in life and in business. He put both hands on her butt and pulls her into him tighter knowing she feels his serious hard on and he is staring into her eyes.

"I am very direct. So, do you really want this career?"

"Yes, you know I do so stop asking me questions you already know the answers to."

Terrence instantly becomes irritated with Katrina for having a smart mouth. If she wants to act like she grown, then she gets treated like an adult. He quickly removes his hands off her butt and pulls her shirt up exposing her breast and bra then slides her bra up fully exposing her breast and starts licking and sucking on her nipples. Slowly, he slides his hands inside her spandex pants from the back grabbing her butt feeling her cheeks since she is wearing thong panties. He caresses her butt while moving his fingers closer between her legs.

Katrina was not expecting him to do this and she knows what is next but she can't let this happen now. Yes, she loves to flirt with guys using her body to have her way but she is still a virgin and now she is very nervous knowing she's got this grown man excited and what he is expecting from her now. She leans away from him.

"Terrence, you know I want my career but don't do this, not now. Let's get to know each other better." She said with a trembling voice.

"No, you want to play games. I don't play games I told you that." He slides his hands lower on Katrina's butt between her legs feeling the entrance to her wetness. "I want you and I know you got some good tight hot pussy and I can't wait to slide this hard dick inside you." He starts sucking on her neck then looks into her eyes. "You want this dick baby?" Doing all this just to irritate her.

Katrina has never been touched by any man like this and part of it feels good causing her body to tremble and making her wet at the same time but she quickly realizes how wrong all of this is and snaps. She slaps his face hard.

"No, Terrence stop please let me go. I can't do this, stop it."

Terrence is no dummy and he quickly let's Katrina go and backs away from her and then starts laughing. Katrina is staring at him with confusion and anger in her eyes.

"What is so damn funny? You think forcing yourself on me is funny. I thought you were different Terrence. A gentleman but you are a dog just like all the rest. I am finished with you." She adjusts her clothes and walks towards the exit door.

Terrence quickly steps in front of Katrina holding his arm out towards her.

"Relax Katrina. I did all of this to teach you a lesson for your personal life and business. You are a young girl trying to play in the big leagues. If you present ass, you better be ready to give up ass because real men or women do not have time to play games. Girls like you come and go in this industry fast. They get lied to and used." He steps closer to purposely intimidate her. "Don't play me or yourself and save those little girl games that you play for little boys. I get women throwing themselves at me daily and I could give a damn about that. Pussy does not make me I make money which makes me a real business man and I don't have time for foolishness. If you want to leave do that but don't come back. If you stay, then get serious and act like a professional and stop wasting my time." He walks over to the exit door pushing it open staring at her. "So, what will it be little girl I don't have all damn day."

Katrina feels so stupid and embarrassed because she knows she played herself and got caught. She walks over and extends her hand out to him.

"I will be a professional."

"No problem." Shaking her hand. "Get some rest and come back when you are ready."

"Thank you, Terrence, for not giving up on me and I will not let you down."

"Time will tell about that it always does, little girl." He smacks her on the butt.

Katrina looks at him smiling.

"You just can't help yourself can you Terrence. You like touching this young round tight butt, don't you?" She winks at him and walks out of the door thinking... *yea, I played myself today but*

RONALD GRAY 25

I know you really want me. Young and fine with curves for days, drives young and old guys crazy. Men are so weak for ass.

Terrence watches her walk away smiling to himself knowing he will be bending her over soon it's only a matter of time. Get them to trust you then get what you want, when you want. He laughs and walks back to the sound board and sits down.

Katrina gets in her car and hits the dash board with her hand out of frustration.

"I am sick of this cracking voice of mine; no matter what it takes I am going to get it right. No matter what." She drives away more determined than ever.

Chapter 5
Doctor Eyes

Doctor Eyes lives in the country in an old house in Beaufort, South Carolina. He is dark skinned, six feet six, two hundred eighty pounds with salt and pepper hair. Doctor Eyes is known as a very powerful root worker who has a reputation to get anything done that you request and people come to visit him from all over the nation. If you come to his house on certain days, you will see a long line of cars with people waiting to see him. He lives off a main street down this long dirt road that takes you about a minute to drive just to get to his house.

No one really knows just how old he is but he has been around a very long time. The people that come to see him don't care how old he is as long as he does what he says he can do. It's very simple, you come to him and make a request and then pay him. Whatever he tells you to do, you must do it just that way with no deviation and you cannot tell anyone what you are doing or it will not work. His reputation is so good at getting things done, people from other countries visit him. There is a debate about who or what he is. Is he a Christian doing the work of God or is he evil doing the work of the devil?

Doctor Eyes lives in a very old three-bedroom wooden house that is surrounded by woods. There is a small graveyard and a creek nearby. He has an old raggedy pickup truck and an old station wagon parked in his yard. There is a story with him and his pickup truck. One day he drove to a gas station in town and one of the mechanics saw this old guy moving very slowly getting out of his truck so he offered to help him. The mechanic noticed how good the engine sounded in his truck. He asked the old man could he look at it but he did not know at the time that he was talking to the great Doctor Eyes. He smiled at the young man and said, "Sure".

As the mechanic was opening the hood to the truck the engine cut off. His mouth dropped open and he quickly stepped back because there was no engine in the truck just a big empty space where the engine should be. He quickly slammed the hood and watched the old man laughing while he went into the station to pay for some gas then walked back out, pumped it and got into the truck. The truck started again and he drove away. The young man was never the same after that because he had a nervous breakdown.

On this day, Doctor Eyes is laying in his bedroom asleep. On top of his night stand is a small black box. His eye lids open but his eyes are missing and he sits up.

"Yes, talk to me." His head turns in the direction of the black box and the lid of the box opens. There are two eye balls in the box that are blood red except for a yellow dot in the middle. The eyes float out of the box and land in his hand and he puts the eye balls in his eye sockets. "Doctor Eyes once again, alive and well. Yes, another one is coming to see me, they all do who choose not to wait on the Lord. They all seek me out for help and I give them what they all want because I am Doctor Eyes. I am the world's Master Deceiver." He laughs and lays back down.

Chapter 6
Attorney Stevens Office

It is afternoon and Lewis Stevens is in his law office in north Raleigh sitting behind his desk. Lewis is a nice looking white man five feet eleven one hundred ninety-five pounds. He is wearing dress shoes, dress slacks, long sleeve white shirt and a tie. Tashianna Jones is sitting at her desk and she is Lewis' legal assistant. She is black twenty-four year old five feet seven one hundred thirty-five pounds very attractive with a tight body and a figure that turns heads every day no matter where she is. This girl is super fine and she knows it and is a big flirt. Tashianna is wearing heels, low cut form fitting dress that comes just below her knees that shows her curves very well. Breasts, hips, and butt for days. She walks to Lewis office and knocks on his door frame although his door is open so she walks over to his desk.

"Lewis, you know I like my job and I like working here but business has been real slow. You need to make yourself more known by doing some advertising or something baby because I need a raise. Lord knows I am fine and have it going on but I need more money Lewis, more money baby." She put her hand on her hips looking at him.

Lewis is looking at Tashianna up and down. Although he loves his wife dearly and she is attractive, Tashianna would make any man lust but he has never disrespected her in any way and has always conducted himself in a professional manner.

"You are right business has been slow and you do deserve a raise. I don't know what I would do without you and you look okay." He said this knowing it would get a rise out of her.

"Okay." She does a full turn in front of him. "Do you need your eyes checked? Baby when I walk down the street ladies are slapping their men because they are staring at me so hard. I am what is known as a *FULL SEVEN;* gorgeous in the face, small in the waist, real pretty breasts, sexy lips, pretty painted finger tips and I got hips and ass for days." She pats her butt. "This ass of mine ain't no butt implants or injections Lewis, no all of this fine body that you see is one hundred percent real. Tight and I emphasize tight, body. You could sit a cup on this ass." She stares at him smiling.

Lewis starts laughing.

"Okay, you would make a fine Instagram model. I get the message you are very attractive and every man's dream."

"What! Instagram model." She waves her hand at him. "I was going to say something to you Lewis but I need my job. Anyway, no disrespect intended but I have seen the way you try not to look at me and you keep adjusting your crotch because you don't want me to see you walking around here with a hard on. Shame on you and you need to stop eye stalking me, Lewis. It's okay baby, I understand you can't help yourself." She starts laughing.

"Yeah well whatever. I have tried so hard to improve business but so far at this point nothing has worked out so I am willing to try anything."

She stares at him.

"Interesting words. Look there is someone who can help you. I don't know him personally and I don't want to but he has helped a few people that I know and they all got what they wanted. As a matter of fact, they all swear by the man."

"Who is he and where is he?"

"They, call him Doctor Eyes and he lives in South Carolina."

"Doctor Eyes, who in the hell is that?" Leaning forward in his seat staring at her.

"He is a root worker and they say he is the best and is nothing to play with."

Lewis quickly stands up.

"A root worker." He starts laughing. "You have got to be kidding me I don't believe in that garbage."

"Okay I understand that but go see him and find out because you have tried everything else. I will find his address and get it to you." She points her finger at him. "Don't mention my name."

He laughs.

"Yeah okay and you are right what do I have to lose."

"Good question." She walks away purposely shaking her butt knowing he is looking at her.

Lewis tries not to but he can't help from staring at her because she is incredibly attractive. He mumbles.

"Lord have mercy." He shakes his head adjusting his crotch underneath the desk.

Tashianna looks back at him.

"I heard that, don't hurt yourself baby." She keeps walking and sits at her desk.

The office door opens and Veronica Stevens, Lewis' wife walks in wearing a long dress and heels. She is attractive, five feet seven one hundred twenty-four pounds and a Christian.

"Miss Stevens, come on in it's good to see you." She stands up and walks toward her.

"Hi Tashianna, you have such a pretty name." She shakes her hand. "Is Lewis busy?"

"He wishes he was; business has been slow and he is a little frustrated but he will be glad to see you as always."

"I have been praying for his business and I know the Lord will bless him."

"Well something needs to happen and happen fast. Love is very powerful and priceless but love don't pay the bills."

"Very true dear very true." She looks at Tashianna in that tight dress. She has never liked the fact that a very attractive young girl with such an incredible body works for her husband. She is not stupid, she knows what men like and this girl has it all in the looks department. She knows Lewis lusts over her but then again, what man would not. Secretly she always hopes she quits or gets fired. She stares at her butt and hips thinking, *This young girl got a body, she has got to go.* "Tashianna you look very nice but don't you think the dress you are wearing is too tight, revealing and inappropriate for work in this corporate professional field?"

"No I do not. I always carry myself in a respectful manner and never allow anyone to disrespect me regardless of how I am dressed. And Mom said if you got it flaunt it and it docs get the attention of men in more ways than one." She walks back to her desk and sits down. She looks at Veronica knowing like so many other women she is just hating on her because she is so fine with a body that men lose their mind over. She wishes she had a body like this, with her flat butt self. No wonder Lewis be eye stalking me.

Veronica steps closer to Tashianna's desk.

"Mom also said if it's not for sale then take the sign out of the window." She smiles and walks towards Lewis office and knocks on his door.

Tashianna watches her walk trying to shake that flat butt. She shakes her head and mumbles.

"Hater."

Lewis looks up from his desk and sees his wife.

RONALD GRAY

"Veronica, hi this is a nice surprise, please come on in." He walks toward her.

"Hi Lewis, I miss you and wanted to see you sweetheart." Thinking, *and come see how things are going with you and Miss lust walker.*

"Your timing is perfect." He hugs and kisses her. "I have been missing you and this body." Pulling her closer kissing her again while rubbing her hips. "You feel so good and I want you."

Veronica lightly pushes him away.

"Lewis not here, I desire you too but this is not the place." Staring at him. "And why are you so horny anyway?"

Lewis steps back and looks at her.

"We use to have so much fun at one time but ever since you gave your life to the Lord nothing has been the same. You are constantly judging me and sex between us is not the same. No more blow jobs and I can't even hit it from the back any more. A little kissing here and there and then the missionary position for sex. I adore you but that has gotten boring." He moves closer to her. "But this is the right place and time so why don't you let me slide that dress up and bend you over my desk and make you scream my name." Smiling at her.

"Lewis Stevens don't talk to me like that. Yes, I am your wife but I am a child of God not some hooker on a corner that you picked up, respect me. Anyway, I don't believe it's me that is making you so horny all the time. It's probably that Jezebel assistant of yours and the foul lust spirit that she operates in. Wearing skin tight revealing dresses showing her body. Exposing her breast and the shape of her butt which sticks out. It doesn't make any sense Lewis. Only a slut dresses like that and you know it." Pointing her finger in his face. "I know you are lusting over her Lewis and don't you lie to me." Staring at him.

"I don't have time for all of this. Are you going to give me some ass or not? No! I didn't think so. Business is bad enough and I can't even get any loving from my own wife. Life sucks. No blow jobs, no ass and no business and God has not helped me." He stepped closer to her while looking into her eyes. "Miss tight panties." Looking at her with disgust.

Veronica is standing there looking at Lewis with her mouth open because she has never heard him talk like this. She points her finger at him.

"I rebuke that devil spirit that you are operating in Lewis Stevens, in Jesus name. I am going home to pray for you."

"Oh wonderful, now I am the devil. Well I am going to pray to, pray I get some ass from my wife and my dick sucked." He walks back to his desk and sits down.

"I can't believe your attitude right now Lewis. I love you but you need to put Jesus first in your life and let God bless you." She walks over and kisses him then walks toward his office door.

"Veronica thanks for coming by and you look nice in that long dress with your hips shaking, I watched. Those hips call my name saying; come get me Lewis, get these panties, good." He starts laughing.

Veronica turns around looking at him shaking her head.

"Grow up Lewis. I am going to pray for your mouth and mind because it's dirty and you need to be delivered".

Lewis stands up and grabs his crotch.

"Can you deliver me now? I need it bad. Deliver me. Get your lips wet really quick." He starts laughing.

"You are totally disgusting and obnoxious at times but the devil is a liar. You are too much Lewis." She walks out and stands in front of Tashianna's desk and points her finger at her. "And you need to be delivered as well." She walks out of the office.

Tashianna stands up and walks toward Lewis office and stands in front of his desk looking at him in bewilderment.

"What was that all about and what do I need to be delivered from." Spoken with a nasty attitude.

Lewis waves his hand.

"Never mind all that just get me this Doctor Eyes address. I am sick of all this and I will do anything at this point to help my business, anything."

Tashianna walks out of his office knowing he is very frustrated so she does something just to make him smile. She rubs and shakes her butt a little more while walking away and Lewis eyes are locked on her body and every step she takes.

"Damn that girl got a fat ass and if only for one night. No wonder why men cheat, damn." He says softly to himself.

Tashianna heard him and turned around.

"I heard what you just said. You need to stop visually massaging me Lewis before you hurt yourself." She winked at him and kept walking back to her desk.

Chapter 7
The Mall

It is night time and Jacob and Crystal are walking through the mall with shopping bags in their hands. Jacob is wearing jeans and tennis shoes and Crystal has on the same but her jeans are tight.

"This summer has started off great. I have a new car, new clothes, Daddy's credit card and money in my pocket. What more could a girl want."

"We have a lot to be thankful for. Mom and Dad have worked very hard so we can have nice things and live a good comfortable life without financial struggles."

"True, we have never known poverty and have never wanted for anything. We eat the best food, wear the best clothes and we live in a baby mansion, we should never complain."

A young attractive girl walks by wearing tight jeans with a nice figure.

"Hi Jacob." She winks at him and keeps walking.

Jacob stares at her butt.

"Hi, you look good in those jeans, nice butt." He smiles and licks his lips.

Crystal pinches him on his arm.

"Don't talk like that around me and she has a very bad reputation at school. That girl has more miles on her than Greyhound, with her nasty self." She shakes her head.

"Just let me add to those miles, don't hide it, divide it, don't play around, lay it down." He laughs knowing his sister does not like how he is talking but said it just to irritate her

Crystal grabs his arm and they stop walking and she stares at him.

"Stop talking like that around me. Your mind is filthy but you are going to act like you have some sense around me and not like some dog in heat, and I mean it, so stop."

Two young guys wearing sweat suits walk over to them. Crystal and Jacob recognize them from school and they are known for being trouble makers.

"Hi Crystal, what's up Jacob?" He is looking at Crystal up and down.

"Hi." Crystal said smiling knowing they are not her type at all but she does not want to seem stuck up.

"Yeah, what's up?" Jacob said with attitude.

"Crystal, since you are already out and looking really good in those tight jeans let me take you to the movies and we can get something to eat after the show. Who knows where we will end up after that?" He said while smiling and looking at her lustfully.

Jacob drops his bags and points his finger in his face.

"She ain't going nowhere with you fool." Mean mugging him.

Both guys step back and lift there sweat suit jackets up to show they have guns stuck in their pants.

"Back up preacher kid. I was just being nice to your sister. So, don't get laid down in the mall."

The other guy steps closer to Jacob.

"That's right, just because your Dad is a big-time preacher and you know that karate garbage, you ain't bullet proof. So, don't meet Jesus today, preacher kid." Mean mugging Jacob as well.

Crystal steps in between them.

"Look we don't want any trouble so why don't you two trouble makers go ahead about your business." Speaking with confidence but was nervous on the inside.

The two guys look at each other and laugh.

"Let's go, she aint worth it." He turns to his buddy and they dap up.

"No problem, Crystal, you and that tight little ass should save some of that hot loving for me." He looks at Jacob. "See you around preacher kid." They both laughed and walk away.

Crystal turns and looks at Jacob.

"You need to watch that temper of yours; you could have gotten yourself killed."

"What! I am trying to protect you and you are fussing at me? You females don't know what you want. I am leaving you and go find miss tight jeans with the butt." He steps away from her.

Crystal grabs his arm.

"No, you are not. We came here together and we are leaving together and if you leave me I am going to tell Dad and you will be grounded for the whole summer." Staring at him with a blank look on her face.

"Oh, so now you are going to snitch on me. Have it your way but after tonight, I am never coming to the mall with you again."

"Yes, you will, because you love me." She smiles and kisses him on the cheek. "Anyway, you can do much better than her. If you are going to ride a horse, at least get a fresh one. Now let's go spend some more money." She hooks her arm inside Jacobs. "Come on dear." Smiling at him.

Jacob looks at her and smiles.

"Yeah okay but you better be glad you are my sister." He picked up the bags and they walked away.

Chapter 8
The Richardson House

Raymond is outside in his backyard practicing his jump shots and dribbling on the court which is well lit by the many lights around the yard and it happens to be a full moon. James walks out.

"Hi Dad, I hope my dribbling and practicing did not disturb you and the family."

"No, you did not but it's late and I just wanted to talk with you, throw me the ball."

Raymond throws him the ball and James dribbles it and shoots, making the basket.

"Are you ready to go one on one?" Smiling at his son.

"Dad you probably had a game back in the day."

"What, I have a game now and I can take you but just not tonight."

Raymond laughs.

"You got a winner Dad but I have to practice, practice and more practice. I will play for the Charlotte Hornets one day. You preach it on a regular basis remember. Call those things which are not, as though they were."

James steps closer to him.

"Very true son. I know that is your dream and you want it very badly but you are missing something. Put God in your life, make him your Lord and Master and all things will be added to you according to his will for your life."

Raymond is dribbling the ball then stops and looks at his Dad.

"I tried that Dad but it does not work for me, it just did not happen. All that praying and for what, people are still poor and suffering and having problems every day. I mean just look what is happening all over the country Dad. This is two thousand and sixteen but racism is still very much alive. So much corruption going on and the police are killing black men like it's their job to exterminate us but are not properly punished for all their wrong doings. How can you still have faith and believe in God with all of this taking place, and more?"

"Son, of course I see all of the tragedies that take place in this world and yes, it's heart-breaking but living for God is not a part-time thing. Yes, people will have problems with or without God but he said in his word, *"Many are the afflictions of the righteous but the Lord will deliver them out of them all."* Son we all have to endure until the end, no matter what."

He picks up the ball and shoots.

"Okay Dad, you keep praying for the world and me but right now I want fame and long money no matter what. Dad I was M.V.P in high school all three years and I made excellent grades but the coaches said my dribble and jump shot needed work. At this point college, does not interest me because I can go to school at any time. But I need to be my best when I am finally able to try out for the team so for now it's practice and more practice."

James walks towards him and put his hand on his shoulder.

"Son there is nothing wrong with having a dream and pursuing it but you must not let it possess you, yes you may get it but at what cost?"

Raymond stepped back and looked at James.

"Dad, I want to play pro ball and I don't care about the cost. Whatever it takes, I am going to play."

"Son, that statement sounds just like how the devil works. He gives people what they want and unfortunately people don't care where it comes from as long as they get what they want, when they want it. I know your mind is made up but please remember this.

Only what you do for God will last. Everything else is temporary. I am going to bed, good night son." He walks away.

Raymond continues to shoot then he slams the ball down. He dribbles some more and he slams the ball down again.

"I am sick of this. I keep practicing and practicing but I still can't get my jump shot right and God won't help me. Damn will somebody help me? Anybody! I don't care what it cost." He grabs the ball and sits on it in total frustration just staring out in space until he hears the voice crystal clear speak to him. *"I can help you."* He quickly looks around the yard thinking one of his brothers is playing a trick on him but no one is there. He hears the voice again. *"I can help you."* He stands up and walks around looking for anyone but again no one is there. He hears the voice again. *"I can help you, come to me."* He feels like he is losing his mind and starts walking towards the house when seemingly out of now where an address for South Carolina comes to his mind. He pulls out his cell phone and puts the address in it and puts the phone back in his pocket. Afterwards he feels happy, like his whole life is about to change. "Man, suddenly I feel good and I am going to this place in South Carolina. The sooner the better. Yeah, this is an omen for me. Good things are about to happen to me. It's my time." He walks inside the house smiling.

The voice that he heard is it a voice from God or the devil?

𝕿𝖍𝖊 𝕮𝖍𝖆𝖕𝖙𝖊𝖗 9

𝕯𝖔𝖔𝖗 𝕺𝖕𝖊𝖓 𝖇𝖚𝖙 𝖇𝖞 𝖂𝖍𝖔𝖒

It is a nice summer afternoon and the garage doors to the body shop are open. Raymond, John, Jimmy, and Shawn are all working on cars. A dark grey GTC4 Lusso Ferrari pulls up to the shop and this well dressed white man steps out of the car. Everyone in the shop stops working to look at this car

"Now that is what I call a car." Jimmy said staring at it.

John is staring at the car shaking his head.

"With a car like that I can pull more girls than a convict can pull time, seven days a week and seven different pairs of panties."

Raymond steps a little closer.

"Yeah the car is great and that man looks familiar to me."

Jimmy and Shawn walk towards him.

"Good afternoon sir. Can we help you?"

He extends his hand.

"I hope so. My name is Steve Collins and I am in this area on business but I want my car completely detailed inside and out and this shop came highly recommended."

Shawn steps forward and shakes his hand.

"Nice to meet you sir and word of mouth is the best advertisement. My name is Shawn and this is my partner Jimmy." He points to Jimmy. "We own the shop."

Jimmy shakes his hand.

"Nice to meet you. That is a very nice car you are driving."

"Thank you it was a gift to myself and now it needs to be professionally detailed. Can you handle it?"

"Absolutely and when do you want it back?"

"I am in no hurry and today being Friday, I would like to have it back by Monday afternoon. Do you have any problems with the car sitting here over the weekend?"

"It's not a problem sir. We have a state of the art security system and our business including the cars on the lot are covered up to five million dollars. You are welcome to see the paper work if you like. It will only take me a few minutes to show you the file on the computer." Shawn said.

"That will not be necessary this shop has an excellent reputation."

John and Raymond walk towards the car.

"Nice ride." John said.

"I thought you looked familiar you are Mr. Steve Collins, Charlotte Hornets head basketball coach." Raymond said staring at him.

"Yes sir, I am, and you are?" He extends his hand to him.

Raymond shakes his hand.

"My name is Raymond. You met my brother Jimmy and this is my other brother John, the best body man in the country. It's my dream to play for the Charlotte Hornets and I feel it's only a matter of time before it's my turn."

"How old are you and what position do you want to play?"

"I am eighteen now. I have been out of school for a year and I was MVP all three years in school and I graduated with a 4.0 GPA. I want to play guard."

"My suggestion to you would be to go to college and get more experienced then try the pros. Unless your skills right now are exceptional dribbling and jump shot including a good attitude to match which is equally as important as the physical skills"

"Mr. Collins, are you a man of your word and honor sir?"

"Yes sir I am. It's my foundation. Why do you ask?"

"If I fit your description of an exceptional ball player would you give me a serious try out?"

"Son, if your skills are truly that good and your attitude matches. Then yes I would give you a try out for my team and if everything else checks out then you would be wearing a Charlotte Hornets jersey." He reaches into his pocket and pulls out a business card. "Here is my card with my private number on it. When you are ready, call me." He extends his hand to him.

Raymond shakes his hand.

"Thank you sir, thank you. I will call you. Great car." He walks away toward the shop smiling.

"That was very nice of you Mr. Collins. Playing pro ball is my brother's dream. That's all he talks about." Jimmy said.

"Well I haven't done anything yet but I have a strong feeling about that young man, he just might be the one. Now back to business. If one of you will ride with me back to my hotel we can sign some papers and you can bring the car back here."

"I will take care of that Mr. Collins just let me go and get my paper work." Shawn walks towards the office.

"Excuse me sir how much does a car like this cost?" John said.

"The asking sells price starts at $300,000 can you handle that?" Smiling at him.

"I wish but my Dad and mom can."

"Who are they?"

"Sherry and James Richardson. My mom owns the largest Lexus car dealership in the state and my Dad use to sing R& B but now he is a pastor and a professional gospel singer."

"Yes sir Mr. James Richardson. I do know the name well but who doesn't. The man is legendary and who hasn't heard of your mom. What couldn't they buy?" Smiling at John.

Shawn walks back out with the paper work in his hand.

"Mr. Collins, If you are ready, I'm all set to go."

A black Lamborghini Aventador drives up next to the Ferrari.

"Mr. Collins no disrespect but move over Ferrari, man look at that." John said.

Raymond walks closer to the car.

"Talk about nice."

Mr. Collins is looking at the car admiring it as well when Alexandria Brown steps out and Theresa Goodman of the driver's side. Both are wearing tight shorts and halter tops. Theresa is twenty-three years old five feet six and hundred and twenty-five pounds. She is a very attractive blond with a nice figure who is almost identical to Alexandria's except she has a more hips.

"Nice car." Theresa said looking at the car then at Mr. Collins.

"Thank you and likewise. Maybe we will meet on the highway sometime." He tries hard not to stare at Theresa's body.

"Hi baby. Are you leaving?"

"Alex, hi and you look great. Great car and yes I have to go but I will be back." He walks towards her.

"Shawn this is Theresa and I need to talk with you."

"Hi Theresa, this is some car you are driving. Baby I have to go so we will have to talk later." He hugs and kisses her and caresses her butt then whispers in her ear. "I will finish this tonight." Smiling at him.

She rolls her eyes at him.

"I am tired of this."

He kisses her.

"I love you too sexy." He turns and looks at Mr. Collins. "Let's go Mr. Collins."
They both get in the Ferrari and drive away.

"Hi Alexandria be patient with him. It really is tough running a business like this and the guy does love you."

"Hi Jimmy. If you say so. This is Theresa my best friend and Theresa this is John and Raymond his two brothers."

"Hello Theresa." Raymond said

"Hi, you look familiar. Have you been on TV?" John said.

"I am a model and I have done some commercials."

"Now I know where I have seen you, you are very attractive and you look even better in person."

"Thank you that was sweet of you to say." She turns towards Raymond. "So, Raymond who is spoiling you these days?"

"Alexandria, it's good to see you again and Theresa it was very nice to meeting you but I have work to do." Jimmy turns and looks at his brothers. "You too Raymond and John."

John is staring at the two ladies.

"Alexandria, Theresa very nice and I am not talking about the car." He looks at them up and down and smiles then he and Jimmy walk back inside the shop.

"Don't take all day Raymond we have work to do." Jimmy yells and keeps walking.

"Raymond, you never did answer my question."

"No one at the moment. I am focusing on my basketball career which is about to improve. The man in that Ferrari was Mr. Steven Collins the head coach for the Charlotte Hornets. We briefly talked and he gave me his private number and said for me to call him when I am ready and he would give me a try out for the team."

"I thought he looked familiar. What college do you go to?"

"I don't. I finished high school MVP and I am going straight to the pros."

"You must be very good." Theresa said with a lustful tone while staring at him.

"I am wondering is basketball the only thing he is good at." Alexandria said looking at his crotch then his face.

"Alex, you are so nasty and such a flirt."
Raymond's eyes are moving back and forth between them trying to decide who looks the best.

"You two could cause an accident just walking down the street, very nice."

Jimmy steps in front of the bay doors.

"Raymond, its work time." He yells.

"Alright I am coming." He yells at him. "Ladies I have to go. Theresa, it was nice meeting you and good luck on your modeling career."

"Same to you and I hope you make the team." Extending her hand to him.

They shake hands.

"Raymond take care of yourself and I do hope you make the team as well."

"Thank you." He steps closer and whispers in her ear. "You know how to get in touch with me." He very lightly caresses her butt and steps back.

Alexandria is staring at him surprised he rubbed her butt and it peaks her interest in him even more.

"Interesting but remember this. Ladies want romance as well as great sex, longer than twenty minutes, if you can."

"I am not Shawn. Bye Alexandria. Theresa, drive safely and don't let all that power in that car get away from you."

She steps closer to him.

"I like power, I ride well and I know how to hold on." She caresses his face.

He stares at her and walks away. Alexandria and Theresa get in the car with Theresa in the driver's seat.

"He is tall and fine and I really do hope he makes the team. He can try out for me any day." She starts laughing.

"Now look who is talking. Sex on the brain. But the question is, is he romantic or just another five-minute humping like a dog bust his nut and roll over and go to sleep type of guy."

"Sounds like Shawn is a quick sex and sleepy lazy dog. You need to be caressed and made slow passionate love to, then sexed to the max. Are you hungry baby?" Smiling at her.

"Would you sleep with Raymond Theresa?"

"Don't ask me a dumb question. Yes, I would and so would you. Shawn or not."

"Yeah, you are right I would and repeatedly if he is as good as he looks. Maybe we could have him at the same time." Winking at her.

Theresa is staring at her because she has wondered about Alex sexuality for years since they have known each other. Wondered if she was into women because she would notice how Alex would look at her when they were in the gym showers. Secretly it always turned her on. Now she knows.

"Yeah, maybe we could." She leans over and kisses Alex on the lips and stares at her. "Soft lips." She rubs Alex leg and drives off.

Chapter 10
Red Lobster

Jocelyn Mitchum drives up to Red Lobster in her black custom seventy-nine Cutlass with dark tint on the widows and a set of deep inset silver and gold rims with grey soft leather interior and a fifteen hundred-dollar sound system. Jocelyn is truly stunning, a *FULL SEVEN* to the fullest. She is black twenty-two years old brown skinned five feet six and a hundred thirty-five pounds. She has been known to cause car accidents just walking. When she walks, she looks like she is floating on air. She parks on the side and steps out wearing tennis shoes, tight shorts and a T-shirt tied in a knot in the back showing off her tight flat stomach and she is carrying her uniform.

Jimmy drives up in his Corvette and parks next to Jocelyn's car. He gets out of his car wearing dress shoes, dress pants and a short sleeve Egyptian cotton shirt. He is walking behind Jocelyn.

"Good God almighty, girl you got a serious body. You know you are breaking the law but probably do not care."

Jocelyn stops walking and turns around.

"Excuse me. I am not breaking the law in any way and do I know you?" With a nasty attitude in her tone.

Jimmy steps closer to her.

"You are very pretty and no you do not know me yet and yes you are breaking the law by carrying a concealed weapon. You got a permit for all of that, let me see it?"

She stares at him and laughs.

"That is so old and corny but you made me laugh and I needed that. What is your name?"

"My name is Jimmy and I don't mind carrying your uniform, opening the door for you and I have no problem with begging."

She laughs again.

"Jimmy, you are something else and you have made my day. Are you always such a gentleman and so direct?"

"Yes, and yes. Now can I open the door for you and will you be my personal waitress? Don't say no and hurt my feelings."

Staring at him trying to read his character because she is use to guys coming on to her talking about a lot of nothing but she knows they have only one thing on their minds.

"Yes, and yes."

They walk toward the front door and a couple walks out and the guy has his arm around her waist but as they past Jimmy and Jocelyn the guy turns his head and looks at Jocelyn's butt. His lady slaps him.

"Really, you are going to directly disrespect me. Your arm is all around my waist but you turn around and look at another girl's butt like I am nothing. Very typical, a dog. You can forget about getting some tonight and as a matter of fact, just take me home and then leave." She walks away from him.

"Baby wait, you are over-reacting." He quickly walks faster to catch up with her.

Jimmy and Jocelyn laugh.

"See, now look what you have done. I said you are carrying a concealed weapon and you got that guy in trouble." Smiling at her.

"If you say so."

Raymond opens the door for Jocelyn and as she walks in he is staring at her butt.

"Damn, Lord forgive me for my X-rated sinful thoughts."

She turns her head towards him.

"I heard that and you need to repent." Smiling at him.

The place is full and all heads turn to look at Jocelyn. One of the waitresses standing by the cash register is staring at Jocelyn and Jimmy as they walk in.

"Hi Jocelyn, you need to hurry up and change into your uniform before you cause a riot in here."

"Jocelyn, a concealed weapon. Hurry up and get that permit." He smiles knowing his words are silly but it makes Jocelyn laugh.

"You two have made my day." Stepping closer to the waitress then points at Jimmy. "Can you seat him please and I will change and wait on him."

She points at Jimmy.

"This fine-looking gentleman, absolutely. Right this way sir." Jocelyn walks away and the waitress shows Jimmy to his table then takes his order and walks away. Jocelyn comes back in wearing her uniform and once again all heads in the place look in her direction. The top to her uniform does very little to hide her ample cleavage, a skirt that shows off her sexy legs and does not hide the curves of her hips and the butt shaking with every step she takes. She walks over to Jimmy's table.

"Did you miss me? And what can I get you, that is on the menu, and don't say anything smart or nasty."

"Yes, I missed you and I would like for us to get to know each other. Let me keep it real with you. You are too fine and you have guys popping game at you all day, every day but I don't play games. I will treat you as good as you treat me and I have my own business and I will spoil you Miss Jocelyn and you will spoil me back."

Jocelyn is looking at him feeling that his words are true and he is a nice-looking guy.

"Oh really. You are very direct, bold and nice looking. I tell you what, give me your number and if I don't call you in two days. I won't call."

"Works for me. Your body shakes real nice when you walk but can you work that body on the dance floor?"

She put one hand on her hip.

"I can dance better than you and I can sing. Now, what do you have in mind, that's not X-rated?"

"Oh, you got jokes. Anyway, it has been a long time since I have been to the club how about you and I go tonight and we will both see who can do what on the dance floor."

Another man sitting at a table calls Jocelyn.

"Excuse me miss."

"I will be right back handsome." She walks over to the other guy's table and takes his order and walks around checking on other customers then walks back to Jimmy's table.

Jimmy was watching her every move. He has seen many attractive ladies before but it's something about Jocelyn that draws him to her and it's not just her physical beauty which is outstanding. The woman is truly stunning and carries herself with class.

"You are one classy, stunningly beautiful lady. What about tonight and I missed you when you left my table." Staring at her face smiling.

Jocelyn smiles while studying his face.

"I was not gone that long. Jimmy you seem to be nice and a gentleman so I will give you the benefit of the doubt. Give me your number and we can make plans to meet at the club tonight."

"Red Lobster has never been so good to me." He reaches into his pocket and pulls out his business card and Visa Black card and hands them to her. "My home number is on the card and now it's time for me to go back to work."

She put his business card in her apron pocket.

"Walk with me to the registry."

They walk to the registry with Jimmy walking behind her shaking his head and smiling. Jocelyn looks back at him knowing the affect she is having on him but keeps walking. She rings up his bill and hands it and his credit card to him. He signs it and hands it back to her.

Jocelyn looks at the bill.

"You gave me a twenty-dollar tip. Are you trying to impress me with money?" Mr. Visa Black card?" Looking at him.

"That's a weak man's move and I would not insult myself or you. The tip is for the service and your pleasant company that I appreciate, nothing more. So, put your claws back in and give me a call."

"I respect that and I thank you for the tip but you have not seen my claws yet. Anyway, don't work too hard the rest of the day. I don't want you to use work as an excuse as to why you can't hang with me on the dance floor. I will call you tonight." She gives him the warmest smile.

"You are something. I always did like Red Lobster; now I am overwhelmed." Looking at Jocelyn from head to toe. "Yes Lord."

Jocelyn starts laughing.

"Get out of here flirting with me."

Jimmy laughs and walks out and gets in his car and drives away.

Chapter 11

The body Shop

It's in the afternoon and John drives up to the body shop in a 2016 Z06 Corvette. The bay doors are open Shawn and Raymond are sitting down eating lunch. John steps out and walks towards them with his hands in the air.

"So, what do you think about the car is she nice or what?"

"The car is real nice. What are you doing with it?" Shawn said.

"Test driving it and I am thinking about buying it with Dad's help."

"You must be drunk if you think Dad is going to buy you that car. An eighty-thousand-dollar car. You're dreaming."

"All I need is ten thousand more dollars from Dad or mom to add to what I already have as a down payment and the car is mine because my credit's great and I can afford it."

"John even if and I say if you get mom or Dad to give you the ten grand, the payments on that car will be ridiculous."

"Look, I am not boasting but I am probably the best body man in the state. I can take an old rusted out car and make it look new. People from all over bring their cars in here so I can fix it, me. Metal, fiber glass I can do it all and well."

"He speaks the truth he is good, very good. Even now he is averaging two thousand dollars a week." Shawn said.

"My brother is good but I didn't know he was making that much. Well the only thing that I can say is, good luck on getting that ten grand."

"Thank you. Now come look at the car and don't hate."

All three walk towards the car and stand beside it.

"It's a beautiful car but too much for you."

RONALD GRAY

54

"The car is just right. It's pretty, fast and comfortable just how I like my women."

Raymond starts laughing.

"Boy, you haven't had any ladies with that bumpy acid face of yours."

"Raymond that was cold man." Shawn is looking at him with disgust.

John is looking at Raymond like he could kill him.

"You know where you can go Raymond. Yeah, I have bad skin but I am a diehard romantic and I know how to treat the ladies well. I am a gentleman with a pearl tongue and even Keith Sweat can't beg like me." He gets in his car and drives off.

"Your brother is something."

"Yeah he is and I should not have said that about his face, man I need to get away from this town for a while."

"Perfect timing, ride with me to Miami. We leave today and come back some time Sunday night."

"I can go for that. What car do we take?"

He points to the Ferrari sitting in the shop.

"That one."

Raymond looks at him like he is crazy.

"You must be out of your mind. Mr. Collins would have us locked up and if anything were to happen to that car we could kiss it goodbye."

Shawn raises his hands.

"Hold up, relax, my mind is made up I am driving the car with or without you and I take full responsibility for it. Anyway, I am protected, nothing can happen to me. So are you coming or do I ride alone and party in Miami without you?"

"Well since you put it that way I am coming with you. I don't know what you mean about being protected but I need a break from Raleigh for a while, so Miami it's."

"Perfect, now let's finish up in this shop and we can leave." They walk back in the shop and stand by the Ferrari. "Look out ladies, it's time to drop the panties."

"What about Alexandria I thought you love her. The girl is fine and she is crazy about you."

"Yeah, I do love her but what she does not know won't hurt her. What happens in Miami stays in Miami, Raymond." Staring at him.

He is looking at Shawn thinking how much of a dog he really is and the respect he just lost for him.

"If you say so."

They work on some cars in the shop for a while and finally finish and then shower at the shop and put on sweats. Shawn park the Ferrari outside the shop and closed all the bay doors so they could leave. Then Jimmy drives up in his Corvette and steps out. Raymond walked out of the shop and stood next to Shawn.

"I was hoping we would be gone before he got back here." Shawn said.

"Yeah me to because I know my brother and see it coming."

"What's up, where are you two going and why is the Ferrari parked out here?"

"What's going on partner? We are going to Miami for the weekend and I am driving the Ferrari and we will be back some time Sunday night."

Jimmy steps closer to them.

"What! You must be crazy. Yeah okay you and Raymond can go to Miami but the Ferrari stays here. There is no way," he points to the car. "There is no way that Ferrari is leaving this shop."

"Jimmy calm down we will take care of the car." Raymond said.

"Relax and I take full responsibility for the car. I can afford it very easily and you know it. Besides half of the business is mine don't forget this."

Jimmy got instantly irritated.

"Tell me something that I don't know and speaking of business, It is bad business to take customers cars for a joy ride and if anything were to happen to that car it would hurt our business and reputation."

"Jimmy, I am covered the car is covered and I could replace the car in a day so just relax and have a nice weekend."

Jimmy walks closer to Shawn.

"Shawn this is a bad move partner don't take Mr. Collins car, it's truly bad for business and we can't afford it."

Shawn put his hand on Jimmy's shoulder and looks at him.

"I can. We have known each other for years have I ever let you down?"

"No, I can't say you have."

"Good, you two can do the best friend bonding thing later. Miami is calling us."

"Yes, it's and it's time for us to operate in lust Raymond."

"No doubt. Asses shaking and popping." He laughs while looking at Jimmy because he knows his brother is highly irritated but he needs to loosen up a bit anyway.

Jimmy points at Shawn and Raymond.

"Well, while you two are watching asses popping and shaking don't wreck that car."

Raymond shakes Jimmy's hand and gets in the car. Shawn shakes his hand and gets in the car and drives off. Jimmy is standing there watching the Ferrari speed down the road and he is shaking his head and walks toward the shop.

Shawn is driving on Interstate 95 south doing a hundred miles an hour and music is playing.

"Shawn this car is nice but actually this is a waste of time. It will take us about eleven hours to drive there but we can fly to Miami in a fraction of time instead of all this driving."

"Yeah we could but it wouldn't be nearly as much fun and it will not take us eleven hours." He quickly increases speed to a hundred and thirty miles an hour.

"As my Dad would say, yes Lord." He starts laughing.

They both laugh as Shawn accelerates to one hundred and sixty miles an hour passing cars like they are standing still.

Chapter 12
Recording Studio

That night James Richardson is in the recording studio along with his record producer William Cox who is working the sound board and his assistant. James is in the recording room singing a gospel song and then he stops.

"William I don't like the way the song sounds so let's take it from the top."

William laughs because he knows his friend well and how particular he can be but he is right about the sound.

"You read my thoughts the song is not bad but you need to put more feeling into it mind, body and spirit. You have been doing this a long time and we both know if people can't feel what you are singing, then it's not real."

"True that my friend you are right. I will start over." He sings the song all the way through. "How was that?"

"Only because I know you so well, I can still notice a little emotional distraction on your part when singing but the song is good. We can wrap it up for tonight so come on out so we can talk."

"Sounds good, I am a little tired anyway."

William turns to his assistant.

"Thanks for all of your help tonight but you can go ahead and leave and I will see you tomorrow."

"All right William, you take it easy and I will see you in the morning." They shake hands and he walks out.

James walks in the sound room.

"The last time you did the song was much better but again I know you. What is on your mind my friend?"

"I am fine just trying to concentrate on this song."

"Have a seat. Look, this is me that you are talking to and I know your gift very well and you never had to concentrate on singing a song this hard, it just comes out of you, because it's gift. We go back many years long before you were a Pastor and singing gospel music, back when you were singing R&B music and the ladies were throwing themselves at you but you still could sing the roof off a building. So, what is really bothering you?"

James looks at his friend and smiles.

"You always could read me well." He looks down and rubs his head then looks at William. "Actually, my mind is on my daughter Katrina and her overwhelming desire to be a big-time singer."

"I wonder where she got that from. She is just like you were many years ago, very determined and nothing or no body was going to stand in your way. Can she sing?"

"Yes, she can sing well but her voice becomes a little scratchy at times but if she would just wait on the Lord to touch her voice, I know he will bless her to sing for his praise and glory."

"Okay, so what is the problem?"

"Katrina does not want to wait on the Lord and she does not want to sing gospel music at all, only R&B music and her mind is focused on money and fame."

"Now I fully understand the situation knowing what you went through and how you were almost destroyed by the industry and running from God. Is your daughter as determined as you were?"

"Probably more so and she already has a manager who is also her producer. His name is Terrence Washington. Do you know him by any chance?"

"Not personally but I know of him and he is good and very persistent concerning his business but he also has a reputation for being hands on with his female clients. He does have a lot of contacts in the industry for getting things done but by any means necessary and then some."

James stands up frowning and his entire demeanor changes for the worse.

"I appreciate the information and I will continue to pray for my daughter and entire family but right now it's time for me to go."

William stands up as well looking at James.

"We have been doing this a very long time my friend and we know how crazy this business can be and the waters are infested with sharks. But you keep praying, preaching, and living a Holy life and let the Lord use you."

"Amen to that by the way when are you going to give your life to the Lord and stop taking his grace for granted?"

"Man, don't start with that I go to church and my brother you sure can preach. I pray, read the bible and give plenty of money to the church."

"You can't buy God and going to church and bible reading will not get you into heaven. You must be born again of the water and spirit, you must ask Jesus to forgive you of all your sins and come into your heart and walk in the spirit of obedience of his word. Not just on Sunday's but every day."

He raises his hands up.

"Okay you got me; I am living foul so pray for me. But the women are so fine my brother everywhere you look nothing but pretty faces hips and butt for days just walking down the street. And the lovin, oh my goodness, next to a pocket full of money sex is the best thing. I know you love the Lord and all that but you can't tell me you don't ever see a woman and just lust because she is so fine and you know you want to hit that. Let's keep it real my friend. Any man will look at a beautiful woman with a fat ass walking by. You aint that Holy." He starts laughing.

James can't help but laugh.

"We all sin and have to repent daily but the point is I want to obey the word of God but I also deeply love my wife and I am very attracted to her. With that being said, I am going home and eat. We will finish this song later."

"Point made. You are a true friend to me."

"I appreciate that but God desires to be your best friend. They shake hands and James walks out.

Chapter 13
Appreciating Home

James was doing some serious thinking when he left the studio and was thanking God for all his blessings and asking him for wisdom to make the right choices concerning his family and life. He pulls into his drive way and walks towards his front door but stops and look around his yard and stares at his house then looks up.

"Lord Jesus I thank you for blessing me with your grace, my wife, family and lovely home and so many more blessings oh Lord that only you can make happen by your mighty hand. I thank you." James walks in the house and looks around not seeing or hearing anyone so he raises his arms up and yells. "Alright Daddy is home, somebody needs to come and give me a hug and act like you love me just a little."

Sherry walks towards him smiling.

"I love you and stop yelling in this house sir I will be glad to give you a hug."

"That's what I am talking about. Come over here and put that sexy body of yours on me and let me taste your lips and rub your hips." They hug and kiss. "Soft lips and I feel the love baby, I feel the love. And don't act like you don't want it."

"James don't start, you really are something and how did things go at the studio tonight?'

"Not bad but it was a little hard to concentrate on my music because my mind was on Katrina, speaking of which where is everyone?"

"Well, Jacob and Crystal are in the living room watching TV, Katrina went to the movies and is spending the night at her friend's house. Jimmy went out to the night club and Raymond went with Shawn to Miami for the weekend and John is..."

John walks towards them.

"Right behind you Mom, hi Dad. I am glad you are home there is something that I want to talk about with you."

"Absolutely, I look forward to talking with my wonderful children because there is never a dull moment in the Richardson house, so what is on your mind great child of mine?"

"James, are you hungry baby?"

"No I have already eaten but I thank you for such a warm offer from such a beautiful woman." He smiles looking at her up and down.

"Yes Lord." Sherry kisses him on the lips and walks away.

James watches his wife walk then looks at his son.

"So, what is on your mind son and make it short and plain if you do not mind because it has been a long day."

"No problem Dad. I test drove this car today that I want very much but I need ten thousand more dollars for the down payment and the car is mine and this is where you come in."

"The best part of the story me and money. It must be some car and how much is the total down payment son and what kind of car is it?"

"Twenty grand down but I have ten and the car is a 2016 Z06 Corvette. Yes, the payments are a little high but I can afford it very easily with the money I make at the shop so will you help me?"

"A Corvette, son that is a lot of car for a nineteen-year-old but before you give me that, Dad don't lecture me look. Just let me think about it and pray on it and I will let you know before the weekend is over, fair enough."

"Fair enough Dad." They shake hands and walk in the living room where Sherry, Crystal and Jacob are sitting watching TV."

"Hi Dad." Jacob said.

"Hi Dad." Crystal said.

"Very heartfelt warm greeting I just received. That must be some TV show that receives more attention than me. I did get hugs at one time when I came home, Crystal."

"I still love you Dad but I will hug you later." Crystal said looking at him smiling.

"Times sure have changed, children don't love you like they once did, no hugs, nothing. Back in the day when I was growing up..."

John throws his hands up.

"Oh Lord, here we go with that, when I was growing up speech." He looks at Crystal. "Crystal see what you did, you hurt Dad's feelings."

"Oh God, not again this is the only family in America that if you don't hug your parents every day they don't feel loved. I am coming Dad." She gets up and hugs James and kisses him on the cheek. "There, you got a hug and a kiss. Are you happy now Dad?"

"It depends. Did you do it with a cheerful heart, did it come from way down deep, and did you feel some love on the inside, did you?"

"Go ahead and preach Dad. Say it one more time." John claps his hands and laughs.

"Mom, please get Dad, hug him do something because you know how he gets."

Sherry walks towards James holding out her hand.

"Come on James stop playing and picking on your children." She grabs his arm and whispers in his ear. "I have something that you can play with." She kisses his lips smiles and walks away.

James watches her walk with a big smile on his face and then looks at his children.

"I am glad somebody loves me." He raises his voice. "I am coming baby just don't leave me, don't leave me baby. I will do you right." He laughs and walks after Sherry. "Yes Lord."

John sits down shaking his head.

"You know what, I think it's very special that after all these years' Dad and Mom still flirt with and love each other so much. They act like high school sweethearts."

"All that praying and fasting Dad does and rebuking demons, Mom could not do better and I know they are still getting busy." Jacob said.

"Yes Lord, as Dad would say." John said laughing.

Crystal stands up and hits both of them across the head.

"Oh my God, you two are so disrespectful talking about Mom and Dad like that. Both of you have lust spirits and need to be delivered, your mind and heart are filthy, you make me sick." She pushes them and walks away.

They both laugh then dap hands.

"We love you too sis." John said.

Chapter 14
The night Club

Jimmy walks in the night club which is full. He walks around and sees Jocelyn on the dance floor and Tashianna is with her and they are both dancing with guys. The song goes off and Jocelyn sees Jimmy and all four walk towards him. Jocelyn is wearing a long skirt with a slit in the middle and a revealing top.

"Jimmy, it's about time you got here." Jocelyn hugs and kisses him on the cheek and then turns to the guy she was dancing with. "Thank you for the dance but my date has arrived."

"Thanks for your time and the dance was my pleasure." He and the other guy walk away.

"Jocelyn, you look absolutely gorgeous and some things are worth waiting for."

"You remember that." Slowly caressing his face with her hand and then looks at Tashianna. "This is my best friend Tashianna".

She is wearing very tight jeans that show the curves of her hips and butt very well and a low-cut top revealing cleavage.

"Hi Jimmy, I heard some very nice things about you."

"Thank you and you have a lovely name and you look good. Hopefully Jocelyn will enjoy my company and allow me to spoil her."

"There must have been some connection with you two because you just met and you are already talking about spoiling her. Do you have any brothers?"

"Girl you need to stop flirting. We have a table so let's go sit down."

Jimmy reaches over and lightly touches Jocelyn's arm.

"I need another hug before we sit down and a kiss would be nice as well." Looking at Jocelyn smiling.

"Jocelyn I see it already you met a spoiled man. Handle your business please hug and kiss him so we can go and sit down, my feet hurt."

Jocelyn was staring at Jimmy and thinking...*I am drawn to him for some reason but I do not want him to get the wrong impression of me and think that I am an easy mark for him. But he is so damn fine.* She steps closer and hugs Jimmy and lightly kisses him on the lips.

"Now can we go?" Smiling at him and embracing his arm.

"As my Dad, would say, yes Lord." All three walk towards their table and Jocelyn was holding Jimmy's hand.

Alexandria and Theresa are walking towards them and both are wearing tight short miniskirts and revealing tops.

"Jimmy, I am surprised to see you here." Alexandria said while looking him up and down smiling.

"Hi Jimmy, this is a surprise, you look good."

"Alexandria, Theresa hello, you two look very nice. It has been a while since I have been here." He points to the girls. "This is Jocelyn and Tashianna."

"Hello." Jocelyn said with a slight attitude.

"Hi." Tashianna spoke with much attitude and did not mind showing it.

"Alexandria, you did not want to go with Shawn to Miami?"

Her entire demeanor instantly changed and she was trying to suppress her building anger.

"Miami? He told me he had business to take care of this weekend. He did not say anything about going to Miami."

"Busted, you men are no good." Tashianna is looking at Jimmy with disgust.

"Tashianna please don't start." Jocelyn said staring at her.

"I assumed that you knew Alexandria."

Alexandria stepped closer to Jimmy.

"Jimmy, I know you two are best friends and business partners but please don't lie. Did he have some slut with him when he left and how did he leave? Yes, I know I am putting you on the spot but you know how much I care about him."

"Yeah I know you are crazy about the guy but he left with my brother Raymond and they drove the Ferrari."

"Who could forget your brother Raymond, tall and fine." Theresa said with lust in her voice and eyes.

"Tall and fine. When is he coming back from Miami?" Tashianna said while looking at Jimmy.

"Thanks Jimmy. As good as I am to that man and he takes off to Miami without me. No problem I have something real nice for Shawn. I am rocking this man's world and he still mistreats me, okay I will deal with him later. Thanks Jimmy you are a sweetheart, take care of him Jocelyn."

"I intend to." But the look in her eyes spoke the loudest. Alexandria and Theresa walk to their table.

"That girl is something and it sounds like Shawn is in trouble but he should be." Tashianna said.

"Big time and she looks like the revengeful type. Jimmy, are you upset because you had to tell on your friend?"

"I don't like being caught in the middle of anything. Anyway, right now I would rather concentrate on you."

"Smart man, now let's go and sit down." All three walk to their table sits down and orders drinks.

RONALD GRAY

69

Alexandria and Theresa are sitting at their table talking.

"I know you are upset and I just wanted us to have some fun tonight but I would not mind being in Miami with Raymond or anywhere else for that matter as fine as he is."

"He is very nice looking and he has a very bright future ahead of him unlike Shawn and his dirty business that he thinks I don't know about.'

"What do you mean dirty business?"

"Never mind but I am tired of Shawn's foolishness but I know exactly what I want."

"What! I have seen that look in your eyes before."

"Not what but who? Raymond, and it's not just a game I am really interested in him. Besides I noticed the way he was looking at me and the feeling is mutual."

"Who doesn't look at you but you are playing with fire. Jimmy and Raymond are brothers and Shawn is his best friend and business partner. You leave Raymond alone and I will take care of him for you, my pleasure."

"No way, I saw him first. Tall, fine and a bright future that is a powerful combination which is not my desire to pass up. Besides I know Shawn and even as we speak he is probably trying to get in some nasty slut panties, damn dog."

Chapter 15
Miami

Shawn and Raymond are in a night club in Miami sitting down at a table with two ladies name Chris and Anita. Both are very attractive and wearing short skirts and low cut tops. The club is very nice and the music is great with many people on the dance floor doing their thing.

"Shawn how long will you and Raymond be in Miami?" Chris asked.

"We will leave on Sunday."

"Do you two have any plans for the rest of the weekend?" Raymond said.

"That depends on how busy you and Shawn will be while you are here and how well we enjoy each other's company." Anita said while slowly caressing Raymond's arm with her fingers.

"Raymond and I came here to relax and enjoy ourselves. We don't have a schedule or any particular place to go, so we are all yours."

"Interesting words." Chris said staring at Shawn.

"Raymond, besides looking good can you dance?"

"Anita, you will never find out by sitting there so let's dance."

"Come on Anita, it's show time."

All four of them walk to the dance floor and spend the next thirty minutes dancing and having fun and then walk back to their table and sit down.

"Raymond I am impressed because most tall guys are clumsy on the dance floor but you move very well, smooth and nice." Anita said while flirtatiously looking at him.

"Shawn, obviously you have not spent all of your time in a body shop because you also dance well." Chris said.

"Thank you even though you were grinding all on me."

"You did not seem to mind or do too much backing up."
A waitress stops by their table and they order drinks and she leaves.

"While we are waiting on our drinks this would be a good time for Chris and I to go to the bathroom. Come on Chris and we will be right back."

The girls stand up to leave and Raymond and Shawn stand as well.

"You two are a breath of fresh air. Dressed very nice, polite, well mannered, gentleman ways and good looking. You both need to move to Miami and then we could really show you around Miami." Chris said. Both girls kiss the guys on the cheek and walk towards the bathroom as Raymond and Shawn watch them.

"Sexy, and they both look good and curves in all the right places. Not exactly a *FULL SEVEN* but still very attractive. Maybe we should move to Miami." Raymond said still looking in their direction.

"Forget that, we are in Miami for fun and they are just demographic booty, hit it and go, so here is the plan. You take the Ferrari and take Anita with you to the hotel and I will ride with Chris back to the hotel as well. Then we will hook up in the morning and swap sex stories."

"Sounds good to me but what about Alexandria, you can't dog her like that, the girl loves you man and probably would like to marry you."

"I love Alex too she is my baby but I am sick of hearing about all of this romance, that stuff is played out. Ladies talk so much about wanting to be romanced but what they really want is for you to put some stiff hard dick in them and rock that body. That's it. All of that courtship and long conversations ended in the seventies, no one is doing that anymore, that's dead."

"Shawn my friend you are living in the dark ages. Laying pipe is fine but all ladies like to be treated special and romance is never dead and it's always a major priority and not just in the bedroom."

"Yeah okay, I tell you what Mr. Romantic, you do all the romancing, candle lights and begging and I will make money. All that romance is for songs and books. While all of you, so call romantic types, are out here being all nice and sweet to the women playing Mr. Romantic. Spending money you suckers cannot afford to lose. That same girl is spending time with men like me that is laying straight pipe, hard and quick and we got that long money. Look around you Raymond people don't marry for love or romance anymore; they marry for fame and money. Don't no lady want a broke man. A lot of money and a lot of dick, that's it, end of story."

Raymond shakes his head looking at Shawn feeling his pain as he was talking realizing he must have gotten emotionally hurt very badly in the past to be this messed up.

"Okay Shawn but just like all men are not dogs all women are not gold diggers either and love, real love, is the most powerful force in the world. You will learn but for tonight you got a winner. But me, even if I just met a woman it's still romance in the bedroom and I am doing it all. I am a romance freak specialist." He could not help from laughing.

Shawn laughs but is looking at Raymond like he just lost it.

The waitress brings the drinks the same time Anita and Chris are walking back to the table. Shawn pays for the drinks and she leaves as the girls sit down.

"Thank you for the drinks. Did you miss us?" Anita said.

"Absolutely." Raymond said as he stares at her.

RONALD GRAY

"Perfect, look I don't believe in wasting a lot of time with words and Anita and I already discussed this. So, would you two like to spend the weekend with us?"

Shawn and Raymond look at each other smiling then look at the girls.

"Chris, I look forward to it." Shawn said smiling because he knew what these two were about from the beginning and Raymond is talking about all this romantic stuff, yeah right. These girls want to get their freak on.

"Like wise Shawn."

"Anita I would enjoy your company very much."

"The feeling is mutual Raymond."

"Good, since that is out of the way let's go dance some more." Chris grabbed Anita's hand and they walk towards the dance floor.

Shawn points his finger at them as he and Raymond are walking behind them.

"Now that is what I call poetry in motion butt and hips shaking as they walk and they are doing it on purpose. I told you, romance is dead. The only thing these two want is to have a good time dancing and some good dick later, that's it. I wonder what Alexandria is doing right now." Shawn said while he and Raymond met the girls on the dance floor.

Chapter 16
The night Club

Back at the night club Jimmy, Jocelyn, Tashianna, and Haley a guy she was with are dancing. Three songs later they walk off the dance floor toward their table but as Tashianna is walking close to Haley she stops walking and touches his arm. Jimmy and Jocelyn keep walking.

"I really enjoyed dancing with you but now I am tired and need to rest my feet."

"Okay but can I take you to get something to eat later?"

"You are sweet but when I leave here my friend and I are going home but I do thank you for the offer maybe some other time." She leans forward and kisses him on the cheek and then walks back to her table.

Haley watches her walk away adjusting his penis trying to hide his erection.

"I almost had that girl. She is thicker than a Hershey big block and most definitely, a FULL SEVEN. Pretty in the face, slim in the waist, hips, lips, pretty painted finger tips, big butt and pretty smile." He walks away shaking his head adjusting himself.

"Jocelyn, you should be ashamed of yourself dancing all up on Jimmy like that, you know men can't handle all of that pressure." Tashianna looks at Jocelyn and then Jimmy.

"Not a problem, I can handle it." He looks at Tashianna smiling then stares at Jocelyn with confidence.

"Oh, you can." She taps Jimmy on his arm then looks at Tashianna. "Look who is talking, I saw how you were dancing with that guy. You had your butt pressed into that man so close, he probably had an accident on himself."

Tashianna started laughing.

"You know I thought I felt something."

"Girl that is disgusting and you are too much."

"Tashianna why is he not with you now?"

"Jimmy, he is good looking and he can dance and he did ask me to go out to eat later but I had to say no."

"Why is that, you two look like you were having a nice time."

"I was Jocelyn and wanted to go but Haley's breath smelled like garbage and when he was talking to me I thought I would vomit."

"Wow, that is cold." Jimmy said.

"That is foul Tashianna. You could have mentioned to him in a nice way that he needed a breath mint instead of teasing the guy like you did and giving him false hope."

"Girl I was not teasing him and one breath mint wouldn't do it and I was not teasing him. Okay I am lying, yes I was but he was all on me."

"I wonder why with you and those skin-tight jeans you are wearing."

"It's not the jeans baby but all this fine tight body in these jeans." She looks at Jocelyn smiling.

"Tashianna you really are something and it would take the right man with the right touch to put a little water on that fire of yours."

"You better be glad Jocelyn saw you first or I would be driving you crazy. Oh, and just for the record I do not need a man to water me down, I need a strong man with a loving heart to bring the fire to match mine and after that it's on." Looking at Jimmy seductively then frowning and looks at Jocelyn. "Jocelyn, are you ready to go, I am hungry?"

"Actually I am ready to leave. Jimmy, will you take me home please?"

"Well since you asked me so nicely. I will be glad to."

"Okay, it's like that. You two just go ahead and leave me here by myself." Looking at Jocelyn and Jimmy frowning and then she smiles. "Jimmy I am just having fun you have to get use to me. Jocelyn and I have known each other for a long time and we are use to each other's ways."

"It's good to have a true friend Tashianna and hopefully Jocelyn and I will get to know each other better, step by step."

"We just met Jimmy but I am interested in getting to know you and I had a nice time tonight. Are you ready to go?"

"I am waiting on you."

All three stand up and see Alexandria and Theresa walking towards their table.

"Jimmy I am glad I caught you before you left and wanted to say thank you for being honest with me about Shawn."

"No problem but don't be too hard on the guy because he really does love you, this I know for a fact."

"Well he has a funny way of showing it." She looks at Jocelyn and Tashianna. "Anyway, it was nice meeting you two, and Jocelyn, don't let Jimmy get away."

"I won't and it was nice meeting you two as well."

"Same to you." Theresa said.

"Nice meeting you both." Tashianna said giving them a fake smile.

Alexandria and Theresa turn to walk away but Alexandria stops and turns around.

"Jimmy tell Raymond I hope he makes the team and I look forward to seeing him again, real soon." She and Theresa walk away shaking their butt hard.

"Those two are something else trying to shake that little butt and I know what is on Alexandria's mind. Jimmy, you tell your brother to call me before Delilah gets to him."

Jimmy is still looking at them walk away and he is thinking; *both of them are fine and their butts are not that little. If Shawn was not in the picture I would get with both of them.*

"Yeah okay. One thing is for sure I need to have a talk with him very soon.

"You really are something girl. Tashianna are you going straight home?"

"I am going to stop and get me something to eat and then go home, I will call you."

"Okay and stay out of trouble." She hugs Tashianna.

"Jimmy it was really nice meeting you and you take care of my sister and don't forget to tell your brother to call me. Alright give me a hug and don't grind on me either." Smiling at him.

"Jocelyn is right you really are something." He hugs her. "Take care of yourself Tashianna."

"Always, bye Jocelyn." She walks away but sees the guy that she was dancing with earlier.

"There is Tashianna's bad breath dance partner, poor girl."

"Having stank breath is an instant deal breaker but anyway enough about her, it's our time."

"Absolutely." She hugs and kisses him on the cheek then looks into his eyes and slowly kisses his lips.

"Very nice and as my Dad would say, yes Lord." He put his arm around her waist and they walk out of the club to the parking lot. He opens the door for her to get in his corvette and he drives away. Jimmy is holding her hand as he is driving.

"Jimmy where do you live?"

"I live in north Raleigh, Governors Club."

"Interesting, you must be rich. Take me to Chavis Heights which is where I live. Does that bother you?"

"I am far from rich and I live with my parents, Mr. James and Sherry Richardson. And no, where you live does not bother me and I can't believe you would even ask me that. Besides those apartments have been totally re-designed and the area is nice."

"Yes, the area is nice now wait, I know that name. Richardson Lexus is the biggest in the state and who has not heard of your Dad. He was a very popular R & B singer but now he sings gospel music and a preacher. Yeah you are rich and I did not mean to insult you but you never know about people."

"Jocelyn, I want us to get to know each other in a way that has nothing to do with material things but just being ourselves."

"I like that." She leans over and kisses him on the cheek.

He continues to drive and they reach Chavis Heights and drive up to her apartment building.

"Well this is home sweet home. I would invite you in but its late and I am going to bed."

"No problem but I would like to hear you sing."

"You will but not tonight now come and open my door please."

"No question." He gets out and opens her door and they walk to her apartment building and stop at the door.

"I had a very nice time with you tonight."

"So did I. Now, where do we go from here?"

"I will give you a chance to spoil me and I will spoil you back but we just need to take things slow, okay?"

RONALD GRAY

"We are on the same page, slow it's."

"Come here." She pulls him closer and they hug and kiss. Jimmy slowly pulls away but she pulls him back kissing him with more passion. "Good night Jimmy and call me when you get home." She kisses him quickly on the lips and walks inside the building.

He watches her every step and walks back to his car and drives away.

"She is fine. I wonder what Raymond and Shawn are doing?"

Chapter 17
Miami

Back at the night club in Miami Shawn, Raymond, Chris, and Anita are all sitting at their table.

"Raymond who is spoiling you back in Raleigh and don't lie?"

"Anita I have no need to lie but at the moment, there is no one."

"I find that hard to believe a tall fine looking guy like you and no woman is all up on you, yeah okay if you say so."

Shawn points to Raymond.

"The guy is all business; you are looking at the next Charlotte Hornets ball player."

"I appreciate the vote of confidence sir and I have not made it yet but it's only a matter of time which is why I am not seriously involved with anyone. It's important at this time in my life to concentrate on my game and career."

"It makes sense and I don't mean to give you a hard time or distract you but I will make it up to you if you let me." Anita said giving Raymond the warmest smile.

"No harm done. Are you ready to leave?"

"You read my mind buddy. Chris, are you ready to go?"

"As a matter of fact, I am. Anita are you ready?"

"Yes I am. Where are you two staying in Miami?"

"We are staying at the Four Seasons Hotel."

"First class one of the best in Miami very nice. Raymond I will ride with you and Shawn can ride with Chris and we can leave."

"Where are we going? Shawn said looking at both ladies but he already knew and just wanted to hear them say it to continue making a point to Raymond about what women really want.

Chris leaned closer to Shawn and kisses him on the cheek.

"To the Four Seasons Hotel and there is no need to even speak on the rest because you know what time it is."

"A lady after my own heart's desire." He looks at Raymond with a silly grin on his face. "Time to ride my friend."

All four walk out of the club and into the parking lot to the Ferrari.

"Nice car is it yours?"

"No, it's not but as soon as I make the team, the price of this car will be lunch money and anything else that I want."

"Raymond, you and Anita wait for us until I get my car please."

She and Shawn walk away and get in her 911 Porsche and Chris drives up to Anita and Raymond standing next to the Ferrari. Chris leans her head out of the window.

"Hey Raymond, other than looking good can you drive?"

"Nice car and I can show you better than I can tell you." He and Anita get in the Ferrari and both cars speed through the parking lot and on to the road toward the hotel.

Both vehicles are speeding down the road side by side having fun on the way to the hotel. They pull in front of the hotel at the exact same time slamming on the brakes getting everyone's attention. All four of them get out of the cars laughing handing the keys to the valet to park the cars. Anita walks with Raymond to his room and Chris walks with Shawn to his and both girls are carrying small purses.

The moment Chris and Shawn entered the room Chris drops her purse on the floor and they are all over each other kissing and grinding. They are kissing passionately while leaning against the bed when Chris steps back from him.

"I have been looking forward to this so sit on the bed and relax because we have all night if you can last that long." She picks up her purse and removes a small bag of weed then drops the purse back on the floor and holds the weed up for Shawn to see.

"You must have been reading my mind, let's roll it."

They both sit on the edge of the bed and roll a couple of joints and start smoking, laughing and playing. Their passions become more intense and they remove their clothes and Chris gets on her hands and knees on the bed but still has a joint in her mouth while Shawn is hitting it from the back. The sex last for about ten minutes and then Shawn kissed her and went to sleep.

Chris is looking at him sleeping and listening to him snoring and she is irritated because her sexual desires has not been satisfied.

"Well, I can handle it myself." She lays down and starts masturbating until climaxing then falls asleep.

In the meantime, Raymond is in his room with Anita and music is playing. Anita is laying on the bed on her stomach naked and Raymond is standing beside the bed in his silk boxers massaging her back with lotion.

"Your hands feel wonderful and you definitely know how to make a lady feel good. I could get use to this and you."

"Relax, I have not even begun to touch you yet but it's coming, very slowly as it should be." He takes his time and massages Anita's body all over front and back feeling and hearing her sexual passions increase which turns him on even more but he remains focused on giving Anita a great massage just to remember him by. Having sex is good but how often does someone say they had a great massage.

"Raymond I can't take this anymore." She turns over holding her arms out to him. "Come here, I want you so badly."

Raymond gets a rubber from his pants pocket then removes his boxers and Anita smiles then sits up and massages his dick with her mouth and tongue as slowly and passionately as he massaged her body with his hands. Not wanting him to cum just yet she stops and put the rubber on him and pulls him on top of her and he slides inside of her. Anita gently bites his lip licking it with her tongue and kisses him.

"Raymond a lady could fall for someone like you."

Chapter 18
Miami next day

The following morning Shawn is in Raymond's room with his bags waiting on him to pack so they can leave.

"Time to go lover boy the highway is calling us. You are one slow packer. Just throw the stuff in the suitcase so we can leave. Folding your clothes making them look pretty is a waste of time my friend. It's like sex, a little hugging, kissing and then you handle your business and go to sleep. All of that caressing and holding each other afterwards is time wasted."

Raymond looks at Shawn shaking his head and laughs.

"Shawn my man you have a lot to learn about women and I don't know how you keep a woman, especially as one as fine as Alexandria. It's not about just banging some woman but making them feel special before you even touch them."

"Yeah okay, I hear all of this same stuff from Alex and we already had this soap box conversation. Bottom line, again you do your thing and I will do mine."

"Works for me."

There is a knock on the door. Raymond opens it Chris and Anita are standing there wearing tennis shoes, shorts and T-shirts.

"This is a nice surprise. I did not think we would see you two again. Hi Chris, hi Anita." He moves forward hugging Anita and kissing her slowly on the lips as he caresses her hips.

"Excuse me but I know you two see me standing here while you are doing all this slobbering on each other and you should have done all of that last night." She purposely bumps into them as she walks into the room towards Shawn. "Hi Shawn and good morning to you." She hugs and kisses him.

Shawn is glad to see her because she was good in bed but he is not in the mood now for all this hugging and kissing. He has business on his mind but fakes a smile.

"Hi Chris and good morning to you as well." He kisses her again and smacks her on the butt a little harder than he should have on purpose just to irritate her so she will become upset with him and leave.

"Ouch Shawn did you have to smack my butt that hard, that hurt." She is staring at his eyes looking for any sign of a mean spirit.

"I apologize for that but I was just playing. It's great to see you." Inside he is happy because now he can leave quicker since she is upset with him.

Raymond and Anita step in the room.

"Shawn what are you doing to my friend?"

"All is well. Hi Anita, you both look great in your tight shorts."

"I could not agree more myself." Raymond walks up behind Anita and puts his arms around her waist kissing her on the neck and pressing his body into hers so she can feel him.

Anita feels Raymond's erection and last night's activities quickly comes back to her which makes her desire him even more now but she knew they had to go so she slowly turns around to face him.

"You are a tease Raymond because you know I desire to be in your arms all over again but you have to leave. So behave yourself."

"That is right Raymond keep your hormones in check and let her go." Chris said while smiling at them.

"All of this is great but we need to be going Raymond. Back to the working world my friend."

RONALD GRAY 86

"True that," looking at Anita and Chris. "Chris you and Anita have our contact information and I would like for us to stay in touch."

"Last night was wonderful Raymond and I will keep in touch but once you become a big time pro basketball player making all of that money and having ladies throwing themselves at you, you will forget all about me."

"I am not like that at all Anita." He pulls her into him and kisses her softly on the lips.

Shawn does not want to but he has to make it look good so he kisses Chris as well and firmly grabs her butt.

"That is much better and I like that Shawn. A warm but firm touch." She hugs and kisses him again. Call me when you get home please."

They all hug each other and walk out of the hotel room to the main lobby and check out of the hotel while the girls are waiting for them leaning against the Porsche 911. Shawn and Raymond hug and kiss the girls one last time saying goodbye and get in the Ferrari and drive away waving at them.

"Chris, how was your night and don't leave out any details?"

"Well, we smoked some weed and then fucked. Shawn was nice and the sex was good while it lasted, all fifteen minutes of it and then he kissed me and went to sleep. The quality was good but he needs more of a romantic touch and longevity. Now how was your night nosey person?"

Anita leans her head back and exhales then looks at Chris.

"Girl, last night with Raymond was beautiful. That man had music playing and he took his time and touched my body in places that I did not know was sensitive. He massaged my body top to bottom and front to back and the sex, girl I never screamed so loud in my life. Oh, he was so good."

"I am envious all ready. What time did you two go to sleep?"

"Sleep, I have not been to sleep. When the sun was coming up Raymond had me on the bed on my stomach and he had his..."

Chris waves her hand in front of Anita's face.

"Okay, I got it. That is too much information for me to visualize right now and I am still horny too."

They both started laughing and got in the car and drove away.

Chapter 19
On The Road

Shawn and Raymond are in the Ferrari speeding down the highway and Shawn is driving.

"Shawn, you are going to get a ticket if you don't slow this car down. I do want to get back home but in one piece and healthy. So slow it down."

"Relax I am covered and I never worry about tickets or the police. Raymond how badly do you want to play pro ball?"

Raymond is staring at Shawn like he is stupid because he knows how badly he desires to play.

"Stupid question. You know how bad I want to play ball. It has been my life dream for as long as I can remember and I will do whatever it takes to make that happen."

"Well, you can laugh about this if you want but I know a way that will guarantee you playing on any pro team that you want. Do you believe in roots?"

"Roots, yeah okay." He starts laughing and hit Shawn on his arm. "You must be crazy and watch too many movies. I don't play with that stuff. I don't believe in it and I don't mess with it either. What do you know about roots, shaking dust and all that foolishness?" He starts laughing again.

"Well I don't pretend to know how it works but I just know that it does and I do business with the most powerful root worker in the country. People come from across the country to see this man or whatever he is but he is very real."

"Even if I believed you. Why would you need a root worker?"

"Glad you asked and I can show you better than I can tell you." He slows the car down and pulls over to the side of the road.

"Shawn what's up why did you pull over?"

"Relax my friend I have something to show you, come on." They get out and walk to the back of the car and Shawn opens the trunk and moves some luggage around then opens a locked suit case. Lifts a towel up revealing some tightly wrapped packages.

"What is in the packages or do I want to know. I got a feeling something really bad is about to happen."

"Don't sweat it. You are looking at ten kilos of cocaine my friend. I have a connection straight from Columbia that I buy kilos for four thousand dollars and I can make sixty thousand per kilo. Do the math Raymond, you are looking at five hundred and sixty thousand dollars. Serious money my brother and how many cars would you have to work on back at the shop to make that kind of money"

Raymond put his hands over his face then stares at Shawn.

"Are you crazy? "He yells. "Oh man, we are going to prison. Lord have mercy you are crazy. No more basketball career, no more ladies. My Dad will kill me. Oh my God." He yells again.

Shawn steps towards Raymond and puts his hand on his shoulder.

"Raymond calm down and stop all that yelling like some woman. Everything will be fine so don't panic I am protected my friend." He reaches into his pants pocket and pulls out a small pouch and holds it up in front of Raymond's face. "This and Doctor Eyes will protect us. He is the root worker that I have been talking about."

"A small pouch will protect us from getting caught smuggling drugs and keep us from going to prison. Now I know you are crazy and doing your own drugs."

"Yeah, I know it all sounds crazy and I don't do drugs but I can assure you that Doctor Eyes and what he can do are one hundred percent real. But I will have to show you my friend. Come on get back in the car." Shawn quickly covers the drugs up and closes the trunk then he and Raymond get back in the car and he speeds off and is doing a hundred and sixty miles an hour.

"Shawn I don't know what you are trying to prove but slow this damn car down before you get us pulled over by the police or killed."

"Relax I know what I am doing and don't start that yelling again like some weak female. Just stay calm and watch."

A highway patrol car is parked on the side of the road and the Ferrari sped past it doing a hundred and eighty miles an hour. Raymond looked back at the police car and hits the side of the car door very hard with his hand.

"Oh God the police. Now we are going to jail because you want to do a hundred and eighty miles an hour in a car full of cocaine, we are finished."

"Perfect, this is just what I wanted. Now you will see the power of Doctor Eyes."

"My life is over. I can't believe you, damn I should have stayed home and practiced my jump shots."

Shawn laughs and slows down so the patrol car can catch up to them. The police car has its siren and lights on as it's following the Ferrari. Shawn pulls over to the side of the highway with the patrol car behind it.

"Relax and don't say a word Raymond and all will be fine. I will do all of the talking."

The patrol officer gets out of his car with his hand on his gun holster. He slowly approaches the driver side door and the window is already rolled down.

"Both of you keep your hands where I can see them. Let me see your driver license, registration and proof of insurance. And move real slow."

Shawn slowly reaches up to the visor and gets the registration and insurance card then gets his driver's license from his pants pocket and hands them to the officer. The officer looks at the registration and insurance card.

"This registration and insurance card say Steven Collins. You stole this car and now I know why you where speeding down the road." He quickly pulls his gun out.

"Officer this car is not stolen." Shawn said boldly and with confidence.

Two more police cars pull up behind them and two officers from each car get out with their guns in hand.

"Shut up Boy. I got you, now both of you get out of the car real slow and if you even breathe wrong, I will blow the back of your heads off. Walk really slow to the back of your car put your hands on the trunk, spread your legs and don't move!"

Shawn and Raymond get out and walk to the back of the car and assume the position but Raymond is so scared his legs are shaking. The officer pats Raymond down then Shawn and he feels the pouch in Shawn's pocket.

"I knew it! Boy, very easy, slide two fingers in your pocket and pull it out…real easy. Don't get shot in the head."

Shawn pulls the pouch out and holds it up.

"What is that, a drug pouch?"

"No it's not."

The officer grabs it.

"The powers of the eyes shall prevail. Doctor Eyes come to me." Shawn says while staring at the pouch.

"What the hell is in this pouch? It's getting really hot!" The officer screams and drops the pouch.

"I am burning up I feel like I am on fire! Get away from me Boy!"

The other officers rush over to help but make the mistake of touching him and this causes all their blood pressure to rise, which causes them dizziness and feeling like they are going to pass out. The police officers are now rolling on the ground screaming and yelling because they feel like their bodies are on fire. The officer who touched the pouch is still screaming but he points to Shawn and Raymond.

"You two get the hell out of here! Get away from me. My hand and body! Oh God I am burning up, ahhhhhhhhh."

Shawn picks up the pouch and he and Raymond get in the car and quickly drive away.

"Wow, I have never seen anything like that in my life. That must be some powerful stuff. Those cops thought they were burning up. Truly unbelievable like something from a horror movie."

"Well you saw it for yourself up close and personal but you haven't seen anything yet. So how bad do you want that basketball career, money and fame?"

"Really bad and after what I just saw I believe in roots and anything else. Let me get one of those root pouches." He is still in shock but manages to laugh.

"I knew you would so now do you want to go see Doctor Eyes and have him get you what you want."

"No question. Where is this guy anyway?"

"He is in South Carolina and we will stop by to see him on the way home and then everything is all yours my friend."

"You can't go any faster?"

"Now you are talking." Shawn presses the accelerator until the car is going two hundred miles an hour.

Chapter 20
The Following Sunday

It is Sunday morning church service and people are still walking in church. The choir is swinging and James is sitting in front of the pulpit. Also in church is Sherry, Jimmy, John, Jacob, Crystal, Katrina, Lewis, Veronica, Mary Stevens who is the mother of Lewis, Tashianna, Alexandria, Jocelyn, Rick Preston and Theresa. Shirley is also sitting next to James. The choir stops singing and sits down then Shirley walk to the pulpit.

"There is no other place that I would rather be than in the House of the Lord. Praise the Lord everybody!"

"Praise the Lord!"

"Giving honor to Jesus Christ, God manifested in the flesh to whom every knee shall bow and every tongue shall confess that Jesus Christ is Lord in this lifetime or the next. Every knee shall bow down before Jesus. Oh, I feel the spirit of the Lord in this place. Hallelujah! Help me choir sing this song."

The choir stands up and Shirley starts singing. She stops singing and the choir sits down.

"Lord Jesus, I thank you for your holy spirit now let thy will be done. Now at this time, I will present to some and introduce to others, Pastor, my brother and dear friend, Elder James Richardson. Let us all greet him by saying, "Praise the Lord!"

"Praise the Lord!"

Shirley sits down and James walks up to the pulpit.

"I greet you in the name of Jesus Christ God Almighty who died on the cross and God raised from the grave on the third day and he is coming back for the church. Not denominations, not skin color,

RONALD GRAY

95

not religious or church going people but those who are born again of the water and spirit. Let the church say, Amen."

"Amen!"

"If you would be so kind to turn with me in your bibles to the book of Matthew chapter ten. My subject for this morning is coming from one scripture, verse twenty-six." He read out loud. *"Fear them not therefore; for there is nothing covered, that shall not be revealed; and hid, that shall not be known.* And my topic is, *the Devil is a Master Deceiver.* It's a dangerous thing to desire something so badly that you will do anything to get it. There is God and the Devil. If you refuse to wait on the Lord, the Devil will deceive you. Open doors that appear Godly but are paths that will carry you to your destruction. Carrying pouches in your pocket, spitting on the floor, shaking dust and working roots can't help you either. The root man, root woman and all their believers and followers are going to hell if they do not repent and turn from their wicked evil ways. It's the spirit of the antichrist and you will burn. Oh, I know you don't like this but it's Holy Ghost Right. Say and do what you want but the word of God is and always has been right. Now somebody shout hallelujah!"

"Hallelujah!"

"Even now I feel that defiant spirit in this place. Somebody is saying, it worked for me. It may have for a season but that is the devil's trap and it's a set up people. Always remember what the devil gives you he can always take it away and more, your life! The devil is a Master Deceiver so chose this day who you will serve. Oh hallelujah, Sister Shirley sing for the Lord." He stepped back.

Shirley walks up to the pulpit. The choir stands and she starts singing. As the singing goes forth and the people begin to praise God even more you can feel the spirit of the church change from bondage to deliverance. The pastor does not have to preach anymore because God is having his way. When church is over James and Shirley are standing on the floor in the front greeting people. Others are leaving and some are standing outside in the front of the church talking. Lewis, Veronica, and Mary are standing close together talking also and Tashianna and Jocelyn are standing close together talking.

"It was very nice and I had a nice time with Jimmy, Tashianna. We talked and I am interested in getting to know him better. He is a very sweet gentleman."

"Okay all that is fine. He is nice, sweet, and a fine gentleman but get to the good part. Is he good in the sheets? Did he make you scream? Is he a ten-minute man roll over and go to sleep? Or did he keep a hump in his back stay up loving you all night long kind of a man."

"Girl, you are so nasty and your mind is lust filled and I can't believe you are talking like that after we just got out of church, you need prayer. Anyway, we just met and you know I did not sleep with that man."

"Okay I need prayer but who said anything about sleeping? I am talking about good hot strong clap, clap sex."

"Oh my God, you are so disgusting. Help her Jesus."

Jimmy walks up behind Jocelyn.

"Jimmy is behind you." Tashianna said.

"Hi Tashianna, Hi Jocelyn."

"We were just talking about you Jimmy."

"Hi Jimmy I was just telling her that we had a nice time."

"Absolutely." He kisses her on the cheek. "Do you have any plans for the rest of the day?"

"Not really. What do you have in mind?"

"We can go to the movies and then you can come home and relax with me and Tashianna you are more than welcome to come, and don't say anything smart."

"Well three is a crowd but sure if you insist."

Jimmy put his arms around Jocelyn's and Tashianna's waist.

"I said I would come with you, I didn't say we would have a freak party. So don't get any ideas."

"You really are something. I like you."

Lewis is walking towards them.

"Excuse me Tashianna can I speak to you for a minute please?"

Tashianna walks toward Lewis and they walk away.

"Do you have that address for me?"

"I am glad to see you too Lewis.' Shaking her head while looking at him but seeing the desperation in his eyes. "Yes, I have the address." She reaches into her dress pocket and pulls out a slip of paper and hands it to him. "You didn't get this from me and don't even mention my name, ever." Shc walks back to Jocelyn and Jimmy.

Lewis walks towards Veronica and Mary.

"Lewis, is everything all right?" Veronica asks.

"Lewis, you do look like you have a lot on your mind, is something bothering you? I can feel your spirit." Mary asks.

"Actually, I am fine mom but there is some business that I have to take care of and I need to drive to South Carolina to see a client."

"When do you have to leave?" Veronica asks.

"Right now, I will be back sometime late tonight."

"Lewis, can't you wait and go tomorrow? I wanted us to spend the day together. Go out some place nice to eat and just relax."

"That sounds very nice but I will let you two discuss this. Lewis, I will see you later." Mary kisses him on the cheek and walk away."

"Your plans sound very nice but we have to do it some other time. As bad as business is I need to see this client today. But when I get home." He pulls her into him. "I will show you how much I miss you."

Veronica pulls away from him.

"Lewis Stevens you should be ashamed of yourself. We are at church and I don't want you to want me just for that which seems to be all that is on your mind, business and you-know-what."

"Sweetheart we have been married for years and I still have the hots for you and I like it and so should you." He hugs and kisses her. "I love you and will see you late tonight." Lewis looks around and then pats her on the butt and walks away.

"I love you too Lewis." Veronica walks away with great sadness in her heart and spirit because for some reason she feels their life is about to change but not for the better.

Chapter 21
Doctor Eyes House

On this sunny afternoon, Shawn and Raymond are driving on this dirt road to Doctor Eyes old house and upon arriving they see a lot of cars parked around the house with license plates from various states with people sitting in the cars, standing outside and sitting on the front porch. Shawn parks the car and they get out.

"Man, look at all these people here ahead of us. We will be here all day and night. This guy must be something."

"The man is the best and we will not be here that long." He pulls the pouch out of his pocket and starts rubbing it between the palms of his hands. "Doctor Eyes, Doctor Eyes come to me." He put the pouch back in his pocket. "It will not be that long now."

"You are really into that stuff and what was that supposed to have been a phone call. Now what?"

"You will see so just be patient." They lean against the car.

Doctor Eyes walks up behind the Ferrari with a White Cane in his hand which is a cane for blind people or visually impaired because he has no eyes.

"Mr. Shawn Black." He walks closer to them.

Shawn and Raymond quickly turn around and the expressions on their face reveals the fear they have for this man.

"Doctor Eyes, where did you come from?" Shawn said trying hard not to show admiration and fear.

Doctor Eyes is standing a few feet in front of them as he is sliding his cane across the ground back and forth.

"Mr. Black, you brought your friend Mr. Raymond Richardson with you. Good, good the more desperate the souls the better."

RONALD GRAY

"How did you know my name?"

"I know all things Raymond. So, you want to play pro basketball but your dribbling and jump shot needs improving. Follow me gentleman." He is tapping his cane on the ground while walking ahead of them.

They reach the house and walk on the porch but the front door is closed.

"Doctor Eyes would you like for me to get the door for you?" Raymond said.

"That will not be necessary." He taps his cane on his feet. "Door obey me." The door opens by itself. "Come in gentlemen."

Shawn and Raymond look at each other and walk in behind Doctor Eyes. The house is very dark inside as they walk through the living room then come to another closed door.

"Door obey me." Again, the door opens. "Come on in you two." The room is dark but in the center, you can see a small table with chairs around it, a dresser with a lot of bottles with different colors of liquid in them and a small box on the dresser.

"Sit down you two." All three sit down and he put his cane on the floor. "No one talk at this point unless I speak to you and no matter what happens do not move from this table or you will die." He looks over at the box on top of the dresser. "Eyes come to me." The lid on the box opens and two eye balls float up and over to Doctor Eyes. He grabs them out of the air and put them in his eye sockets. The eyes are blood red with black veins.

The very sight of seeing two eye balls floating out of a box grip Shawn and Raymond with fear like they have never known and are reading each other's thoughts, run! But their bodies do not cooperate and are frozen to their seats as their legs are trembling and hearts are beating so fast as if they are about to go into cardiac arrest. Beads of

RONALD GRAY

sweat are pouring down their face. Doctor Eyes quickly slams his hand down hard on the table to get their attention and they both jump.

"Pay attention." He yells. "Raymond look into my eyes and give me your hands and do not move boy."

Raymond looks at Doctor Eyes with intense fear but he is at a point of no return now and he feels compelled to continue. Slowly Raymond slides his trembling hands closer to Doctor Eyes resting them on the table. Doctor Eyes grabs his hands firmly and rubs them then gets up from his seat and grabs a small bottle off the dresser, opens a drawer and pulls out a small necklace with a charm on it and he sits down. He hands the necklace to Raymond.

"Raymond this is for you and you need to wash your hands with the solution in the bottle twice a day and do not miss a day no matter what. Come back to see me before you run out. Wear this necklace always and never take it off. Any questions?"

Raymond takes the necklace then looks over at Shawn exhaling heavily and stares at Doctor Eyes.

"What happens if I miss a day of washing my hands with this stuff or don't wear this necklace one day?"

"You will instantly become very sick and your pains will only increase. Now, hold out your hands."

Raymond cannot stop his hands from shaking as he extends his hands to him. Doctor Eyes opens the bottle and pours some of the solution on Raymond's hands and rubs his hands roughly.

"Power of the Eyes obey me. Raymond Richardson, you will play pro basketball and you will be the best player in the entire NBA. Now put this necklace on your neck and tell no one about this or it will not work. Pay me one thousand dollars, now."

Raymond stands up and reaches into his front pants pocket pulling out some money and counts it on the table.

"I only have six hundred dollars on me."

"Shawn has two thousand dollars in his pocket don't you Shawn." Pointing his finger at him.

"Yes I do and I will not ask how you know." He stands up and pulls the money out of his pocket and counts four hundred dollars and lays it on the table then he and Raymond sit back down.

"Very good. Raymond always remember what was spoken and done here, remains here. Not a word to anyone. Shawn is there something more that I can do for you."

"No everything is fine with me and business is great."

"Of course it's, because I am in the driver's seat. Oh, by the way did you like what I did to the cops that stopped you on the highway. They became a little warm." He laughs then Doctor Eyes demeanor quickly changes to seriousness. "You two may leave now."

Raymond put the necklace on and stands up and put the bottle in his pocket then he and Shawn walk out of the house towards the car stopping next to it.

"Oh my God, I almost had a heart attack and died in that room when those eye balls started floating across that room and he put them in his eye sockets. I have never been so scared in my life, Lord have mercy." Raymond said while looking at Shawn.

"Yeah this man or whatever he is does some incredible things but you have not seen anything yet this is just the beginning. Money, power and fame are coming your way my friend. Time to ride."

They get in the car and drive away and for hours they ride in complete silence until Shawn notices the highway sign reading national park and takes the exit.

"Shawn what's up man where are we going now."

"Relax partner. It's Doctor Eyes power show off time."

"Yeah okay if you say so."

They drive to the park and see a basketball court and look at each other and smile then park the car and get out. Shawn opens the trunk and grabs a basketball and hands it to Raymond.

"I did not even know there was a basketball in the trunk. Where did it come from? Never mind I already know and all this stuff is beyond creepy but if I get what I want, then so be it."

"You said it. Now go to the court and do your thing."

For the next hour, Shawn watches Raymond dribbles and shoot jump shots from anywhere on the court like he has never done in his life. His dribbling speed and moves are incredible and not only does he make his jump shots but his leaping ability has increased to an awesome level. Raymond finally calms down and walks over to Shawn with a huge smile on his face while spinning the ball on one finger.

"Unbelievable Shawn. I did all that and it feels like a dream, wow."

"It's a dream, a dream come true for you. Wait until the NBA gets a look at you."

"Oh yeah, because here I come." He hugs Shawn and they get in the car and drive away. Raymond is sitting in the car just smiling knowing better days are ahead of him for sure.

Chapter 22

No Turning Back

It is night time Lewis Stevens drives up to Doctor Eye's house and people are still in their cars and sitting on the porch waiting to see him. Lewis gets out of his car and stands next to it looking around wondering how did his life get to this point to even believing someone can do all the things this man is supposed to be able to do and be here now.

"I can't believe I am here and all these other people. I must be crazy, out of my mind and very desperate."

The front door of the house opens and Doctor Eyes walks out and points at Lewis then waves at him to come forward. Lewis stares at Doctor Eyes then walks toward him and stands on the front porch staring at his eyes which are completely black and he can feel the coldness in his entire demeanor.

"Mr. Lewis Stevens it's good to see you sir. It's always good to see those who are willing to cross over to my side."

"I don't know exactly what that means but you must be Doctor Eyes and how did you know my name?"

"The spirit I operate in knew your name and so many others the day you were born. The rest is just me waiting until you all get frustrated and turn to me for help which I gladly embrace everyone that comes to me. Please come in Mr. Stevens and tell me all about how badly you desire to become a very successful attorney."

Lewis walks in the house behind Doctor Eyes and the door quickly closes by itself and Lewis looks back wondering did he make a big mistake by coming here. They sit down at the table and on top of it's a law book that Doctor Eyes opens.

"Do exactly as I say and how I say. Place your hands, palm down on top of the book and repeat after me. The law of the land is my God and it I will serve and obey"

Lewis almost wanted to bust out laughing because all of this seems so ridiculous but the demeanor of this man prevented him from doing it.

"The law of the land is my God and it I will serve and obey."

"Good." He reaches into his pocket and pulls out a ring and hands it to Lewis. "Put this ring on wear it at all times and never take it off."

Lewis is hesitant but there is an overwhelming compelling force in the room that moves him to do so. He puts the ring on and it feels warm but he can also feel a powerful presence from it which makes him emotionally excited.

"Now your career is in your own hands. Obey and you will become successful beyond measure. Now pay me fifteen hundred dollars and then get out of my house. I will see you soon soul."

He put the money on the table and walks out the house towards his car smiling while turning the ring around repeatedly on his finger. Lewis can feel the spirit of excitement building within and he does not care about not being able to explain it but he knows his life is about to change for what he desires. He gets in his car and drives away smiling.

Chapter 23
𝕿𝖍𝖊 𝕽𝖎𝖈𝖍𝖆𝖗𝖉𝖘𝖔𝖓 𝕳𝖔𝖒𝖊

James, Sherry, Jimmy, John, Jacob, Crystal, Katrina and Jocelyn are all sitting at the dining room table in the Richardson home enjoying dinner. Jimmy and Jocelyn are sitting next to each other and food is spread out on the table.

"Mrs. Richardson, thank you again for your wonderful hospitality and the food is delicious. You are a very good cook." Jocelyn said smiling at her.

"Thank you sweetie and I am glad someone appreciates my efforts and does not take it for granted." Looking at the family with a smirk on her face. "Husband and children."

"Baby you know we all adore you and your cooking every single day." James said while looking at Sherry with a mischievous grin on his face. "Yes Lord, I appreciate you with no question."

Sherry lowers her head smiling trying to hide her own facial expressions so her deep inner desires for her husband does not show and embarrass her.

"James don't start that we have a guest so behave yourself." Smiling at James with a twinkle of love in her eyes.

Jimmy looks at Jocelyn smiling and nodding his head.

"Yes Lord the spirit of appreciation is priceless."

"James see what you have done. Jimmy remember who you are." She looks at him frowning then smiles and looks at Jocelyn. "Jocelyn my son must really like you because he has not brought anyone home in a long time. You are a very attractive lady but I know there is so much more to you than just physical looks in order to have my son's attention."

Thank you mam. Jimmy is a gentleman and he treats me well and he is very direct to say the least which caught my attention quickly and he's very handsome."

Jimmy nods at Jocelyn then slowly slides his hand under the table caressing her thigh.

"I appreciate the compliment Jocelyn. Dad, Jocelyn has mentioned to me several times that she can sing but I have not heard her yet. Don't you think this would be a perfect time?"

"Jimmy, I can't believe you would put me on the spot like that." Looking at him scornfully but playfully then slides her hand under the table and pinches his hand and removes it from her thigh.

"With this family expect anything at any time Jocelyn but I would like to hear you sing." Katrina said looking at her smiling.

"Well thank you for the heads up but I also heard that you can sing as well." Jocelyn said.

"She can sing and is pursuing her career and I am very proud of her for that. Many people have dreams but they never really try to achieve them. All they do is talk." John said.

"Very true faith is powerful but you can't accomplish anything in this world by just talking about it and waiting for it to happen. You have to put in work and continue to work hard and smart until you reach your goals. Faith without work means nothing." Sherry said while looking at everyone in the room.

"Yes, you must work for the things that you want in life but God also said, *"no good thing will he withhold from them that walk uprightly."* Make Jesus your Lord and master and all good things will be added unto you, according to his will and time." James said with the authority of someone walking in the spirit of faith and obedience.

"Amen to that Dad." Jacob said while looking at James with admiration.

"True that. Faith without works is dead but anyway Jocelyn, I would love to hear you sing something." Katrina said and was trying to take the attention off her.

"So would I." Crystal said.

"Alright Jocelyn you have us all in anticipation so let us hear this gift that God has blessed you with." James said with eagerness in his tone.

Just then Raymond walks in the house and in the dining room.

"Family, I am home so show the brother some love."

"Hi Raymond, we missed you and I hope you had a nice trip. Now sit down and join us." Sherry said with as much love in her voice and eyes as any mother can have.

Raymond has been looking at Jocelyn since he walked in the room with lust in his eyes and everyone at the table notices it.

"What's up Raymond." Jimmy said looking at his brother with cockiness knowing he is staring at Jocelyn and all her beauty.

"Hi son, I am glad to see you and we have guest. Now sit down and stop staring at her." James said looking at Raymond feeling his strong instant lust spirit.

"Yes Lord, we have guest. Who is this beautiful lady sitting next to my ugly brother?"

"Raymond don't be disrespectful. This is Jocelyn, Jimmy's lady friend and she was just about to sing for us until you came in making all that noise. Now sit down and be quiet so we can hear her sing." Sherry smiled at him.

"Yes mam." He grabs a chair and sits down.

"Jocelyn the floor is yours." She waves her hand at Jocelyn.

Jocelyn looks at Jimmy giving him a fake smile.

"Jimmy I am going to get you for this." She clears her throat and starts singing the song, *Un-break My Heart* by Toni Braxton. You could hear a pin drop as she was singing and everyone's eyes were on her. Jocelyn's voice was incredible and you could hardly tell that it was not Toni Braxton singing. She was now standing up as she was singing because her emotions are so into the song. When she finished, Jocelyn sat down with a slight spirit of shyness because she knew they all are staring at her. Everyone started clapping their hands giving her many compliments. Jimmy was in awe of her to say the least.

"Wow, you said you could sing but I did not know you could blow like that, good Lord girl you can sing." Jimmy said.

"Jocelyn, you have a beautiful voice." Sherry said.

"Girl you can sing we need to talk" Raymond said while smiling at her.

"I am impressed. God has really given you a wonderful gift to sing and I pray that you use it for his glory."

"Thank you and coming from someone like you Mr. Richardson that means a lot me. You're R& B songs are still very popular and your gospel music is very nice."

"Jimmy, she is fine and has a voice waiting for a contract. You better hold on to her because I see star material my brother." Raymond said with sincerity and a little jealousy.

"Thanks Raymond but I see more than that. It's my desire to continue to spend quality time with Jocelyn so we can get to know each other better, spoiling her along the way."

"I am feeling you as well Jimmy and as far as you spoiling me, well time will tell." She put her hand under the table and rubs his leg and smiles at him.

"That is what I am talking about Jocelyn, make him put some work in." Katrina said, making a face at Jimmy but at the same time she is a little jealous because this girls voice is very good and she is receiving the admiration from her family that she wishes.

Everyone laughs and continue to talk and eat. About thirty minutes later Jocelyn squeezes Jimmy's leg under the table and they walk outside and sit on the front porch.

"You are very blessed Jimmy and you have a wonderful family in many ways."

"Thank you but I am sure some people think it is strange that in this day and time and at our ages we are all still living together, praying together, eating together and when we can and going to church together. But we still deal with family issues like all families do. What about your family? Are you all close?"

"Well I am originally from Harlem New York but I moved here some years ago to be with my Mom. She left the city years ago. Anyway, she became ill and I started taking care of her and along with that, we had some very difficult times financially, then my Mom passed away." She lowers her head and emotionally fights within to hold back the tears because the pain is still there.

Jimmy can feel her hurt and put his arm around her shoulders to comfort her.

"Wow, that is a lot to deal with Jocelyn. But what about the rest of your family? Where are they now?"

"My Dad died years ago because he refused to stop smoking cigarettes and he would constantly say, it's just cigarette smoke and I am strong. Well, he got lung and throat cancer. My two brothers and sister died in a car accident by a drunk driver. So, now it's just me and I know my voice is the ticket to a better life for me, better place to live, better life style and away from poverty. I really don't care about the fame or popularity I just love to sing and need a break so I can do my thing."

"Your story is heart breaking Jocelyn and if I could take away all of your pain I would but you are right about your voice being the blessing for you. I do admire your persistence to walk in your vision for your life. My sister is working on her music tracks so you should talk to her. Maybe the two of you could do something together but the person you really should talk to is my Dad. He still has serious connections in the business."

"Thank you and I will talk to your sister and your Dad but I will also greatly appreciate if you would talk to your Dad for me as well and put in a good word for me. You never know what may happen."

"No problem my entire family heard you sing so I know my Dad will do what he can to help you especially with me speaking on your behalf. But I need some persuasion." He leans over pulling Jocelyn closer to him kissing her on the lips.

Jocelyn wants to resist him but his touch warms her heart and stimulates her body at the same time so she welcomes his tongue and hands caressing her breast. Not wanting to but she slowly pushes him away and they both stand up facing each other.

"You are something. Jimmy I am glad we met regardless of what your Dad or sister can do to help me and I am very attracted to you but we need to take things slow and really get to know each other and not just sexually. Two people having sex is the easy part but I desire us to get to know the real person and that takes time."

"Not a problem and we can take it as slow as you want and I will show you the utmost respect in the meantime." He smiles and pulls her into him placing both of his hands on Jocelyn's butt kissing her.

Raymond walks out on the porch and sees Jimmy kissing Jocelyn and his hands on her butt and is thinking how lucky his brother is right now to have someone so fine next to him.

"Am I interrupting something?" He speaks with a voice a little louder than usual just to annoy them.

Jocelyn and Jimmy both look at Raymond and step away from each other and Jocelyn's face instantly becomes flushed. She is embarrassed by Raymond seeing Jimmy's hands all over her butt because she does not want him or any of his family members to think she is a tramp or gold digger. She turns her head away and looks at Jimmy giving him a mean look.

"Brother Raymond as usual your timing is bad. You can be late for work but on time for everything else."

"Better I came out than Mom or Dad and catching you two trying to get your freak on and do the nasty on the front porch." He shakes his finger at Jimmy. "Shame on you Jimmy for trying to corrupt this nice young lady to succumb to your nasty desires." He starts laughing.

"Hi Raymond and Jimmy is not nor could he corrupt me thank you very much." she turns to face Jimmy. "Jimmy, it's getting late so will you take me home please?"

"No problem."

"Jocelyn before you leave can I have a hug. I feel so, so lonely." He holds his arms out towards her and smiles knowing his words will irritate them both.

Jocelyn gives Raymond a very mean look.

"No, you may not hug her." Jimmy said with attitude.

"It was nice meeting you and your family Raymond but no I am not hugging you."

"What, no hug I am deeply hurt and emotionally traumatized behind this moment of rejection and I might need counseling now." Smiling.

"You need help Raymond."

"Bye Raymond."

Jimmy and Jocelyn walk away holding hands. He opens the door for her to get in but she gently places her hand on his chest looking directly into his eyes.

"Jimmy, you know I am into you but that was embarrassing for me. What your family thinks of me is important so I need you to keep the affection to a minimum when we are around your family or in public. Yes, I am very affectionate as well but there is a time and place for all things. Okay?"

"Consider it done."

As Jocelyn gets in the car Jimmy gently caresses her hips and closes the door laughing as he walks around to get in the car. Jocelyn punches him in the shoulder and he drives away laughing.

Raymond is still standing on the front porch staring out in space with his thoughts. He claps his hands smiling.

"She is fine but tomorrow is show time Doctor Eyes." He walks back in the house feeling confident and ready for a change.

Chapter 24
Lewis and Veronica

Its late but Lewis finally made it home. He just came out of the shower wearing a robe and the ring is on his finger. Veronica is on her knees next to the bed with a robe on praying. He stops walking and is standing directly behind her looking down at her butt.

"And Lord Jesus I thank you for your grace and mercy, Lord touch my husband and deliver him from darkness and into your Holy light, and..."

"Yeah okay, I am glad you are praying but you sure look good in that position on your knees and right now speaking of delivering, I want to deliver you over and over all night, so get up from there."

Veronica exhales to control her emotions but she stands up with a serious attitude and steps closer to Lewis.

"Truly I thank God for you Lewis and my salvation and I pray for you so hard. But you know I do not like you making sexual comments towards me so often. Lewis, is that all I am to you now, just your sex partner? You really hurt my feelings with your constant degrading of me." Holding back her tears.

"I do not mean to hurt your feelings Veronica and you know that I am seriously in love with you and what is so wrong with me desiring my own wife? Stop all the emotional negative drama. You women can be something else at times. If we men do not pay enough attention to you then you complain, if we are not sexually playful with you, then you complain. If we don't make love to you long enough, then you complain. It's always something."

"Of course I am glad that you sexually desire me and what wife would not want her husband to desire her. But I don't want you to

RONALD GRAY   115

see me just in that way. You put more emphases on this part of our relationship than anything else. More than your own salvation Lewis. I am a child of Jesus so respect me and get right, Lewis."

"All right, don't start that Jesus stuff, just calm down and take that robe off and get on the bed in that same position you were in when you were praying. On your knees but with your head down and ass up." He laughs knowing she is about to go off on him.

"What!" She yells at him then points her finger in his face. "Lewis, are you crazy? I told you I am not some hooker that you picked up off the streets. I am your Christian wife and I rebuke that foul spirit that you are operating in right now in Jesus name."

"Not again, I was just playing with you so don't take it so personal and relax with the rebuking me and Jesus stuff, I don't feel comfortable around you when you start talking like that. I am not the devil. Now come here." He gently pulls Veronica into him. "You will always be my sweetheart." He kisses her neck while firmly grabbing her hips.

Veronica pulls away from him frowning and stares at the ring he is wearing.

"Lewis where did you get that ring?"

"Why? It's just something that I bought for myself because I thought it looks nice and it fits me. Do you like it?"

"Actually, I don't like it at all, it gives me the creeps."

"Well don't think about it because in a few minutes my ring will be the last thing on your mind." He removes her robe letting it fall to the floor while admiring the nakedness of his wife's body. Lewis takes his time and begins kissing and caressing Veronica's body all over front and back while she is standing there leaning her head back enjoying his every touch.

Veronica can't help from climaxing from Lewis skilled hands and mouth but she can feel that something is not right about his ring, it feels so evil and it makes it difficult for her to totally relax with him. But things have been a little difficult for them lately and she does not want them to argue tonight about anything so she allows him to have his way. Veronica has never been into a lot of different sexual positions but for some reason she has made up her mind to allow Lewis to have his way this night and do whatever he wants to do with her. She feels compelled for some reason and does not know why.

Lewis was feeling his wifes uneasiness when he first started touching her but can now feel the spirit of relaxation in her. After her two orgasms, he carries her to the bed and intends to take advantage of the cooperation he is receiving. He makes love to Veronica gently and slowly like she is use to but after she climaxes again he is all nasty.

Veronica can't believe how she is allowing her husband to sexually treat her this night and is enjoying it for some reason. She sucks his dick with passion which she usually does not do and allows him to put her body in various sexual positions. Up against the bed, on her knees with him hitting it from the back, sixty-nine position and so many more. Lewis has her in the buck position and she is not complaining but taking it with pure lust.

"Oh Lewis, yes baby don't stop ohhhh Lewis. Ahhhhhhh, I am cummming, ahhhhhhh Lewis." Veronica grips the sheets hard as she explodes over and over but hearing herself is truly surprising. After holding each other for a while they get up and shower together and lay back down. Lewis is asleep but Veronica is quietly crying trying to figure out why this night was so different and wondering what has come over her but feels very strongly it has everything to do with the ring Lewis is wearing. Regardless of that she deeply loves her husband and gently rubs his shoulder and softly kisses him on the cheek. This wakes Lewis up and he kisses Veronica on the lips sliding his tongue in her mouth. This causes Veronica to instantly desire Lewis again and she rolls over on her stomach.

"Lewis, love on me like you really want to, please baby."

Her very words and actions excites Lewis too an instant erection and he slowly starts kissing Veronica from the neck down then back up to her butt kissing and licking it.

Arching her back seems like a natural reaction to Veronica because his touch feels so good and she was feeling extremely compelled to allow him to have his way. She rolled over on her back allowing Lewis to slowly lift her legs up and back.

"That's right Lewis, just like that, now fuck me." The very second, she allowed those words to come out of her mouth, shocked her to the core. Never in life did she talk like that but she wanted more. So Veronica grabbed his hand with the ring on it and started sucking on his finger with passion.

Lewis was shocked to hear his wife talk and act the way she is now but to say that it turned him on is an understatement. He slid inside her moving slowly at first but felt his wife's deep inner sexual desires to be dominated so he did what she wanted. They were no longer making love at this point but were trying to fuck each other into submission. An hour later after so many sexual positions and sweat Veronica was climaxing so hard and crying at the same time because she felt like she was going crazy. But Lewis was loving every second of it and all smiles.

Chapter 25
Lewis new beginning

Monday morning Lewis is at his law office sitting behind his desk wearing a new suit and singing to himself. Tashianna is sitting at her desk wearing a blouse, dress slacks and heels. She walks to Lewis office.

"Lewis, you have been in a good mood ever since you came in this morning. Singing and smiling to yourself, extremely happy. I can assume your trip went well."

"Yes, it did. A very weird but productive business meeting." He stands up smiling at her. "And I have you to thank for what I know will be a much better life for me and my wife. She is my sweetheart, with her sexy self."

"Well, I am happy for you Lewis but I do not want to hear anything about the business with you and that man. And you men are all alike you can always tell when you get some booty and that is why we woman have always been in control. Oh, the car may be yours but we hold the keys, always have, always will." She walks back to her desk purposely putting a little extra in her step knowing Lewis was staring.

A man walks in the office wearing a suit and carrying a briefcase.

"Yes, sir may I help you?"

"Yes, I need to see Mr. Stevens please."

"Do you have an appointment?"

"No I do not but it's extremely important that we talk. My name is Mr. Lambert."

"Okay, excuse me." She picks up the phone. "Yes, there is a Mr. Lambert here to see you...Yes Sir." She hangs up the phone. "Will you follow me please." She walks towards Lewis office door.

As Mr. Lambert is walking behind Tashianna staring at her he is shaking his head and whispers to himself.

"This girl is fine and got body."

Tashianna heard him but smiled and kept walking. She knocks on Lewis door and walks in with Mr. Lambert behind her.

"Mr. Stevens this is Mr. Lambert."

He stands up behind his desk.

"Mr. Lambert please have a seat. Thank you Tashianna."

"Yes Sir." She walks out closing the door behind her and sits back down at her desk.

Mr. Lambert is sitting down holding the briefcase in his lap.

"I will be very brief. My name is not Mr. Lambert but I am representing a client who is in jail on a murder charge and he has no bail. All my client desires at this point is for you to get him a bail."

"Without knowing the details to his case even if I could get your client a bail it would be very high."

"The price does not matter how you do it does not matter but the time factor does. My clients name is Todd Baxter." He opens his briefcase and pulls out a stack of money and lays it on the desk. "If you can get Mr. Baxter a bail in one week I will pay you twenty thousand dollars, ten now and then when the job is done."

"Interesting and I know of Mr. Baxter and his case. A wealthy business man and suspected drug dealer accused of killing a well-known call girl. I know the prosecutor handling his case and I will see what I can do."

Mr. Lambert grabs his briefcase and stands up.

"Very good and I will be in touch. If you can get this done there are many clients I can send your way."

Lewis stands up.

"I would appreciate the business. If you stop by my assistant's desk she will give you a receipt for the money."

"Thank you but there is no need for the receipt. I know the money was given to you and you know, that is all that matters."

"This is true Mr. Lambert." He stares at him and then shakes his hand. "I will walk you out. He grabs the money off the table and they walk out of his office and Mr. Lambert leaves. Lewis stands in front of Tashianna's desk and holds the money up so she can see it. She looks up and smiles

"That is a very nice sight that any women would enjoy seeing. So, I can assume that you have a new paying client."

"You assume correctly my dear. Twenty grand just for a bond reduction. He gave me ten now and the other ten when it's done. I could hug and kiss you for your help because I know Doctor Eyes is behind this and I have you to thank."

"Yeah okay but I told you do not mention that man's name to me please and you want to hug me anyway which is understandable because I got it going on like that." She stands up and walks closer to Lewis slowly turning around in front of him showing off her great figure. "You keep your root doctor business to yourself. Don't tell me anything and when you get more money I would like more money, Lewis."

Lewis kisses the money and holds it up in the air then quickly grabs Tashianna pulling her against his body picking her up turning around several times smiling and laughing. Because of his excitement and without really thinking while twirling around he gently kisses Tashianna and she kisses him back pressing her body into him even more and Lewis wraps his arms around her body tighter allowing his hands to slide down her hips and butt caressing it. He quickly snaps out of his lust moment and put Tashianna down then backs up.

"I am truly sorry for what just happened it was just me getting caught up in the moment. God, I can't believe I just kissed you, damn what is going on with me." He lowers his head feeling instantly remorsefully for his actions.

Tashianna waves her hand in his face.

"Relax Lewis and don't sweat it dear. I fully understand you got caught up and all excited." She is looking down between his legs sees the contours of his erection then looks at his face smiling. "Yeah, you got real excited. Okay, we hugged and kissed, so what it happens in life. It never happened so just relax and go make us some more money please."

Lewis looks at Tashianna smiling then counts one thousand dollars and hands it to her.

"No smart comments or questions asked please just accept the money.

She looks at the money and then at Lewis smiling.

"No problem! My mom didn't raise no fool. Thank you, Lewis." She takes the money and put it in her pants pocket. Kisses Lewis on the lips while gently caressing his erection then sits back down at her desk. Lewis walks back to his office adjusting himself along the way and closes his office door behind him.

What they did not know was Veronica wanted to surprise Lewis with an office visit but she saw them hugging and kissing from outside through the glass. She walked away with tears flowing from her eyes, angry and heartbroken.

Chapter 26
Raymond's Time

Raymond, Jimmy, John, and Shawn are at the park early in the morning standing close to the basketball court and a few people are already on the court playing ball.

"We should be at the shop working, not at the park. I can't believe I let you all talk me into this. Oh, and Jimmy thanks a lot for telling on me, Veronica is very upset with me because of you." Shawn said.

"You can't blame me because you got caught sneaking off to Miami and I was caught in the middle of you and Raymond's conspiracy. Speaking of which, Raymond was it worth all that driving going to Miami?" Jimmy said.

"As our preaching Dad would say, "Yes Lord", in more ways than one my brother." Raymond said looking at Shawn smiling.

"All this conversation is not putting any money in my pocket. I have a Z06 Corvette with my name on it. So, Raymond do what you are going to do so I can get back to work."

"No problem." He rubs his necklace.

Two guys on the basketball court stop playing and one of them walk towards Raymond and yells.

"Hey, it's your game man."

"It's show time." He walks on the court rubbing his necklace. "Doctor Eyes come to me."

It's four on four on the court. Jimmy, John and Shawn see Theresa in her Lamborghini and Alexandria with her driving up to the park close to the basketball court.

"Hey Shawn it's time for you to do the Keith Sweat and start begging and suck up really good." John said, pointing toward the Lamborghini.

"Amen to that, romance Shawn romance." Jimmy said smiling. Alexandria and Theresa get out of the car walking towards Shawn wearing heels and short tight dresses.

"Lord have mercy that don't make no sense." John said while staring at the girls.

"Relax John I am driving all of that." Shawn said looking at Alexandria smiling.

The girls stop walking close to Shawn while Raymond is playing ball.

"Hi Alexandria, Hi Theresa. You two look great." Jimmy said.

"Hi Jimmy, John." Alexandria said smiling.

"Hello." Theresa said.

"Hello yourself and Jimmy is right. You two look great." John said while staring at Theresa.

"Hi Theresa, Hi sweetheart." Shawn hugs Alexandria and tries to kiss her but she pulls away from him.

"It's not that simple Shawn and you know it so don't act like everything between us is just perfect because it's not. I am still very upset with you and we need to talk."

"We will talk as soon as we check Raymond out on the court. I am glad that you came out here. I have missed you and you know that." He kisses her.

They all start watching Raymond play and he is playing like a pro with serious years of skills on the court. Fancy dribbling, fast breaks to the basket, making all his jump shots from anywhere on the court. He does a three sixty and dunks the ball hard.

"Wow, is that my brother playing like that." Jimmy said.

"I knew he was good but not that good. Jordan, there is another star on the rise and his name is Raymond Richardson." John said with much pride in his voice.

"He must have really been practicing because the brother is good." Shawn said knowing the truth.

"He is definitely pro material right Alex?" Theresa said looking at Alexandria smiling.

"He truly is and in more ways than one." She looks at Shawn hoping her statement made him jealous and sticks her tongue out at him.

Raymond continues to play exceptionally well and with every move that he does on the court it only seems to improve each time. The game is finally over and one of the guys Raymond was playing with walks over to him.

"Brother, you did not have to totally embarrass us like that and I know just like everyone else on this court knows that you play pro ball somewhere."

"I appreciate the compliment but I don't play pro ball at least not yet but I will. It's only a matter of time."

"Brother, you got the skills and then some to dominate the court anywhere. Later to you and hope to see you on TV one day. What is your name?"

"My name is Raymond Richardson and thanks again for the game." He walks away towards his brothers. "So, what do you think family? Do I contact Michael Jordan so he can sign me?"

"Raymond after seeing you just now on that court, it's show time and we all know it. Do what you have to and call the man or whoever so you can get paid." Shawn said with eagerness.

"Hi Raymond, you did look really good out there." Theresa said.

"Yes, he did, Hi Raymond." Alexandria said giving him a look that said, if only you knew.

"Ladies, Hello to both of you. Thank you and you two look great just standing there wearing those tight short dresses. You could get somebody hurt." Raymond looked at them back and forth but he is staring at Alexandria visualizing the things he would like to do to her over and over. Then he turns towards his brothers. "Jimmy and John what do you think?"

"My brother you were great on that court and I don't know how you got so good so fast but whatever you did it worked, so keep doing it." John said.

"The only thing that I can say is brother make that call." Jimmy said patting him on the shoulder.

"Yes Lord." Raymond said looking at his brothers and starts laughing.

Shawn's phone beeps because of a text message sent to him. He looks at it and frowns.

"It's been great but I have to go and I will see you all back at the shop." He looks at Alexandria knowing what is coming.

"Shawn, we have to talk." Alexandria said moving closer to him. "Whatever it's can wait because your business matters are not more important than our relationship so you better not leave me now and I mean it." Staring at him with coldness in her eyes.

"You are right but there are priorities and this is very important and I have to go, I love you." He hugs and kisses her then steps away pats Theresa on her butt then runs towards his car.

Alexandria turns looking at Shawn running away and yells at him.

"Shawn come back here. I will not forgive you for this." She turns back around with tears in her eyes. "Damn him."

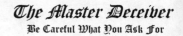
"Alexandria I know you are upset and you have every right but I know Shawn means well and he does love you." Jimmy said.

"Yeah right, sometimes I wonder just how he feels about me."

"I don't want to seem rude but the body shop is calling me and I have work to do, we all can't be basketball stars." John said.

"Very true and we have work to do. Raymond, I loved the show my brother you know that but until you get on the team, it's time to go and do some car work." Jimmy said.

"Thanks for the support. You and John go ahead I will be behind you."

Jimmy looks at Alexandria, then Raymond knowing what was on his mind and giving him a mean look.

"We have work to do Raymond so don't take all day. I am sure you will make the team but you have not made it yet."

"The team is made and I said I will be there, Daddy."

Jimmy looks at Raymond and points his finger at him then looks at Alexandria again. He and John walk towards the car and drives away.

Theresa steps closer to Raymond.

"Raymond, you played very well today and you should have no problem making any team. Anyway, I think Alex wants to talk with you so I will be over by the car."

"Thanks I appreciate that."

Theresa kisses him on the cheek and walks away with Raymond staring at her.

"Do you see anything that you like?" Alexandria said with attitude.

Raymond turns to look at her.

"Do you? Walk with me to my car if you don't mind. What is on your mind Alexandria?"

"I think you already know. I don't want to put you in an uncomfortable position but to be very direct I am very interested in you and desire to get to know you better."

"You are right on both accounts and I am also interested in you as well but there is my brother and Shawn your man. It's a tough situation for you and me."

"So are you saying no and we should leave things as they are."

They reach his corvette and stand next to it as he looks at her.

"Yes, we should leave things as they are but I don't want to and it's far more than just a physical thing, we can get that anywhere. I like you and want us to become closer."

"I am glad you feel that way and you are right it's far more than physical but we do have to be careful. So, where do we go from here Raymond?"

"Well, right now I have to go to work but we will make time for each other and see how things go."

"I like that but before you go can I have a hug?"

"No problem but I am still a little sweaty."

"I don't care."

Raymond steps closer and hugs Alexandria then kisses her on the cheek and steps back while she is staring at him, she pulls him into her and slowly kisses him on the lips and he wraps his arms around her waist caressing her back and butt. Alexandria can feel his erection growing and pressing into her. Never has she desired someone so badly both emotionally and physically and if they were in the right place it would be on.

"That was very nice. I have not been kissed like that in a long while. Shawn definitely does not do it."

"It only gets better." He kisses her on the lips and get in the car rolling the windows down. "By the way, I am not a twenty-minute man." He drives away.

Alexandria walks toward Theresa who is leaning on her car.

"I saw you kissing and pressing your body all into him. Girl, you are playing with fire."

"I know but there is something about him that is very appealing to me and he can kiss. The chemistry between us is incredible."

"Yes I can see that. You two were all over each other and I am jealous but you are still playing with fire."

"And you know what, as soon as I get him in bed I am going to let him do whatever he wants to me, many times and over. Oh, I want him."

"You are nasty but keep me informed. He is so fine."

"Fact is after Raymond and I spend some quality time together in and out of the bedroom, you can join us Theresa." Smiling at her.

"Yeah, right. We both know if you get him in bed you will not share him with me or any other women, so keep it real."

"I really thought you knew me better than that. Yes, Raymond does interest me greatly but we have been friends for years and we can share him."

Theresa just stares at Alexandria not sure what to really think.

"Okay if you say so."

They both laugh and get in the car then Alexandria rubs Theresa's leg and kisses her on the lips.

"Let's go back to my place."

Theresa did not expect that from her but it only increases the suppressed sexual desires she has for Alexandria.

"Okay!" She kisses her and they drive away.

Chapter 27
The Body Shop

Jimmy, Raymond, Shawn and John are at the body shop working on cars and the bay doors are up and music is playing. Shawn and Raymond are working on one car together and John and Jimmy are working on the other. Raymond stops working and looks at Shawn.

"Shawn, did you see how I played today. It was unbelievable, it was like I could do no wrong on that court homie my dribbling and jump shot were outstanding. My hands felt like they were magic, Charlotte Hornets here I come."

"Raymond, I was standing there watching your every move and yeah you played like a pro. You know who you have to thank for it. I told you the man is the best but this is only the beginning, good times and pay day is coming real soon."

"I owe you Shawn, big time." Stepping closer he shakes Shawn's hand smiling and feeling great but he still wants to get with his girl. Then he walks toward Jimmy and John. "My brothers what do you think of the show that I put on today at the park?"

"Again, you were great Raymond almost too good but I told you to call Mr. Collins and set a time so he can check you out. You must have had a great time in Miami." Jimmy said.

"It was a trip that I will never forget."

"My brother, you were fantastic out there and it looks like your dream is about to come true but I wish mine would. A fine looking well paid brother like me with this bumpy acne skin. I hate it and would do anything to have smooth skin." John slaps the top of the car he is working on with his hand and then walks to the bathroom.

Raymond and Jimmy watch John walk away both feeling his heartache then Raymond looks at Jimmy

"Let me go talk to him and at least give John some encouraging words." He walks toward the bathroom.

John is inside putting some cream on his face when Raymond knocks on the door and walks in. John gives him a look of total disgust.

"What do you want Raymond? I am not in the mood for your stupid comments so you can turn around and walk right out the door just like you walked in.'

"Relax my brother I just need to talk with you about something but you have to give me your word that this conversation goes no further because this is very serious and it can help you." He stares at John.

John turns to look at Raymond trying to decide if he is running some type of game on him but he sees the seriousness in his eyes, so he extends his hand out to him.

"You have my word. So now talk to me." They shake hands.

"I had some help with my game. Do you believe in roots?"

"Come on man don't insult me with this and who has not heard about it? No, I do not believe in that garbage. Why do you ask?"

"I can't go into details about it and can only say so much no matter what. I saw a man in South Caroline on the way back from Florida. He is a root worker and is truly unbelievable. He is responsible for my show on the court today. Anyway, you saw my game my brother. I am good but not that good." He reaches in his pocket and pulls out a business card and hands it to John. "This is his name and address. Go see him because I know he can help you concerning the acne on your face and so much more. But remember we never had this conversation." He pats John on his shoulder and walks out of the bathroom towards Jimmy.

Jocelyn drives up in front of the body shop and gets out the car wearing her work uniform.

"Wow, I have to talk to her." Shawn said and steps toward Jocelyn.

Raymond is staring at Jocelyn then looks at Shawn quickly grabbing his arm.

"Slow your walk Shawn, you are a little late my friend."

Jimmy points towards Shawn.

"Slow your roll dog in heat, she is already spoken for." He mean mugs Shawn then walks towards Jocelyn smiling.

John walks out of the bathroom and sees Jocelyn.

"A Red Lobster uniform never looked so good. She could have been mine. That girl is fine."

Raymond and Shawn turn and stare at John and say at the same time.

"Yeah right."

Jimmy is standing in front of Jocelyn.

"Hi, gorgeous Red Lobster should pay you extra just for wearing that uniform and to say you look good in it's an understatement. This is a nice surprise."

"Hi Jimmy I could get use to your compliments, come here."

"Absolutely." He moves closer hugs and kisses Jocelyn.

"Stop attacking that girl like that Jimmy." Raymond yells and then laughs.

Jocelyn steps back from Jimmy and laughs as well.

"I am on my lunch break but I just wanted to see you and bring you something."

"It's a nice surprise and I thank you, what did you bring?"

"I brought you and the others some food from work." She walks to the car and pulls out some Red Lobster bags and hands them to Jimmy.

Jimmy takes the bags and turns around holding them up.

"Hey guys lunch time."

All three of them quickly walks towards Jimmy. Raymond takes the bags.

"Hi Jocelyn and thank you for the food. You look great even in that uniform, Jimmy you better treat her right."

"Hi Jocelyn and thanks for the food. If this guy mistreats you, let me know and I will take care of it for you." John said while looking at her up and down.

"You are welcome for the food and I will let you know if he mistreats me. This must be Shawn the man that did not tell his lady that he was going to Miami for the weekend, shame on you Shawn."

"Oh, so you know about that? I wonder from who." Looking over at Jimmy. "So, big mouth introduce me to your lady friend, who is truly lovely."

"My pleasure, Jocelyn this is Shawn my best friend and business partner, Shawn, this is Jocelyn, the finest waitress in the state with a voice to match."

Shawn steps forward and shakes her hand.

"It's nice to meet you Jocelyn and you are very beautiful."

"Nice to meet you Shawn and thank you. I met your girlfriend at the club and she is very pretty. You have some sucking up to do to get on her good side again."

"You are right and that is my goal. Thank you for the food Jocelyn." He, John, and Raymond wave bye and walk in the shop and begin eating.

Jimmy turns to them and yells.

"Save me some food greedy people."

"Well, it has been nice to see you but I have to get back to work."

"Thanks again for coming by to see me and for bringing the food which was not cheap." Reaching in his pocket he pulls out a wad of bills. "Please allow me to pay for it."

Jocelyn smiles and places her hand on top of his.

"I appreciate the offer but it's not necessary and what I want from you and desire to give you all the money in the world can't buy, friendship! Come over for dinner and bring Raymond with you because Tashianna wants to meet him and we can spoil each other."

"I look forward to it and by the way, I don't have a curfew."

"Interesting thought." She hugs and kisses him and they walk towards her car holding hands. Jimmy opens the car door for her and she gets in and starts the car then sticks her head out of the window waving her finger at him. "Come here you."

Jimmy steps closer to the car.

"For you, absolutely."

Jocelyn sticks her head out of the window further and puts her hand around his neck pulling him closer slowly kissing him.

"Bring a toothbrush." Smiling at him she drives off.

Just as Jocelyn drives away Sherry drives up in her Lexus, Katrina is in the car with her and a roll back tow truck is behind them with a new Z06 2016 Corvette on top. James is in the passenger seat of the tow truck. Shawn, Raymond, and John stop eating and walk towards Jimmy. Sherry and Katrina get out of the car as James and the driver of the tow truck get out as well. Jimmy walks closer to Sherry.

"Hi Mom, what are you, Katrina and Dad doing here?"

"I will let your Dad tell you." Sherry said.

"John come over here." Katrina said waving at him.

James walks closer to them.

"John come over here and hurry up because I am in a hurry Son."

"Hello Mrs. and Mr. Richardson, Hi Katrina." Shawn said.

"Hi Shawn, it's good to see you again you haven't been to the house in a while." Katrina said smiling at him.

"Mom, Dad hi. What's up Katrina." Raymond said.

"Dad, that's my Corvette." John said with much excitement in his voice. "Hi Mom, Katrina." Smiling at them.

"It's your car now Son. Your mom and I took care of the paper work for you and the down payment. The car is all yours and you better drive like you have some sense."

John starts dancing and jumping up and down.

"Yes, yes." He hugs James. "I love you Dad, thank you so much."

"Yeah, yeah I know you do."

"What about my hug Son, I helped with the car and far more important, I helped bring you into this world, you spoiled brat."

John quickly hugs Sherry.

"I love you to Mom." He looks over at Katrina and walked over and picked her up kissing her on the cheek. "Sis, I love you too."

"Stop boy. John put me down. Mom, Dad, get him."

John put Katrina down and walks over to the tow truck and the driver is moving the car off the truck and James walks over to the truck. The driver is moving the car off the truck and James walks over to the truck as well, pulling some keys out of his pocket handing them to John.

"Son listen to me."

"Yes sir."

"Your Mom and I got this car for you because you have always been a hard worker and very responsible so don't change now. The ten grand that you were going to use as a down payment, hold on to it. The insurance is in your name and it's paid up for one year, now I have to go."

John is staring at his Dad and shakes his hand.

"Thanks a lot Dad."

Sherry walks over to James.

"John, enjoy your car and drive safely because that car is very fast, so easy on the gas pedal Son."

"No problem Mom and thanks for everything." He hugs her.

The Corvette is on the ground and John is looking at the car smiling. The driver of the tow truck walks over to James.

"Mr. Richardson, are you ready to go sir?"

"Yes I am."

The driver gets in the tow truck.

"James will you be home for dinner?" Sherry said.

"No, I will be home a little late because I have to go to church and seek God in prayer about some things. I will eat later." He hugs and kisses Sherry. "I will see you tonight." Then turns and looks at John. "Hey John, no speeding tickets."

"No problem Dad."

James and the driver get in the tow truck and drive away. Sherry walks over toward Katrina, Raymond, Shawn and Jimmy who are standing close together talking.

"Well, it has been nice but Katrina we have to go baby and your Dad will be home late so we can go shopping, fat stores here I come. I hate being fat, truly hate it."

"I want a better voice more than anything and I have been praying but it aint happening." Katrina said while holding back tears.

Raymond looks at Shawn and Shawn nods his head. Raymond steps towards Sherry.

"Mom I need to talk to you." They step away. "We never had this conversation but I know someone who can help you." He reaches into his pocket and pulls out a business card and hands it to her. "Forget shopping go see this man because I know he can help you, he is very good."

Sherry looks at the card then stares at Raymond.

"I have heard of this man and I know people who have been to him and he has helped every one of them but Lord have mercy son." Staring at Raymond, then looked at Katrina. "Katrina time to go."

"I am ready." She walks toward Sherry then looks over at John. "Bye John."

John can't help but look at the Corvette with inner anticipation of getting behind the wheel. But he looks up at Katrina and Sherry.

"Bye Mom and thank you for all that you and Dad have done."

"Just be careful in that car son and I will see you all later."

Shawn, Jimmy, John all say bye. Sherry and Katrina walk to the car and get in.

"Mom are we still going shopping?"

Sherry was deep in thought thinking about what she would do.

"No, we are driving to South Carolina for you and me, no questions asked and we never took this trip." She drives away.

Raymond, Shawn and Jimmy are talking then Raymond walks over to John.

"My brother this is a dream come true now if I can just get rid of this acne face of mine."

"You can, get in your new car and go see the man we talked about."

"Oh yeah, I got so excited about the car that I forgot about that, see you later." John smiled at Raymond then got in his car and drove away spinning tires and laughing.

Raymond walks toward Jimmy and Shawn.

"Where is John going in such a hurry?" Jimmy said.

"He said he had some place very important to go."

"Yeah well, I just hope he slows that car down. This has been some day and it isn't over yet." Looking at Raymond then the shop. "There better be some food left." He said grinning.

The three sit down in the shop and finish eating then Shawn and Raymond walk away and Shawn steps closer to Raymond speaking quietly to him.

"Raymond are your Mom and John going to see Doctor Eyes?"

"On the road as we speak."

"Good, really good. It's just the beginning my friend, just the beginning."

They slap hands and walk back to the shop and continue eating.

Chapter 28

The Switch

Jimmy was home in the backyard with Raymond watching him practice. Jimmy has been doing some deep thinking about him and Jocelyn who he really likes a lot but something was bothering him and he could not figure out what it was for a while until he prayed about it. He knew deep down in his heart that he would not be the man for her future or she would not be the woman for him. He knew this woman was a very gifted singer and it was only a matter of time until she got her business break and be very busy singing and traveling all over the country. This is not what he wanted for his life and in a lady but he would never want to do anything to hold her back. He laughed to himself. The fact is with Raymond's path of being a pro athlete and Jocelyn's a professional singer they would be a better power couple. Wow I must be losing it to let her go so easy but although it would bother me to do so, it would bother me a lot more to live a lie just to have someone in my life. Anyway, plans were made for he and Raymond to go over Jocelyn's place for dinner tonight and Tashianna will be there as well. He had to admit that she was extremely attractive from head to toe and he is drawn to the fire in Tashianna's personality but would not admit it to himself until just now. He shook his head and laughed because life can be something. He looked at Raymond practicing and thought about how badly he wanted to play pro ball and how he has dedicated himself to his life goal. He loved his brother and wanted the best for him.

"Raymond, stop playing for a minute I need to talk with you about something very serious my brother."

He bounced the ball over to him and sat down wiping his sweaty face with a towel.

"What's up my brother and make it quick because you know I have to get in my practice." Laughing as he said it but when he looked at Jimmy he saw the seriousness in his eyes. "Jimmy, talk to me what's up man. You got something you need us to handle? Somebody giving you hard time? Talk to me."

"No, I appreciate the love but it's nothing like that. Just here me out okay."

"No problem."

Jimmy went on to explain everything to him in detail about his feelings for Jocelyn and what he thought would be best for her life and Raymond's life as well. All Raymond could do is just stare at Jimmy thinking this was a joke but when he saw the tears come to his eyes as he was talking, he knew then that he was very serious.

"Wow Jimmy, I don't know what to say to all of this. I do know that I am not having no falling out with my blood brother over no female so I can't step to her like that after you two have already been together. She is just a female but you are my brother for life."

"Thanks my brother and much love. I know all of this sounds crazy and I appreciate the respect you know that but even if you don't step to her I am calling it off between us. And no, we have not been together sexually if that is what you were talking about."

At the exact same time, Jocelyn was having the same conversation to herself about her feelings for Jimmy but thinking about Raymond so after a while she called Tashianna and told her everything about how she was feeling. Tashianna was shocked but oddly she has been thinking some things about Jimmy but would never betray Jocelyn like that. So she agreed to still come over tonight for dinner and see how things went.

It was very hard for Jocelyn to do but she called Jimmy and told him everything and he did the same. They both agreed this was for the best regardless if her and Raymond connected or not. She mentioned to him that Tashianna would be calling him to talk before they came over and that she was going to call Raymond as well so things would not be so very awkward when all four of them get together tonight.

Jimmy and Raymond arrived at Jocelyn's place and even though they talked in detailed beforehand it was still awkward when Jocelyn opened the door. She hugged Jimmy.

"Hi, Jimmy come on in." She was dressed casual but still looked great. Jimmy walked in and Tashianna was standing there with some conservative shorts on and a nice top but looked great. She hugged Jimmy as well.

"Hi Jimmy."

Raymond and Jocelyn locked eyes as he stood in the door way not sure of exactly what to say or do but the chemistry between them said it all.

"Hi, Raymond come on in."

As he walked in he saw Tashianna and said *wow* to himself. He extended his hand.

She shook his hand and quickly looked him up and down and said to herself, *this tall brother is fine* but she is still very much attracted to Jimmy as well because he was also good looking.

"Hi, Raymond it's nice to finally meet you."

"Likewise, you look very nice."

"Thank you and so do you."

RONALD GRAY 141

Jocelyn has a nice two-bedroom apartment and to make things better she suggested that they talk alone for a while first to get to know each other better. She and Raymond went in one of the bedrooms and Jimmy and Tashianna remained in the living room.

Jocelyn was feeling a little uncomfortable being alone in the room with Raymond because the chemistry between them was intense but it was not just sexual, it just felt right although she could not explain it.

"Raymond please don't get the wrong idea because I will put you out but can I hug you?"

"Absolutely."

When Raymond put his arms around her it took everything she had not to give in to her own desires for him. Jocelyn looked up to his eyes as they embraced and saw so much care in his heart. Raymond did not want to get slapped or put out but this woman had him, so he slowly leaned forward to try and kiss her and to his surprise she kissed him. The moment their lips touched they knew they had to get to know one another. She allowed Raymond to kiss her with more passion than what she was prepared for and accepted his warm tongue caressing her lips into her mouth. Jocelyn could feel his growing physical excitement and having his strong hands caressing her butt was not helping matters at all.

Raymond has never wanted someone as badly as he wanted Jocelyn right now but he knew this was not the time or place so he removed his hands stopped kissing her and slowly backed up. They both looked at each other and said at the same time.

"Wow."

They laughed and this was the ice breaker that allowed them to sit on the edge of the bed and talk.

Tashianna and Jimmy were having a great time talking about various subjects and she found it a lot easier talking to him about personal things than she thought. She had a deal breaker list like everyone does and one of them was a bad kisser so she had to find out if they connected.

"Jimmy, I am not one for pretending and wasting life's precious time so I need to find out something about you."

"Okay, I am the same way so what is it?"

She stood up and so did he and it was then that he knew exactly what she was talking about so he walked closer to Tashianna slowly pulling her into him and kissed her. Their kiss lasted for a minute and within that minute they knew this could be something special. Tashianna backed up from him smiling.

"That was some kiss and no we are not going any further so you need to relax yourself." Looking between his legs seeing the print of his erection then smiling.

"Yeah okay, no problem." He smiled as well then sat down on the sofa to hide his condition.

Tashianna sat down next to him and rubbed his back.

"Poor baby, you will be alright." Just to make him laugh she said something silly. "Not tonight dear I have a headache." They both started laughing then Raymond and Jocelyn walked out and sat down.

"It looks like you two are getting along well."

Raymond and Jimmy looked at each other to get the brother okay that all is cool. They both smiled and held up their hands at each other felling all is well. The four of them talked and laughed for a while and then helped Jocelyn in the kitchen to prepare dinner.

Chapter 29
The Church

Shirley and James are in church tonight by themselves kneeling at the altar praying.

"Oh Lord in Jesus name thank you father for blessing us to come together. Now Lord guide and instruct us for your glory." James spoke with great confidence.

"Yes Lord, your Holy word say, where two or three are gathered together in your name there you are in the midst. Father speak through us and for us directing our paths by your Holy spirit." Shirley said.

"Lord we are touching and agreeing that thy will shall be done, in the mighty name of Jesus, Amen."

"Amen." Shirley said as she was patting James on his back.

They stood up and walked toward the front pew and sat down. Shirley turned and looked directly at James.

"James what is wrong? When we spoke on the phone your voice was so emotionally and spiritually burdened and I felt your heavy spirit."

"Yeah you are right, I am. Everything in my life and family is great and God has truly blessed us abundantly but the Lord has been talking to me in my prayers and recently it's always the same, prepare yourself, a storm is coming."

"Did God tell you what kind of storm is coming and how to prepare yourself James?"

"No, he has not and I have been seeking him diligently in prayer but the Lords reply is always, *seek me early and trust my word, prepare yourself!*"

"Well, the Lord has spoken so just prepare yourself with continued prayer and fasting." She looks up. "Hallelujah, James the Lord has just quickened my spirit and said prepare for the battle of your life because the devil will attack your family and your faith in a big way but you must hold on no matter what."

"I felt the Lord's anointing and received his word. The devil cannot hide from God or anything that he does. The heavenly Father's word is; *For there is nothing covered that cannot be revealed, neither hid that shall not be known.* My strength is in my Lord Jesus."

"Praise the Lord my brother for the God that we serve our Lord and savior Jesus Christ God manifest in the flesh. Even the grave couldn't hold him because he has all power in heaven and earth, no matter what it seems."

"Preach sister. The same God that brought Lazarus back from the dead even after Lazarus lay in the grave four days, that same God shall deliver me and my family. This I am sure."

"Amen to that my brother. Death and life are in the power of the tongue, and they that love it shall eat the fruit thereof. You continue to speak to the storm and let God guide you."

"Thanks a lot sis and I really appreciate you, the encouraging words, the blessed relationship that we share and your tight walk with the Lord is priceless." He stares at her then hugs and kisses her on the cheek.

"Thank you and I pray that we will always be close and humble ourselves to God so he can continue to use us in a mighty way."

"Amen and I receive that. God can use those the greatest who humble themselves the most and he can teach those the most who admit they know the least."

Shirley smiles and gently pats James hand.

RONALD GRAY

"Amen right back at you. Now let's close this conversation out in prayer."

They get down on their knees and lean on the pew.

"Lord Jesus, we thank you for your blessing and for speaking to us. Lord you allowed Job to be attacked by Satan but it was for your glory, now Jesus God almighty prepare me for this battle and protect my family."

"Yes Lord, we plead the blood of Jesus against my brother's family. He who laid his life down on the cross, rose from the grave on the third day has all power to overcome the forces of darkness. If God be for you, then who can be against you. Let thy will be done oh Lord."

"Thank you father, now unto him that is able to do exceeding abundantly above all that we ask or think, according to the power that worketh in us. Unto him be the glory in Jesus name, Amen."

"Amen."

They stand up and hug then sit back down.

"We make a great team sis."

"Yes we do. God has blessed you to be pastor and me the assistant and we will continue to stand in the gap for each other, you stay strong James, God shall prevail."

"Yes he will." He gently grabs her hand. "So, what is going on in your life Miss Prayer Warrior?"

"So are you asking me about my personal life because if you are, you are being nosey." She stares at him then starts laughing and punches James on his arm. "Just kidding with you. But I do have something to tell you."

Chapter 30
Family Secrets

John drives up to Doctor Eye's house late at night but he arrived here faster than he thought. A few cars are parked in front of the house with people sitting in them. He parks his car and turns off the engine but the radio is on and the song is playing, *"Got To Be A Special Lady"* by Ray, Goodman, & Brown. John is looking around and wondering what he is doing here.

"I can't believe I am doing this but just being here is making me feel like something big is about to happen in my life." Flipping the car visor down he looks in the mirror. "Especially when this ugly acne on my face disappears then there will be a special lady, just for me." He smiles then turns off the radio and steps out of the car looking at this strange looking man walking out of the door.

Doctor Eyes walks slowly out of the door and points at John.

"John Richardson, come here boy." He yells.

John can't help but stare at him for some reason then speaks softly to himself.

"That has got to be him but how did he know my name." He looks up. "Lord help me." Exhaling slowly, he walks towards the house following Doctor Eyes into this dark room that is not well lit and has old ugly furniture. They sit down at a table and Doctor Eyes is just staring at John with blood red eyes.

"So, you want to get rid of the acne on your face but you have tried everything and nothing has worked for you."

"Yes I do and yeah I have tried many products with no results. How did you know this?"

"I know all things so let's not waste time discussing trivial matters. Now back to your temporary problem. Reach into your pocket and hand me a hundred-dollar bill."

"How did you know I had…"

John never got the chance to finish his sentence because Doctor Eyes slams both of his hands on the table and leans towards him.

"Be quiet boy; just do as I say and you might live."

John reaches into his pocket and pulls out the bill and hands it to him all the while staring at Doctor Eyes looking at him like he is crazy for talking to him like that.

Doctor Eyes takes the bill then stands up and walk to his desk full of bottles. He grabs one and sits back down putting the bottle on the table and lays the hundred-dollar bill on the table as well. He stares at John.

"Hand me your left hand and no matter what I do or say, do not talk."

John extends his left him to him. Doctor Eyes opens the bottle and pours a small amount of the liquid on the hundred-dollar bill then he removes a needle from his shirt pocket and sticks John's first finger until it bleeds and squeezes some of his blood on the bill and spreads the blood on the bill with Johns finger and puts the bill in his shirt pocket.

"Take this bottle with you and put some of the liquid on your face in the morning and at night and your face will become very clear and remain clear as long as you do this." He pours some of the liquid from the bottle in his hands and wipes it on John's face and holds his hands on his face. "Power of the eyes, obey me and do my bidding." He removes his hands and put the top back on the bottle. "It's done."

"Now what? What do I do?"

Doctor Eyes points to a mirror on the wall.

"Look for yourself."

John stands up and walks towards the mirror staring at his face in awe at what he sees.

"Oh my God, I don't believe it, my face it's clear, my face is clear." He raises his hands over his head. "Yes, yes finally my face is clear unbelievable. Look out ladies here I come." He turns around and looks at Doctor Eyes. "How much do I owe you, name your price?"

Doctor Eyes smiles and picks the bottle up from the table and stands up.

"You yelled, oh my God. Very interesting words but the question is, which God, interesting. When you get home bury two thousand dollars in your back yard and I will be by later to pick it up. Now take this bottle with you and do as I said and leave." He hands the bottle to him.

John takes the bottle smiling.

"No problem, this is truly unbelievable. Doctor Eyes I owe you, I truly owe you."

"Yes you do, just don't forget to put the solution on your face in the morning and at night and your face will remain clear and come back to see me before you run out."

"No problem and thank you again." He walks out of the house towards his car and get in and stares at himself in the mirror. "I always knew I was handsome but now I am super fine. I have waited years for this day. Well paid, good looking and hungry for living a real life. For me it's nothing but gorgeous ladies and I am talking about ladies that are a **FULL SEVEN** that are willing to give that ass up with the quickness. Yes!" He smiles and blows a kiss at himself and starts his car and drives away quickly.

Two hours after John left Sherry and Katrina arrive at Doctor Eye's house. She stops the car and turns off the engine. No other cars or people are around.

"Mom I can't believe we are even here and considering doing this but I want my voice to be perfect so bad that I am willing to try anything."

"Well believe it dear because we are here now and I have tried everything to lose weight and prayer aint helping so whatever or whoever will help me, I want it."

"I know how you feel Mom but Dad is crazy about you and his actions show it because he always wants you. The way Dad acts concerning you he behaves like a teenager in love for the very first time. Always hugging and kissing all over you. A little much at times but okay. Horny man for his wife."

Katrina's words resonate hard as Sherry listens and she thinks about how her husband treats her and his continued devotion. And he has always been very affectionate towards her since day one. She wonders if being here is a mistake but pushes those thoughts to the side because her own happiness is important. She stares at Katrina.

"Child watch your mouth and manners that is your Dad that you are talking about and my husband so don't get it twisted."

"Mom I was..."

"Hush child I am talking. Your Dad is a very special man that I love deeply and yes, he is affectionate to me constantly which is a blessing in various ways. But I need to feel comfortable within and every woman does. Not for someone else but for herself. And your Dad is fine and well, never mind." A huge smile comes over her face thinking about James wonderful fulfilling touch.

"Okay mom no problem. I hope you and Dad remain together for life and continue to be happy." She looks around. "So, what do we do now that we are here?"

Sherry is looking around as well suddenly feeling very uncomfortable about this place but she must remain strong and focused for herself and Katrina.

"Well, we did not come all this way for nothing so let's go to the front door and see this mystery man and he better be for real. Driving all the way down here I must be desperate."

They step out of the car and walk towards the house and when they step on the porch the front door opens and Doctor Eyes walks out wearing old looking dress slacks, white dress shirt and black dress shoes.

"Mrs. Sherry Richardson and her daughter Katrina. I have been expecting you so please do come in."

Sherry and Katrina look at each other then Sherry looks at Doctor Eyes.

"How do you know our names and who are you sir."

"I know yesterday, today and tomorrow and am he who you came to see. I am Doctor Eyes, please come in so we can talk." He walks in the house.

Again, Sherry and Katrina look at each other and both exhale deeply before walking in following Doctor Eyes. All three are sitting at the table in a dark room but several candles are lit on the table and two bottles are sitting on it as well. Doctor Eyes points to Sherry.

"You go to the graveyard at exactly midnight and take this bottle with you. Pour some of the liquid in the middle of a grave and pick up the dirt and throw it over your left shoulder and say, I shall lose weight by the power of the eyes."

"Then what?"

"Then you drink some of the liquid and drink it twice a day and you will lose weight very quickly."

"Okay no problem."

He stares at Katrina purposely trying to intimidate her.

"And you, good clean church going girl. You should be ashamed of yourself for teasing men so you can get what you want, dick teaser shame on you child. And you want to be this great singer but your voice is not what you need for it to be, another one to the list of great singers. Ruthless dirty business the music industry is and so many have come to me wanting the same thing, poor souls. But you are still a virgin and that is sweet but eventually you are going to have to give that butt up soon because it's part of life. You display butt little girl you must give some butt. And in your case because you want what you want so badly you are going to be giving up a whole lot of ass and mouth." He laughs hard. "Anyway, little dick teaser you do the same thing only you say, power of the eyes give me my voice. And tell no one about any of this."

Sherry's anger is increasing by the second as this man is talking so disrespectful to her daughter but she knows to say nothing no matter how angry she becomes. She hates this man.

"What happens if we forget to drink this stuff one day?" Katrina asked with a little attitude while trying to hide her own inner fears of being here and seeing this creepy looking man.

"You two will become very sick until you drink it so don't forget and before you run out come back to see me. Now both of you pay me one thousand dollars each."

They both reach into their pockets and pull out a wad of money and count out a thousand dollars putting it on the table. Doctor Eyes counts the money again while staring at them just to be intimidating and he can feel the fear in them which he likes. He leans across the table staring at Sherry and Katrina while his eyes turn dark black and red at the same time.

"Don't forget what I said. I don't care who it's never tell anyone what you have done and will do or you both will pay a severe price. Now you can go."

They both stand up and pick up the bottles and walk towards the room door but Doctor Eyes stands up and points in their direction.

"Sherry and Katrina." His voice echoes throughout the room.

They both quickly jump and then turn around facing him.

"Sherry that is a whole lot of butt you are working with are you sure you want to get rid of all that fat ass. And Katrina, the dick teaser, that young tight booty you are working with, some guy is going to be all up in that ass. Tongue and stiff dick. Now get out of my house, freaks." He starts laughing and the house begins to shake.

Sherry and Katrina quickly run out of the house and in the car. Both start sweating profusely and shaking and stare at each other.

"Mom, what did we just do?"

"I am not sure honey but it's something we both wanted and we will never discuss, ever. I do know that I hate that evil looking man and I hope we never have to see his ugly face again, disrespectful bastard." She hugs Katrina and then drives away.

The Master Deceiver

Chapter 31

Lewis Stevens

James drives up to Lewis Stevens's house in the afternoon and walks to the front door then rings the doorbell. Lewis and Veronica are in the living room sitting on the couch. A coffee table is in front of the couch with Lewis legal papers on it and he is doing some reading.

"Perfect timing because I need a break from all of this reading but I was just thinking about tasting you." He leans forward hugs and kisses Veronica. "Soft lips. Do you have those high cut panties on that is easy to slide to the side so I can slide in?"

Veronica lightly slaps him.

"Stop it Lewis. I have asked you nicely repeatedly not to talk to me like that. Stop talking and treating me like some whore that you just met. You will respect me Lewis so stop talking to me so dirty and foul, I am truly sick of it, so stop. What is wrong with you?" Giving him a very mean look.

Lewis just smiles and quickly kisses her again.

"I do respect you dear but you need to relax and loosen up a bit like you did the other night which was incredible baby. The real you came out and I was shocked but glad to see and hear your freaky side. Again, if I can't flirt with and be nasty to you, my own wife then who do you want me to give my love to?"

Just thinking about that night makes Veronica have thoughts that are uncomfortable for her to even desire to deal with.

"Lewis I do not want to talk about that night and do not make fun of me or give our love making a cheap name, please." Feeling ashamed and very embarrassed about the whole thing.

"Woman please. Okay, yes, we started out making love but once you allowed the real hidden you to come to the surface. Oh, my goodness, you started fucking your husband good. Sucking my dick damn good. I did not know you love the dick so much, mouth almighty lips for days." He looked at her and could not help but laugh.

"Lewis, stop it." She yells at him. "Stop talking to me like that, you are embarrassing me." Staring at him with anger.

"Yeah okay whatever you say dear. You need to get a grip on yourself woman." He walks towards the front door then looks back at her smiling. "Or let me get a grip on that tight body of yours and stop playing with me. You know you want this good dick." He winks at her and keeps walking to the door.

Veronica points her finger at him.

"Lewis, it will take an act of God to change your very dirty, filthy, mind and mouth."

Lewis opens the door and smiles seeing his friend standing there.

"James, hallelujah praise the Lord come on in my brother." He starts laughing.

"That is not funny and you need to stop doing that because one day you will truly need God and cry out to him for mercy, then what?" James points his finger at him.

"True that and you are right." He closes the door and walked behind James.

Veronica is still sitting on the couch when James walks in the room and she walks towards him.

"Praise the Lord James."

"Praise the Lord Veronica." He hugs her. "It's good to see you. Are you keeping this guy in line?" He looks at Lewis.

"Not by my hand or power but by the spirit of the Lord will Lewis be what God desires him and every soul to be."

Lewis smiles and walks towards Veronica and kisses her on the cheek then pats her on the butt.

"I love you to dear, day and night." Staring at Veronica and smiles while slowly licking his lips.

Veronica quickly smacks Lewis hand.

"Lewis stop that and do not embarrass me in front of James. I have told you repeatedly about your disrespectful ways." Looking at him scornfully.

James starts laughing.

"You and Lewis are something else because as long as I have known you two, Lewis has always been very affectionate towards you and you constantly fuss at him for loving his beautiful wife. Veronica, your husband adores you all day long, so just relax and enjoy it." He points at Lewis. "Go for what you know my brother." He continues to laugh.

"James Richardson, you should be ashamed of yourself and do not encourage him please. Loving me is good but not disrespecting me with crude attitude and actions."

Lewis walks over to James and pats him on the shoulder.

"Spoken like a true friend. I appreciate the words now sit down and make yourself comfortable."

James and Lewis sit on the sofa together and Veronica sits across from them.

"James, it's always a pleasure to see you and fellowship with you or did you come by to discuss something private with Lewis. If so I can leave so you two can talk."

"No, actually I came by to see you both just to spend time with you and see how you are doing."

"James my friend things are great. Business has picked up and I have the best wife in the world even though she slapped me and chastise my deep love." Looking over at Veronica playfully mean mugging her then smiles. "I know the best is yet to come."

"I am happy things are going well for you Lewis but don't forget where your help comes from and Jesus is still Lord of Lords and kings of Kings. Veronica what did Lewis do to cause you to slap him?"

"Nothing, I love my wife and I show it, right baby." Smiling at her.

"James, Lewis knows that I love him tremendously and yes he spoils me but I lightly smacked him because of his continued disrespectful sexual comments and attitude towards me. I am a child of the Lord Jesus and will not be disrespected by my husband. I am not a hooker and will not be treated as such."

"My friend Lewis, I know you and I know that you have it bad for your wife which is a good thing but she walks in Holiness now and you must treat her with the utmost respect."

Lewis attitude instantly changes as he is looking at James with contempt.

"Look James, yeah you and I have been friends a long time and we go way back and no disrespect intended but I don't need you or anyone telling me how to treat my wife. That's mine."

"Lewis, that was uncalled for and you know it. What has gotten into you? James is your best friend but he is also your pastor and I know you love me but I am not your sex toy."

Lewis anger feels like it's ready to erupt but he does not want to disrespect his wife especially in front of James and he does feel bad about talking to his friend and pastor like he did.

"Sweetie you are right and I will tone it down some and James I apologize for the way that I spoke to you, it was wrong."

"No problem Lewis we have been friends for years and know each other very well my brother so we can always be ourselves."

Lewis kind words to her and James touched Veronica's heart so she walks over hugs and kisses him then sits back down with love and admiration in her heart.

"Ahhh, that was so sweet, you love your man, get it girl." James smiled at Veronica.

Lewis was enjoying this because some of it was an act on his part only because he wanted to take his wife in the bedroom and have a repeat of the previous night.

"Yes, that was sweet dear and later tonight can I have another long hug. Love your hugs." He could not help but laugh.

"Lewis, some things about you will never change my longtime friend. Veronica you will just have to love him in spite of it all but he loves you deeply and this I know for sure."

"Yes James, you are probably right he is who he is but I love him anyway. James what is really going on with you and family."

"The family is good and my children are just growing up and becoming adults in this interesting world that we live in. I pray for my family daily for protection and growth in the Lord. But I just have this deep inner feeling that things will change soon and I am not sure it will be for the best."

"Pastor James, no matter what will happen I know you will be prepared because you are the most praying man I know and you actually live it which is why there is so much respect in my heart for you. No faking in you my friend, its Jesus twenty-four seven."

"Thanks Lewis but this is the only way I can be and walk in the anointing that God has for me and all flesh if he so desire. Is it easy? No! But God can do all things at any given time."

"Amen to that James." Veronica said with much respect for this man.

James notices the ring on Lewis finger and through the spirit of discernment he can feel something very wrong and evil about it.

"Lewis I notice that ring on your finger. Where did you get it, it looks expensive?"

"Fact is my knowledge and time paid for this ring. I did some legal work for a client that could not pay me later, so he offered me this ring which I told him no thank you. The man was very persistent and said the ring was worth some serious money, so I took it to pay off his debt. Later I had it appraised and was surprised to find out that the ring is worth eight thousand dollars."

"Wow, that is expensive but I feel it's not something that you should be wearing. You should get rid of it and sell it my friend."

Lewis is thinking. *You must be crazy thinking I am going to sell this ring that is helping my business like never before, yeah, right.*

"You know I respect your opinion and will give it some thought."

"Great idea, speaking of ideas, let's go out to eat somewhere right now. We can stop by and pick up my wife."

"That is a very good idea and Sherry and I can talk."

James walks out the door first then Lewis and Veronica which Lewis slides his hand on her butt caressing it just to irritate her.

Veronica quickly stepped to the side and smacks Lewis hand down harshly whispering in his ear.

"Stop it Lewis and behave yourself for once."

"No, I want some booty, now." He whispers back to her and laughs then walks out holding Veronica's hand.

James prays when they are all in the car and drives off. While driving, he looks in the rear-view mirror and notices Lewis being himself by flirting with Veronica and although she is irritated by his actions at times, he can also see the love in her eyes for him.

Lewis slowly caresses Veronica's hip while sitting so close to her in the back seat and she smacks his hand again and whispers to him.

"Lewis I am going to scream if you do not stop and embarrass us both, I promise you this, stop it."

He leans closer to her and whispers in her ear.

"No, you stop. Stop resisting and give me this hot booty and shake it when we get home." He laughs knowing she is irritated with him now.

Veronica stares at Lewis for a while trying to hold back her tears and hurt but something in her just snaps and she emotionally gives up. She whispers in his ear.

"I give up fighting with you Lewis and maybe it's me. I am sure many wives would love to have their husbands all over them like you are to me. So, if that is what you want from me, then so be it. Lewis I will be your private in house freak." She kisses him on the cheek then just stares out in space feeling empty and defeated.

Lewis looks at her seeing the great distance in her eyes and not sure if what she just told him is a good thing or bad but he is determined to find out when they get back home tonight.

Chapter 32

Raymond's Deal

One month later on June 24th early Saturday morning is the day for the NBA draft for the Charlotte Hornets at the Time Warner Cable Arena. Many others on this day have desires to make the team and live their dreams but on this day Raymond is confident that this will be his day for sure. He has been practicing hard and doing a lot of running to be in excellent shape. Because of his new exceptional ball playing skills Raymond has been traveling a lot playing in games wherever he can just to get the exposure and each time the event was posted on *YouTube* for all to see. Word has spread quickly throughout the USA and internationally because of the internet. Raymond has over ten million followers on his *YouTube* channel, and over five million on *Twitter*. His nick name is Raymond the regal Richardson aka Triple R because he does have an elegant look in all his moves and personality along with being very respectful to everyone. He even has his own website named; *Triple R* to the NBA and a message board on the site so anyone can leave messages and comments. Mr. Collins did give him a tryout to see for himself Raymond's skills and what he saw in person was incredible. He walks down the street now and people recognize him because of his exposure. Raymond's ball skills are above great and everyone knows it and he has met many of the current and past NBA players who encourage him to remained focus and continue to believe in himself.

All his family members are there along with Shawn, Theresa, Alexandria, Tashianna, Jocelyn, Lewis and Veronica. James and the rest of the family are very happy for John concerning his face finally becoming clear of acne and for Sherry for losing weight. But James also wonders about this but keeps his thoughts to himself. Raymond and Jimmy already sat down with the family to explain the situation concerning Tashianna and Jocelyn so everyone would understand. James told his sons that he was very proud of them and that they both made a very mature decision, a difficult one but wise beyond their years. When no one else was around John and Jacob told Raymond and Jimmy that both girls were fine and they could not go wrong anyway. They all laughed and said, yeah you right but they knew it was much more than that for them but appreciated their brothers love.

Waiting for his name to be called is the hardest part for him and yes in the back of his mind he wonders, what if they don't call me because Raymond feels this is the biggest day of his life. After so many people are called it's down to the last few names and teams when Raymond's name is called. All his family members and friends jump up shouting but Raymond is just sitting there in a daze after hearing his name called for a member of the Charlotte Hornets team. Jocelyn is sitting next to him screaming his name and then she hits him to wake him out of his daze. Raymond finally jumps up and shouts.

"Yes, yes." He hugs Jocelyn very tightly and kisses her then walks up to the front and stand behinds the podium. "Wow, all of this seem like a dream for me and I thank God and my family members and friends for supporting me through it all. Thank everyone for supporting me as well by helping get the word out through social media and thank the Charlotte Hornets for accepting me and giving me an opportunity to live my dream. Wow!" He has to hold back his tears because all of this is so emotional for him.

When Raymond was kissing Jocelyn, Alexandria became a little jealous but in her mind, it's only a matter of time to get her hands on him. Everyone came back to the Richardson home to celebrate Raymond's great opportunity.

This was Raymond's day and he was loving all the attention he was receiving and having Jocelyn by his side was perfect but he could feel Alexandria's eyes on him and her sexual desire. Even though he had strong feelings for Jocelyn he could not dismiss his feelings for Alexandria. He wanted to spend time with her but did not know how or when he just knew it was a strong desire that needed to be fulfilled. Raymond opened the door coming out of the bathroom when Alexandria appeared in the doorway and pushed him back in closing the door behind them.

"Alex, what are you doing, are you crazy? All the people in this house, we are going to get caught."

She presses her finger against his lips.

"Be quiet Raymond, I know what I am doing."

Alexandria dropped to her knees quickly unzipped his pants and pulled his dick out and gave him the best and quickest blow job ever.

"Damn Alex."

For the next four minutes Raymond felt her hands, lips, tongue, and hot mouth on his dick until he could not take it anymore and exploded. Alexandria sucked every drop like her life depended on it then zipped his pants back up, opened the cabinet grabbing a toothbrush out of a pack, quickly brushed her teeth and kissed Raymond.

"Now, you remember that Mr. Raymond Richardson, pro ball player." She kissed him again squeezed his dick and walked out smiling.

All Raymond could do was stand there and watch her leave.

"Damn, I am messed up now." He adjusted his clothes and walked out to find Jocelyn. He hugged and kissed her but saw Alexandria looking at him smiling and winked at him.

Raymond was signed to a one-year contract for five million dollars to see how things go but he also signed various endorsements deals for a total of twenty-two million dollars and was ready to start living his life after so much work and sacrifice. Raymond Richardson became a millionaire overnight which is a truly a dream come true for him.

Chapter 33
Katrina's Rise

Katrina was eighteen now and so happy for Raymond and all the great things that was happening for him. At the same time, she wanted to see her life dreams come to pass. She knew now was her time because she has been singing and her new voice was incredible. She called Terrence Washington to make an appointment with him so she could come to the studio but he spoke to her with an attitude saying if you are not fully ready then do not come in and waste my time. Normally she would say something smart back to him but she wanted to save her words and blow him away with her voice.

When Katrina walked in the studio she walked in with confidence and was dressed to tease. She was wearing heels and a snug fitting long dress with a long slit on the side with the curves to her young tight body doing all the talking. Even Terrence and his assistant who was working the sound board noticed it was something different about her but kept it to themselves. Although they did whisper among themselves that this young girl was hot.

Katrina sat down in the recording room and started singing Whitney Houston's song, *I will always love you.* Terrence and his assistant had their mouth open in total amazement listening to this girl sing this song. Terrence waved his hand at her.

"Stop, is this some kind of trick? Do you have a hidden recorder on you somewhere because there is no way you can sing like this? I told you young girl I don't have time to play games."

Katrina was loving his reaction and simply remained calm when she spoke but with a little cockiness to her tone.

"Terrence, I don't play games either, so relax and let me sing please or I can leave."

"Fine, go ahead and do your thing Katrina." Shaking his head.

She started from the beginning of the song again and sung it all the way through. Her voice was so phenomenal, if you were blind you could not tell that Whitney Houston was not in that chair singing.

"So, Terrence, what do you think baby?" Katrina was feeling herself now and wanted to get to him.

Terrence and his assistant both looked at each other still not believing what they just heard.

"I don't know how you did it and I really did not think you were coming back but damn girl your voice is incredible to say the least. My business mind is already turning. Oh, we are celebrating tonight for sure and if that voice of yours stays right you can write your ticket in this world. With my experience and connections, you will go to the top and fast." He turned to his assistant giving him a nod for which he knew Terrence wanted him to leave and they would talk later. He waved at Katrina and walked out.

"Come out of that room girl so we can talk some business." His mind was on business but he wanted to test her again as well.

Katrina knew she had Terrence but was aware she needed to be very careful in dealing with him because he did have all the connections and she had none. She walked slowly to him pretending to adjust the dress she was wearing and showing more leg than necessary on purpose. She sat down in front of Terrence showing a lot of leg and thigh with a big smile on her face.

"Terrence Washington, am I ready baby?"

"Girl you are more than ready, damn you ready. You know I am hyped but who would not be? Stand up and give me a hug.

RONALD GRAY

It was all a game but Katrina felt like she was in the driver's seat so she stood up and hugged Terrence who is a very nice looking man with a hard body. He had on some nice smelling cologne and it did feel good to be in his arms which is why she let her guard down and hugged him a little tighter.

Terrence took this as a sign and kissed Katrina on the cheek and without really thinking about it she turned her head to meet his lips and they kissed. She has not kissed a lot of guys but this man could kiss and she allowed his hands to grip her butt caressing it and he slid his tongue in her mouth and she felt his erection. He stopped and moved around to the back of her putting his arms around her waist kissing and sucking on her neck as he slowly moved the slit on the dress to the side and was gently caressing her leg moving his hands higher.

Katrina knew this was wrong and did not plan on letting things get this far but it all felt so good even his erection that was pressed so tightly against her butt. She could feel the wetness building up between her legs.

He knew this young girl was hot but he still wanted to see how far she would let him go so he moved his hands up higher feeling the wetness on her panties and sucked her neck just a little harder. Terrence slid one hand inside her panties from the side using his fingers to caress her lips and wetness.

She arched her head back into him while pressing her butt tighter on him as well.

"Oh Terrence." She wanted this man so badly knowing it would be her first time.

Terrence finger caressed her wetness and she was so wet. He moved his hand and rubbed his finger over her lips and Katrina started sucking on it. This reaction motivated him to slide his other hand inside her panties and his finger slowly move inside her. Katrina jumped and quickly turned around to face him.

"Terrence please baby I am not playing games but I am not ready. Can we take our time and focus on business? You know I like you and we can do some great things together, please let's just work together and take care of each other."

He was surprised she let him get this far but he is patient. He licked and sucked the same finger Katrina was sucking on and was looking directly at her eyes while doing it and then smiled at her. This turned Katrina on even more but she had to remain focused.

"Katrina I would never force myself on you or any woman and yes we can do some serious business. So, let's go out to eat and celebrate. Oh, to show you that I am serious and believe in you I am prepared to offer you a two hundred and fifty thousand dollar signing bonus and a two-year contract. The paper work is in my private office and I can show it to you at any time."

"Terrence, are you serious? Don't play with me. Let me see the contract."

"Not a problem. Follow me."

They walked down a long hallway and came to a door with an electronic combination lock on it. Terrence pressed some buttons and opened the door and they walked in a large room that looked like a very lavish hotel suite. Katrina has stayed in some wonderfully decorated luxurious hotel rooms while on vacation with her family but she was impressed with this. Terrence walked to the desk and picked up the contract and handed it to her.

"I am not rushing you so take the contract and show it to whoever you want and on the day that you agree to the terms I will put a two hundred and fifty-thousand-dollar check in your hand. Then, we can go to the next level in business."

She looks at him and exhales heavily.

"Wow, okay you are very serious and I appreciate and thank you for that. This is great and yes I will take the contract with me. Now let's go eat and celebrate." She smiles and steps to Terrence kissing him on the lips and walks towards the door.

Terrence smiled as well because he knew his time was close to becoming even richer with this girl's voice and getting in her panties was good and she is a virgin.

"Let's eat." He followed her out.

Just when Katrina reached the door she closed it and turned around and removed her dress letting it fall to the floor. Standing there in heels, panties, and bra. She walked over to Terrence and kissed him then placed his hands on her butt.

"I am not playing games Terrence but I believe you will take care of me, so this ass is yours baby. You will be my first so please take your time and make love to me." Looking directly into his eyes.

He is staring at her in amazement and is thinking. *No way did I see this coming but I will do as she asks because this girl is walking millions in the bank and that is the bottom line for me but no way am I turning down this young hot ass.*

"Katrina I will take very good care of you baby."

He picks up Katrina and slowly lays her on the bed. Terrence is all about Terrence but he does have a heart and wanted this to be special for Katrina. Every caress, every lick, every touch was slow and very passionate all over her body.

Even at this very moment Katrina was emotionally torn. Wanting his touch but knowing it was all wrong but with each passing second her mind was being consumed with lust and her body was betraying her. When she felt Terrence tongue between her legs it sent chills throughout her body. Katrina has watched porn and

RONALD GRAY   169

masturbated many times but she has never put anything inside her not even her own fingers. Terrence tongue felt amazingly good and caused her to have an intense orgasm.

Terrence was enjoying the effect he was having on this young girl but he did not want her to have a change of mind at the last-minute concerning penetration so, while she was still having her orgasm he slowly started sliding his dick in and she was tight.

The moment she felt him Katrina gripped the sheets and arched her back. Even though she is very wet, it's a little painful but she had to relax her mind and body to enjoy this very special moment. Then she thought about him not having on a condom. Oh God, what am I doing? The little pain she was experiencing is replaced by pleasure because now it was feeling good. Katrina was now on her hands and knees as Terrence was making love to her. Okay, it's not love but damn it felt good and her confidence level has increased as she was throwing her body back into his with each stroke, taking all his dick which was not small.

"Terrence, it feels good baby please don't stop. Fuck me Terrence."

Watching his dick slide in and out of her was turning Terrence on and her body was tight and sexy. Hot, tight, young pussy and he knew now that he could turn her out with her nasty mouth. He stopped and turned Katrina over on her back. He lifted her legs up then slid back inside but he was close to exploding and he knew it, so he went slow but deep until he could feel her body begin to shake.

"Ohhhhhhh, I am cummming, ahhhhhh, Terrence." She gripped the sheets harder and has never had an orgasm like this before in her life as she is throwing her body into him with force and intention to fuck him good. After climaxing so hard, Katrina relaxes but she knows Terrence is close as well so she throws her body into him even more and decides to taunt him.

"That's it Terrence fuck me. I thought you wanted this tight pussy, so fuck me."

Damn, young girl was talking to him like she's in charge but he loved her confidence. He could really put it on her but that would be stupid and he wanted this nice piece of ass again. He was about to turn her over again but too late pussy is too good.

"Damn girl, ahhhhhh your pussy is good." Terrence squirts every drop of his seed inside her knowing he should have a condom on but damn that. He finally pulls out kisses her repeatedly and then lays next to Katrina thinking about all the money he is about to make. "Girl you are something else, you trying to make a man fall in love." He kisses her again and gets up. "I am going to take a shower would you care to join me."

"I am going to lay here for a minute. I will be in there soon okay."

"No problem baby." He winks at her and walks to the shower.

She watches him walk away and smiled but then reality hits her hard and she rolls over on her side grabbing the pillow crying hysterically.

"Oh God what have I done?" This was so very wrong no matter what and Katrina knows that she will never be the same because she has given away something that is priceless. Her womanhood. She will never be a virgin again and gave it to someone that she does not love or is even in a relationship with. So be it, what is done is done and I can never go back so I may as well use my body and mind to get what I want. Tears still flow from her eyes and she buried her face in the pillow and screamed.

Chapter 34
Living a Dream

So much has happened in one year for Raymond. He purchased a five bedroom, three car garage three-million-dollar home in Myers Park, Charlotte NC. He also purchased a S600 Benz, Bentley, and a Range Rover. His time playing on the team has been nothing but incredible in every possible way. Raymond has broken all records for most points in one game and he made MVP of the year. His nick name, *Triple R* serves him well because he is unstoppable on the court, and because of his value he now has a one hundred and twenty-million-dollar five-year contract with the team and eighty-million-dollar endorsement deals. He is known as the, Two Hundred-Million-Dollar Man.

His personal romantic life has been and still is emotionally tough at times. He and Jocelyn became much closer and they fell in love hard. Not seeing her every day because of the distance was having an effect on him. Jocelyn in Raleigh and him in Charlotte. After much persistence on his part Raymond finally convinced Jocelyn to move to Charlotte so they could be closer but she would not move in with him.

Jocelyn was promoted to manager at Red Lobster when she moved to Charlotte and made it very clear to Raymond regardless of how much money he had she did not want to depend on him or be with him for his money and fame. This caused him to care for, respect, and love her even more. Jocelyn moved in a very nice apartment close to him while still pursuing her singing career. She is now singing in some of the most popular clubs in Charlotte and surrounding cities. Her increased income allowed her to stop working at Red Lobster and sing full time and travel with Raymond when she could according to their busy schedules.

But as much as Raymond loved Jocelyn he was still involved with Alexandria. They would connect on a regular basis all over the country because she could travel at any time to meet him and sometimes Theresa would be there. Theresa liked Raymond a lot but was not in love with him because she saw his situation for what it was. A very young rich ball player doing his thing in life and she would not allow herself to fall in love with him and get her heart crushed, no way. However, the sex she and Raymond had was so good and the threesomes she, Raymond, and Alexandria would have at times was great. Alexandria on the other hand was deeply in love with him as Jocelyn is and she wanted Raymond to leave Jocelyn alone and be with her. Theresa tried telling her many times that this was never going to happen and just enjoy the ride while she can or leave him alone but she could not. She loved him too much.

Today is Jocelyn's twenty-fourth birthday and she was sharing it with the love of her life, Raymond Richardson. It was the off season with the NBA so he made plans to fly him and Jocelyn to someplace private but tropical for this special occasion. He chose Tahiti. Tahiti a place that dreams are made.

They slept a lot on the plane and after two stops and eighteen hours of flying they finally arrived in Tahiti. They checked into the Inter Continental Resort. Their luxurious suite was fabulous with a wonderful view of the ocean. They talked for a while and then unpacked. It's evening time and so close to sunset so they decided to go for a walk on the beach. Jocelyn was wearing sandals and a two-piece bikini with a sarong wrapped around her waist, Raymond was wearing beach shorts and sandals and carrying a beach bag with a large beach towel and water. Of course, he had his necklace on.

Raymond is not a jealous man but he is especially glad on this day that they are on a private beach because he desires to have Jocelyn all to himself looking at her incredible body. They stop walking and he just stares at her.

"What is wrong Raymond and why are you staring at me like that?"

"Baby nothing is wrong and I am staring at you because of how I feel about you, the way you have touched my heart and the intense effect that you emotionally, mentally, and physically have on me. You are one fine sexy looking woman top to bottom." He reaches inside his beach shorts pocket and pulls out a platinum necklace with the initials RR on them for Raymond Richardson and holds it up for Jocelyn to see. "This is for you from my heart for the world to see that you are my baby. I love you Jocelyn Mitchum, happy birthday to you baby." He leans forward and kisses her lips and slowly uses his tongue to caress her lips then puts the necklace on her. He looks at this woman with so much love and guilt because of the things he has done with other women.

Jocelyn can't hold back her tears as she quickly wraps both arms around Raymond's body and just holds him tightly. She slowly looks up at him looking at his necklace that he never seems to take off and she does not like but Jocelyn was not about to spoil this moment for anything.

"Oh Raymond, I love you more than you know." Tears flow from her eyes as she stares at him.

He hugs Jocelyn tightly and rubs her neck with his finger tips and then lightly bites her neck. She jumps and playfully slaps him.

"Boy, you better stop biting me before we get in trouble out here because you know how that makes me feel. Since you bit my neck can you massage it please because it has been a little sore ever since the plane ride. Maybe I slept wrong on it I don't know."

"You should have said something to me earlier because I would have taken care of that. Come on let's go back to the room and I will massage not only your neck but entire body."

"That sounds great Raymond but I want a real massage not you trying to be nasty."

"Woman please, I don't have to try and be nasty I can do that right here." He quickly picks her up kisses and licks her neck, shoulders, and breasts.

Jocelyn is laughing and trying to get away from his grip.

"Raymond put me down before I scream and I want a real massage." Still laughing and playing with him.

Raymond caresses her butt as he puts her down.

"Come on let's go back to the room and I will give you a massage, for real."

"Okay." They are looking into each other's eyes penetrating the mind and heart like physical touch alone will never be able to do and the sun is setting adding to a perfect background and mental picture for them to remember for years to come.

Back in their large suite there are candles lit all around the room and music is playing. The moment Raymond and Jocelyn stepped in their room they could not keep their hands off each other, far too much passion, desire, and love to continue suppressing. For the next two hours, they made love. So much emotional and physical foreplay on the floor, the sofa, the table, the bed and finally in the shower still satisfying each other over and over. Tears of joy and love run down Jocelyn's face as Raymond penetrates her slowly but deeply as he has her up against the shower wall until they both climax together and collapse into each other's arms.

RONALD GRAY 175

Jocelyn is now lying face down on the bed the candles are still lit and music still playing as Raymond is taking his time massaging her body with scented warm oil. His hands feel beyond good to her and he knows just how to touch her sore spots. His fingers and hands easily glide over her body hitting every spot just perfectly and for the next thirty minutes she receives the massage of her life, front and back. His wonderful touch relaxes her so much that she falls asleep and dreams about getting a massage by him. Two hours later Jocelyn wakes up and raises her head thinking it was all a dream but Raymond is asleep lying close to her body with his hand touching her leg. She smiles, kisses his lips very lightly and lays her head back down on the pillow then drifts off to sleep.

Chapter 35
John's New Life

It is eighty degrees outside on this bright summer day and John drives into a park in Raleigh in his new Z06 Corvette and he is enjoying the looks he is receiving as so many people are admiring his ride. There are a lot of people here today and John see's attractive ladies everywhere he looks. Having his face finally rid of the bad acne he has been dealing with for so long is fantastic and has given him an increase in confidence. John has been spending more time in the gym and his tight muscular physique shows it and he has been buying new clothes and jewelry. His reputation concerning the body work he does on cars has increased a great deal which has made him more money. He thought about opening his own body shop but decided against it after having a serious business conversation with Shawn and Jimmy and they informed him about the continued paper work and keeping good records. Forget that because he dislikes doing paper work.

He steps out of the car with sun shades on wearing casual dress shoes, pants and a tank top T-shirt. John came to the park today to relax, show off his car, and hopefully meet a nice girl. In a few months, he will be twenty-one and it would be great to have the right person to share it with. As he is walking John almost trips because he sees three girls that are in the gym on a regular basis and he like every other guy in the gym would love to talk to. All three girls are very attractive with serious curvaceous bodies which is being displayed well in the short shorts and cut off T-shirts they are wearing. But the bad acne on John's face prevented him from even approaching them. That was then and this is now and his confidence level is over the top which must be showing because he sees all three of the girls staring at him but he keeps walking until one of them wave at him.

"Excuse me could you come here for a minute please." Eliza said. She is twenty-three years old five feet seven, one hundred thirty-four pounds.

"No, you are not calling him over here. You are so bold Eliza and I could never do that." Kalani said. She is twenty-two years old five feet four one hundred twenty-eight pounds.

"She has no shame so we should be use to her by now." Aurora said. She is twenty-four years old, five feet eight one hundred thirty-six pounds.

The timing could not be better for John as he approaches the girls with his now flawless skin, wearing shades hiding his eyes so they don't see how hard he is looking at their bodies as he gets closer.

"Ladies, hello to you."

"Hello to you." Eliza said extending her hand. "My name is Eliza and these are my friends Kalani and Aurora." She points to them. "Anyway, we see you in the gym sometimes but you are always so into your work out and you don't really talk to anyone. We just figured you had a bad attitude."

John smiles because he knows where this is really going. Just another story of attractive girls thinking every guy will talk to them which may be true but he can already tell this girl has attitude for days thinking she is all that.

"No that's not me at all. I just want to get done what I need to while in the gym and get out because I am not one of those people that spend hours in the gym. Get it, hit it hard and leave."

"Oh really, so is that your attitude about everything in life? Get it and go, a quickie." Aurora said.

RONALD GRAY

All three girls start laughing.

"If you are talking about sex then it depends on the time and person. Somethings are worth being patient for and moving slow so you don't miss anything." He removes his shades and stares at Aurora then looks at the other two up and down with pure confidence.

"Okay, message received. Nice car you are driving is it yours?" Eliza said while looking at it then looks back at John.

"Thank you and yes its mine."

"What is your name?" Kalani said.

"My name is John. So, what do you ladies do when you're not in the gym?"

"We are independent advertising models that advertise for company products or anyone's for that matter that is not offensive to us. You contact us or we contact you and discuss what you have in detail then we give you our price and hopefully we can do some business. Simple process. What do you do?" Kalani said.

"It's a good business because everyone needs their product advertised in some form or fashion. I work on cars, specifically, I do the body work on any car but my specialty is high-end autos. Family run business."

"Now that is a great business and it also explains the very nice Corvette you are driving. You must be a very good body man." Looking at his crotch. "Wait a minute, you said body shop, family run business. Are you related to the Richardson family?" Eliza said.

This is the part that John dislikes. He was hoping to stand on his own merit and not his family name but he is proud of his parents and all they have done.

"Yes as a matter of fact I am."

"Okay, your Dad was a famous R & B singer but now he is a preacher and your family owns a large Lexus car dealership. It's good to see black people owning something and doing well." Aurora said while smiling at him.

"Yes, that is good and your family name is big, I have been to your Dad's church. That man can preach." Kalani said with excitement in her voice.

Eliza gives Kalani a bad look because she knows she did not call John over to discuss church any preaching. It's about opportunity, money, and having a good time with someone else's money. But she can play the role to get what she wants.

"That is nice and I hope you and your family continue to be blessed. John, we were talking about going to Atlanta this weekend just to relax and have fun if we get paid in time from one of our past jobs. Would you like to join us?" Eliza said knowing it was all a lie but worth a try.

"Atlanta sounds good and I could use the break from work. I tell you what. If you really want to go don't worry about getting there or the hotel cost because I will cover that. I will go online tonight and purchase the tickets and we can all fly out first thing Friday morning. Direct flights are only an hour and a half flying time. We can stay at the Sheraton Hotel and come back Sunday night. What do you think?"

All three girls looked at each other in surprise.

"Wow, you don't have to do all that but it would be great and I know we would have a very nice time." Eliza steps closer to John putting her hand on his shoulder.

"Good, it's done. Now let's walk around the park so we can talk for a while and exchange phone numbers and info."

"No problem John." Aurora said and walked closer putting her arm inside his because she knew Eliza was about to do just that but wanted to beat her to it. Aurora liked the vibe she picked up from John feeling his sincerity to life and thought it would be nice to get to know him before Eliza got to him. Her plan was always to see what she could get out of someone and how much.

John was enjoying walking with all three of them and was on cloud nine to say the least noticing how the guys were staring wondering, *"How did this one guy get all three of these fine girls"*. He came here to hopefully meet one and now three but he is no fool and he knows Eliza is a user and all about the money. The other two he is not so sure. Out of the three, one of them was going to end up in his bed this weekend although he was most attracted to Aurora and not just for her exotic look.

Chapter 36
Atlanta

Its Friday night John, Eliza, Kalani, and Aurora have been having a great time since they got to Atlanta. The accommodations at the Sheraton hotel are very nice. All three girls are in a large suite and John has his own room. They are walking in one of the most popular night clubs in Atlanta, Club 426 and the girls look fantastic. They are all wearing miniskirts and tops revealing flat stomachs and none of them have on a bra. John is wearing Armani dress shoes, slacks, a short sleeve dress shirt and Bulova watch. He hands the security guard at the door a hundred-dollar bill along with his driver's license so he has no problem getting in. The club is crowded and the music is loud. You can feel the lust spirit in the atmosphere. They are sitting in the VIP section that John arranged with a phone call and money of course.

John was sitting across from the girls and trying not be so obvious when looking at them because he could see the prints of their nipples so easily. Their skirts are so short he can see the panties they are wearing when sitting down. John was having a hard time keeping his growing erection hidden. Everyone was drinking and laughing enjoying the night but Kalani kept twisting in her seat and was talking low so John could not hear her.

"I can't believe I let you two talk me into wearing this miniskirt which is too short and I know John can see my underwear. I have no bra on which clearly shows my nipples. The things I have done in my life since leaving God."

Eliza has never really liked Kalani because of her shy ways and weak whining attitude so she pinches her.

"Will you be quiet and stop all your whining and leave the past in the past. Live your damn life to the fullest by getting paid and some good dick along the way. Just relax Kalani and you might get some dick tonight."

"Leave her alone Eliza she has been through enough without you picking on her." Aurora said, giving her a very mean look.

Eliza gave Aurora a fake smile then looked at Aurora's nipples and stared between her legs. Aurora gave her a disgusting look.

Kalani has always been shy and a little insecure although she is very attractive with a great body and was raised in church but became rebellious when she turned eighteen. She became very promiscuous, smoking weed and drinking too much. One night after her nineteenth birthday she was at a house party drinking and smoking and participated in a threesome. While driving home she hit the back of a car killing the driver and badly hurting the passenger. They were twenty-one-year-old newlyweds but Kalani only received probation and a fine because her attorney was able to prove the car she hit slammed on brakes first and Kalani was unable to avoid hitting it. She attended the funeral and broke down crying and the wife who was using a cane at that time told Kalani she will never forget she murdered her husband, slapped her and walked away. Kalani has never been the same since.

"I have to go to the bathroom you two." Kalani said and when she walked away John lightly smacked her on the butt.

"Girl you are wearing that skirt, hurry up back."

Aurora stared at John and rolled her eyes at him showing her disproval of him smacking Kalani on the butt. Kalani smiled at John and kept walking but she made up her mind that this was her last day of drinking. When she opened the bathroom stall door to leave Kalani received the surprise of her life. The guy's wife that she killed was standing there and quickly grabbed Kalani by the throat pushing her back in the stall and closing the door.

"I recognized your sorry ass from the time you walked in and I have been watching you all night. I knew one day our paths would cross again."

"Please don't, I never meant to kill your husband…"

Kalani never finished her sentence because the girl kissed her very hard on the lips, grabbed her butt hard with one hand and then reached in her bra with the other pulling out a razor cutting Kalani's throat from ear to ear. Blood was pouring and Kalani dropped to the floor holding her throat knowing she was seconds away from death but was looking up at the girl. The girl wiped the razor off on Kalani's blouse and then spit on her.

"My name is Teagan Miller. Take that to the grave bitch."

Kalani breathed her last breath looking at Teagan who is just looking down at her smiling then she walked out of the stall locking it from the inside and looked in the mirror to make sure no blood was on her then walked out of the bathroom. She saw the attractive waitress with the sexy lips and hot body who waited on her early that she was going to talk to later and got her attention.

"Excuse me sexy but do you remember me?"

"Of course, it would be hard for me not to with your baby doll looking face and seriously sexy body. What can I do for you besides give you my number?" She reached inside her bra and pulled out a card giving it to Teagan.

Teagan took the card and put it inside her bra because it may come in handy one day.

"Thank you for the compliment and you know I am feeling you as well. Will you give my friends over there this note please?" She pointed to John and the girls and gave her the note then a hundred-dollar bill. Teagan looked around and stepped closer to the girl moving her hand under her short skirt caressing her butt and then whispered in her ear.

"Very nice ass and I will call you." She quickly kissed the girl and smacked her on the butt then walked away smiling.

The waitress looked at Teagan walking away in her sexy tight jump suit and got instantly turned on by her gorgeous looks and aggressive touch. She walked over to John and gave him the note and walked away thinking about Teagan and them hooking up.

John read the note out loud so they all could hear. *Please forgive my rudeness but I ran into someone I know and will be spending the night with him see you all later.*

"Typical of that sneaky girl. Playing that shy role and you guys fall for it every time." Pointing to John. "When will you guys learn." Eliza said.

"Well, I hope she has fun because I plan to." Aurora said looking at John.

They all laughed and went to the dance floor and remained there for two hours before returning to their seats. Eliza had too much to drink so they all decided to leave and John was cool with that because he really was not into her. Aurora was feeling all over him on the dance floor acting like she was his woman and walking arm in arm when they left the club.

Teagan was leaning against her 2017 black one-hundred and sixty-five thousand dollar Audi R8 smoking a joint when Eliza, Aurora and John walked out. John had his hand on Aurora's hip as they were walking and laughing then Aurora looked up and saw Teagan leaning against the car staring at her. Aurora has not been attracted to any girl in a serious way in a long time but this girl stirred her emotions quickly and for brief seconds she had thoughts about going over and talking to her if she was not with John and Eliza but she quickly dismissed those thoughts and kept walking. She will never forget that girls image and how she made her feel.

The waitress that Teagan gave the note to was walking out of the club right behind John and the girls. She was looking around when she saw Teagan leaning against the car smoking and smiled then walked towards her.

"Hi, I never thought I would see you again. Are you waiting on someone?"

"Yes you. I left the club early to take care of some business and came back and asked what time you got off and hear I am. Do you have any plans for tonight?" Holding the joint down to her side.

"Allow me to introduce myself, my name is Rosemary but please don't call me that. I prefer Rose and you are?"

"Hi Rose, my name is Teagan and now back to my question. Do you have any plans for tonight?"

"Well I was just going out to eat with some friends of mine, no big deal." She looked at the joint and stepped closer to Teagan. "Let me have some."

"My pleasure." She took a puff first and then passed it to her.

Rose is looking at Teagan up and down while smoking the joint and got in her face with their lips almost touching and slowly blew smoke in her mouth.

"Very nice car you have. Can we go for a ride Teagan?"

"Absolutely! How about to the Sheraton Hotel? We can talk, smoke some and relax. No pressure, no strife and no promises and we can see how things go."

"Let's ride Teagan." She stares at her. "You are so sexy."

They get in the car and Teagan left the spot doing one hundred miles an hour.

Aurora, Eliza and John sat in the Sheraton lobby for a few minutes talking and making sure Eliza was okay then they walked Eliza back to the room and Aurora went with John to his room. But as they were approaching his room, Aurora saw someone she did not think she would every see again. Teagan and Rose were walking in their direction with their arms around each other and stopped at the room across from theirs. Teagan was equally surprised to see Aurora and wanted to send her a strong message. She placed her hands on Roses butt, leaned against her room door pulling Rose tightly against her body and they kissed very passionately. She then opened the door allowing Rose to walk in first and winked at Aurora as she walked in and closed the door.

This was the last thing Aurora needed to deal with right now especially being with John who she wanted to be with tonight. It took a lot for her not to give John some excuse and knock on this girl's door. She wanted and needed to leave her past in the past and see how things go with her and John.

It's a night John will never forget because the sex with Aurora was great and they talked afterwards until the sun was coming up then fell asleep together. In the morning, John woke up looking at Aurora's incredible naked body lying next to him still asleep and he gently caressed her neck with his fingers and this woke her up. Aurora moved her hand on John's dick which was already hard then turned on her side and backed up grinding on him. He gently slid inside her and remained still just to feel her warmth and then started moving slowly, pleasuring Aurora and himself until they were both satisfied with intense orgasms.

Chapter 37
Back in Raleigh

It is a wet and rainy day as John, Eliza, and Aurora are attending Kalani's funeral along with many of her friends. All three had on all black with both girls wearing long dresses that were still revealing their nice figures. They cannot believe she is dead and was killed while they were in Atlanta partying. The police still don't know who killed her. Although John just met her he feels hurt in his heart because Kalani seemed like a very nice young girl and her shyness made her even more attractive. She had her entire life to live but now all that is gone because she is laying in the ground. It was Eliza who was taking it the hardest as Aurora was holding her up because she was crying so hard mainly out of guilt. Eliza would tease Kalani often about not being aggressive enough in life to go after what she wanted and being so shy all the time thinking it was cute but to Eliza it is a weakness and she would tell Kalani this. What no one knew is deep inside Eliza was jealous of Kalani because she was a sweet girl from the heart despite all the things she had been through and she loved all people. Now she is dead and it's breaking her heart many times over. Aurora was beyond sad to see her friend laid in the ground and would miss her so much. She just observed the people and listened to all the kind words being spoken and everyone doing the polite thing that so many do at funerals. It's all so fake because most of the people that do show up at burials don't really care. They only come to see who else is going to show and to do a lot of gossiping. John, Aurora, and Eliza are walking away towards their vehicles and Eliza is holding on to John like he is her husband, a little too affectionate but this is what she does. She finds anyway she can to get next to a man to get what she wants and this is what makes Eliza not trust worthy. To her, John is a walking gold mine because of his family, their connections and money. Aurora is not a gold digger by any means and she genuinely likes John and the sex was good. She was curious so she did a little research into his family. His Pastor Dad is famous and rich and invested his money well in real estate, stock market and car dealerships. She discovered John is very good at doing body work and has a great reputation. She looks over at Eliza hanging all over John playing the emotionally hurt girl to the max over Kalani's death, so fake. Eliza and Aurora rode together and John drove his own car which was parked close to theirs and he was walking with them to the car. When they got there, she was leaning on him and the car as they were talking.

"John, Aurora and I appreciate you coming to the Kalani's funeral it was very nice of you especially since you really did not know her but being here and supportive just shows how sweet you are. Again, thank you," She started crying while leaning on John even more.

Aurora rolled her eyes at Eliza.

"John I need to talk with you about something please so I will ride with you." Rolling her eyes at Eliza. She walked over to John's car. Watching her being so fake leaning all over John was irritating because it was nothing but an act.

Eliza became instantly irritated knowing John was about to leave her but she hid it well.

"Stay sweet John and thanks again for being here. Call me so we can talk." She pressed her body on his and kissed him on the lips then got in her car, winked at Aurora and drove away.

He saw the bad look on Aurora's face as he walked toward his car. He opened the door for her to get in and he did the same and was getting ready to leave when she hit his leg.

"John, this is not a statement made from jealousy because I know my self-worth but I know you see Eliza for what she is. Yes, we are friends to some degree but her personality is devious so be careful."

John smiled while staring at her because she stimulates his mind and body. He is interested in them spending more time together, starting with today. He leans over to kiss her but she holds her hand up in front of his face.

"Stop, I know you are not about to kiss me with Eliza's saliva still on your lips." She quickly wipes John's lips with her hand and then slowly leaned over kissing him. "Let's go back to my place so we can talk.

"No problem with me." He drove away smiling.

Aurora lived in North Raleigh in a very nice two-bedroom condo with a pool and a two-car garage. When the garage door opened, John saw a blue BMW 760 Li.

"That is a nice car starting at a hundred and forty thousand dollars. You are doing it nicely."

"Thanks, it's just a car. I have learned not to get too attached to any materialistic thing. Friendship and love is much stronger if it's real."

John drove his car in the garage and they walked in her house which is decorated very nicely with expensive furniture all over the place. Aurora leans over to remove her shoes then looked back at John knowing he was staring at her butt. She smiled and walked to her bedroom and called John. When he walked in Aurora was standing there naked except for the heels she was wearing.

"Damn! You are gorgeous and your body is flawless."

"John, I don't want to talk right now. Stay with me today please and I will answer all of your questions tomorrow." She walks over to her king size bed and laid down looking at him.

"Tomorrow it's then." He removed all his clothes and joined her on the bed.

For the rest of the day, they sexually explored each other's body. Sometimes in a very serious manner and other times just laughing and being silly. They ate, went swimming in the pool, drank a little wine and back to bed. Then, fall asleep and wake up doing it all over again.

The following morning John woke up to an empty bed. He smelled food because Aurora was in the kitchen cooking breakfast. Scrambled eggs, French toast, turkey sausage, freshly cut cantaloupe and orange juice. John got up took a quick shower and walked out to the kitchen wearing dress slacks. Aurora was wearing a robe. He walked over hugged and kissed her. His hands are caressing the contours of her body and he discovered she was naked underneath the robe. She smacked his hands and laughed.

"Later lover, let's sit down and enjoy this breakfast I cooked." She kisses him and they sit down at the dining room table eating and talking about many things. With sadness John stares at her.

"Is something wrong John?"

"No, earlier you called me lover. I need to be direct with you. I know we just met and we are doing our thing but I don't want to just be your lover. My interest in you at this point is for us to become great friends and take it one day at a time."

She studied John's face as he was talking and felt his vibe.

"Okay, and I appreciate you being direct with me and I will do the same. You are the first guy that I have brought to my home and I have not been with anyone sexually in over a year and I come from

RONALD GRAY 191

money so material things do not impress me. My Mom, Dad, Brother and Sister are still in Ethiopia but they travel all over the world. I am so far from jealous but I am territorial. What is mine is mine. I am attracted to ladies as well and yes, before you ask, I experienced that a long time ago. You interest me a lot, if not you would not be here. You would probably be with Eliza. Speaking of her, I will go ahead and share this with you so she cannot try and use it against me later." She lowers her head then looks at him. "Eliza and I have been together sexually. It happened one time long ago when we were hanging out one night at a party and ended up at a hotel. It was a heated moment before I got to really know her and she still tries to seduce me at times but I am not interested. How is that for being direct?"

"That is a lot to share and I appreciate it all. So, where do we go from here?"

"Well, we finish eating and go back to bed and make love. Then I'll take you shopping in New York."

John is all smiles and impressed. They finished eating and he walked over and pushed Aurora's seat away from the table, and kneels down opening her robe and bury his face between her legs.

"Oh John." She leans back and enjoys his warm tongue.

Chapter 38

Veronica

Lewis business is doing very well and he has Tashianna to thank for it because if she never told him about the creepy man he would not be doing well at all. He changed Tashianna's pay from hourly to salary and she is making fifty thousand dollars a year now. He would also give her a minimum of one thousand dollars whenever he got paid from a case. But his home life changed for the worse and he could not understand why. Veronica seem to have an attitude often and she stopped having sex with him. She also started spending a lot of time in the gym which he thought was a good way for her to release some stress.

After ten hours at work he walked in the house and sees Veronica standing in the living room wearing some tight spandex pants and a revealing top. Yes, he knows it's what ladies wear in the gym but she has always been so conservative in her dress.

"So is this how you dress now when you go to the gym. Tight pants on and showing your breasts. What is wrong with you? Are you cheating on me Christian Lady?" He laughs because he knows his wife is Jesus crazy.

"Oh, so you think this is funny and you have no room to talk, Mr. Morality. You think I am stupid Lewis and don't know what is going on with you and that slut assistant of yours. Paying her all that money now. I know you two are having sex."

"What! Are you crazy? I am not having sex with Tashianna and never have and I do not know where you are getting all of this. Okay, you don't like how she dresses but she is good at her job and dependable which is hard to find these days, so give me a break with all this nonsense. Look, it has been a long day and I just got home and I do not want to argue with you so just chill with the craziness."

She walks toward Lewis and with each step you can see the anger building up in her eyes. Veronica slaps Lewis so hard spit flies out of his mouth.

"Don't insult me you lying bastard. I wanted to surprise you at work one day and I saw you two kissing and you had your hands all over that fat ass of hers so stop lying to me." She slaps him again and screams. "I know you are fucking her Lewis." She drops to her knees crying.

Lewis reaches down to touch her but she slaps his hand away and quickly stands up facing him with eyes of hate.

"Don't touch me, don't you ever touch me again Lewis and I mean it."

Lewis understands everything now and he feels so bad about putting his wife through this who he loves deeply and no matter how fine Tashianna is and anyone else for that matter, he would never cheat on his wife.

"Veronica please listen to me. I am truly sorry about that and can only say I got caught up in the moment of some good news concerning business. Things at work had been going downhill and I seriously thought I was going to lose everything but on that day, I got some great news. You only saw my reaction that is it, I am not having sex with her or any woman so please forgive me because you know I love you Veronica."

She is staring at him trying to remain angry but she can see the seriousness in his eyes.

"I don't know; I just don't know Lewis. I need time to myself to think about all of this." She walks toward the door.

"Veronica wait." He grabs her arm but she quickly pulls away and slaps him again.

"I told you not to touch me." Veronica is looking at him with such hate. "I need to get out of here before I sin some more. Lord forgive me." She walks out slamming the door.

Lewis walks over to the sofa and sit down. Tears begin to flow and he prays.

"Oh Lord, I am so sorry for all I have done. Hurting my wife and myself in the process please forgive me father. Help me Lord." He lays down on the sofa and falls asleep.

Four hours later, Lewis cell phone rings and wakes him. It's from a previous client of his named Wilson calling to let him know that he saw his wife in the lobby of the Crabtree Valley Hotel drinking and all over some guy. Lewis jumped up and ran out of the house, got in his car, arriving at the hotel in twenty minutes. When he walked in the lobby he saw Wilson sitting down and Wilson saw him and stood up.

"Mr. Stevens I know this is a messed-up situation but you got to be cool man and don't do anything stupid because things are not always as they seem. Anyway, I owe you because you saved me from doing twenty years in prison from the drug charge. I knew you would get it no matter what, so I got the room number for you and the room key card but I am going up there with you to possibly keep you out of prison."

"Okay but I am cool and thanks for the call, let's walk."

Lewis was anything but cool because with each step taken he feared the worse. During the short elevator ride the walls seem like they were closing in on him and walking down the hallway to her room made his heart rate increase. They arrived at the room and Wilson handed him the key card.

"Remember you got to be cool. I did a short stay in prison and it's no fun and you aint built for prison." He laughed to make him relax.

Lewis exhaled slowly, put the key card in and slowly opened the door. He and Wilson quietly walked in but what they saw and heard makes them both stand still. Veronica was on her hands and knees close to the feet of the bed and a tall muscular black guy was standing at the feet of the bed with his hands gripping Veronica's hips, fucking her. She was moaning and screaming.

"Yes, fuck me, fuck me hard, ahhhhhh."

She and the guy turned their heads at the same time and see Lewis and Wilson standing there.

"Oh my God, Lewis." She quickly leaps forward grabbing the sheets to cover up.

The guy quickly reaches for his pants but never made it because Lewis and Wilson leaped on him beating him unconscious while Veronica is screaming stop. Lewis is staring at her and then loses it. He leaped on the bed grabbing her by the throat with both hands choking her. Wilson was able to pull him off and wrestled Lewis to the floor.

"I am going to kill her, let me go Wilson so I can kill her."

Veronica is still screaming and crying while she quickly gets dressed and Wilson held Lewis to the floor until he calmed down. Veronica runs out of the room and Lewis tries to catch her but Wilson grabs him. They sit down and Wilson starts talking to him but Lewis is in such a daze he does not hear a word because the images of what he just saw and heard are burned in his head. Tears come down his face until he can't hold it in any longer and puts his hands over his face and screams from his very gut and soul feeling like he is going to faint. His pain is beyond measure but all Wilson can do is hold him. Two hours later they are just leaving the room Lewis walked toward the guy who is still unconscious on the floor and gets his wallet out of his pants pocket to look at his driver's license. Reginald Grimes. He put the wallet back and they left and walked to the hotel lobby and sat down.

"Lewis, I can say I do know what you are going through because this is how I ended up in prison the first time. Came home from work early one day, walked in the bedroom and caught my fiancée in bed with two guys. Needless to say, neither one will ever walk straight again. I went to prison but the judge was lenient because of the circumstances and only gave me two years. I would not want you to end up there."

"Let me say thanks for everything especially keeping me from probably killing my wife. I am exhausted and just want to go home and sleep. Before you say anything that is the last place my wife would be." He stands up and extends his hand. "Thanks again Wilson I owe you big time."

Wilson shakes his hand.

"Don't sweat it just call me tomorrow and we can sit down and talk."

Lewis hugged him, walked out got in his car and drove home crying all the way. When he walked in the door he is shocked to see his wife sitting on the floor crying and praying. He walked over and picked her up from the floor holding Veronica tightly as tears came to his eyes. He kisses her on the lips then twisted her neck so hard out of pure anger that it popped and her body falls to the floor. Lewis checked her pulse.

"Noooo." He screams because she is dead. "No Lord, I did not mean it. Veronica." He screams her name so loud it hurt his throat and he continued crying while holding his wife's dead body. An hour later after staring out in space Lewis stood up and went in the backyard into the shed and grabbed a shovel. He digs a very deep hole and drug his wife's body out the house dropping it in the hole. He takes all his clothes off putting them in the hole as well, then mixes up some bags of concrete ready-mix pouring it in the hole covering the body. He also put the shovel in then uses his hands to put the rest of the dirt in and plants flowers all over the grave site. He uses the water hose to rinse off and walks back in the house straight to the shower. Lewis fell asleep on the living room sofa.

The following morning, he filed a missing person report for Veronica. Contrary to what so many people say concerning waiting, it's not true. When you believe, someone is missing you can file a missing person report at that time. Lewis received a great deal of support from Mary, James, and so many others after telling them he found Veronica with another guy. Lewis said she probably ran off with him. The police talked to Reginald Grimes but was convinced he was telling the truth and that he had no information as to where Veronica was. Lewis continues with his legal practice and is getting richer every month. At what price? Guilt was affecting him to a point that he was taking pills just to sleep and pills to function throughout the day.

Chapter 39

Sherry Richardson

Sherry is in the bedroom smiling looking at herself in the mirror wearing heels, panties and a bra. She could not believe it and felt like a new woman with all the weight she has lost. It is a dream come true. Not only has she lost the weight but her body is also very tight from working out so hard in the gym with her personal trainer. She thanks Doctor Eyes for doing his thing but of course this is her secret. Sherry now weighs one hundred and thirty-eight pounds and has not been this size in twenty years. Her and James are going out for dinner to spend quality time together because they both have been so busy with their business and the family. They also have been spending a lot of time with Lewis, being a friend knowing he is hurting so badly concerning Veronica's betrayal and disappearance. Sherry did not want to think about all of that now because it's just too depressing. James walked out of the bathroom dressed very nicely and seeing his wife smiling so hard looking at herself in the mirror makes him smile as well. Yes, he is very proud of her for losing the weight although he never stopped loving her or showing her continued affection and genuine care. He walked over and kissed the back of her neck and put his arms around her.

"You look gorgeous Sherry and I am very proud of you for losing the weight because you have been so very unhappy." He caresses her hips while pressing his body against hers.

"James, I thank you for always loving me and treating me so well but the weight loss was for me first and for you because I know you like this tight body you see." She pushes back into him feeling what is her desire. "James I know you want this hot body of mine right now so stop playing. We can go out later baby." Gyrating her body against his. "Much later."

James erection was concrete hard. He wanted Sherry so badly, not because of the weight loss but because he has the hots for her and always has. Tonight, they needed to spend quality time together and not just in the bedroom so he backed up.

"Baby, you know how badly I want you right now but later will be even better for us so let's go out to eat and have some fun. We don't even have to come back here after dinner we can check into a hotel and get buck wild."

"Now that is what I am talking about and the husband I know. We need to spice things up. All married couples do, especially married Christians who get too comfortable in their lives and become boring doing the same thing over and over."

"True that baby. Now get your sexy-self dressed so we can leave." Lightly smacking her on the butt.

"You love this hot body baby because of the freakiness in you that makes me love you even more. Freaky, praying husband, love it." She kisses him and walked away to get dressed.

They arrive at the five-star Saint Jacques restaurant in Raleigh which has great French dishes normally you need to have a reservation to get in but James reputation speaks for itself. He and Sherry walked in holding hands and James always feels good when he is with his wife. However, he does not particularly like the outfit she is wearing. It is a little too revealing for his taste. For years, she has dressed well but in a conservative manner but the dress she is wearing now is far from conservative. It's too tight revealing all her curves and has a low-neck line that shows too much cleavage. He wanted to ask Sherry to wear something else before they left the house but he did not want to spoil the great mood she was in. When

RONALD GRAY

they were escorted to their table Sherry noticed the stares she was getting from the men and loved it but she knew James did not like her dress. He would get over it because she has worked too hard and sacrificed so much to get where she is now. They ordered their food and for the next two hours it was all talk and flirting between them until they finally left and walked to their car. Sherry tapped James on the arm.

"James I just had an idea baby. Let's go to that new Jazz lounge that we have been hearing so much about that opened about six months ago. Yes, Terrence Washington owns it. I know you don't like him that much and neither do I. Just thinking about Katrina dealing with him bothers me but hopefully her career will go well. Anyway, the reviews have been great and it has a dress code which I know you like, so let's go baby because I am in the mood to hear some nice relaxing music."

"Actually, that's a good idea despite who he is. I am not in the mood to go home anyway although getting you in bed is high on my list." He looks around as they are walking then caresses her hips. "Very high on my list, Lord have mercy." He smiled.

"You are something James and I am all yours baby and always have been but you can wait. It will be good for you. Too much of this sweetness might mess up your brain." She kisses him on the cheek and laughed and kept walking.

James is thinking, *Oh, now she is getting cocky talking to me like that but I got something for her when we get home, I am going to teach Mrs. Sherry Richardson a good lesson.*

There is a line in front of the Jazz lounge which is called; *House of Groove* but James and Sherry walk to the front and the attendant working the front door recognizes them. He shakes James hand and they walked in being escorted to the VIP section and sat down.

James looked around the place and had to admit, it's very nice with a classy appeal and the décor is good even for his taste. The band is good and he likes the selection of songs they are playing from various artist; Miles Davis, John Coltrane, Louis Armstrong, Thelonious Monk and Dizzy Gillespie. Song after song is played and James and Sherry are loving it smiling at each other and swaying their bodies to these wonderful sounds. James does not drink but Sherry orders a glass of wine which he gives her the look of disapproval. She hugs and kisses him and continues to enjoy herself knowing how to deal with him later.

Finally arriving home at two o'clock in the morning, they are still laughing and flirting with each other all the way to the bedroom. James waste no time getting Sherry's clothes off but she playfully pushes him away and stands there naked with her hands on her hips.

"So, James Richardson do think you can handle this body of mine and all of my new energy baby?" Smiling and slowly dancing in front of him, dropping it low and coming back up.

He looks at his wife doing her thing and he removes his clothes standing there with a full erection looking down at it and then at her.

"What do you think? Come here sexy."

"No." She waves her finger at him. "You come to me baby."

"My pleasure." He walked to her and for the next hour they made passionate love but Sherry is more aggressive than usual. She talks dirty, using language that she has not used in years and is very nasty during their love making. James just accepts it thinking she is caught up with her new look and confidence and continues to please his wife with intense passion.

If he only knew!

Chapter 40
Katrina's Show

Ever since Katrina came back from seeing Doctor Eyes things for her have been happening very fast. She moved out of the house knowing it would be impossible for her to make the moves necessary for her life and music career living at home. Also, it made it easier for her and Terrence to have a greater private involvement. She was putting out hit songs one after another. Doing small shows at first then selling out everywhere she goes and making a lot of money in the process. Her and Terrence are lovers on a regular basis now and she renewed her contract before it was even close to being over. This was a mistake because Terrence now owns her. In a very short time he has made over ten million dollars from her singing career by being kind to her, paying her on time, and sexing her on a regular.

Katrina was sexually turned out by Terrence. She knew and loved it. She allowed Terrence to do whatever he wanted to her body giving him oral sex on a regular basis and even participated in threesomes at times with him and another girl of her choice. Her and Terrence watched porn together many times which is where she got many of her ideas. She was smoking weed on a regular basis but did not drink. Katrina felt on top of the world but deep inside she felt something was missing and knew what it was, her relationship with God. She suppressed these feelings daily because it hurt to think about it. The relationship with her family is not the same and she knows it's because she hides many things from them. She disappointed her Dad by not listening to him and now it's too late because she is in way too deep to stop and does not want to. She is living her dream and feels it's only going to get bigger.

Terrence would see Katrina in deep thought often and he knew what it was, so to keep her mind where he wanted it he would be extra nice to her, smoking weed and having wild sex. Anything to keep Katrina's mind on what he wanted for her life.

It's Saturday morning the day of Katrina's biggest concert performance so far. It's at the Walnut Creek Amphitheatre in Raleigh, NC which seats twenty thousand people. Other artists are performing but she is the main attraction and appears last. All her family members and friends are here, even Raymond with his busy basketball career. She is nervous and confidant at the same time. Today's concert is a sold-out event and Terrence already has her booked to sing in New York. After the other artists performed it was her turn and all the stage lights were turned out except one that is shining in the middle of the stage. The music starts and Katrina walks out on stage dressed very provocatively wearing heels, and tight shorts showing her butt cheeks and an almost see through top with no bra. She starts singing and dancing and the crowd is enjoying her wonderful voice. As she continues to sing other songs they are on their feet at this point clapping hands and dancing. Katrina's voice is incredible by anyone's standard. She also dances very well and moves her body perfectly to every song and beat. She performed for an hour giving the crowd all that she has before walking off stage to a standing ovation. Terrence was waiting back stage for her and she ran to his open arms feeling great about her performance. She kissed him repeatedly before backing up looking at him.

"Terrence what do you think?"

"Baby girl the show was great but you already know this and so does the crowd, from their response. You did a wonderful job and that voice of yours is beyond fantastic." He hugs her again and is thinking. *That is why I have been making so much money off you and will make millions more.* "It's celebration time for us but I know all of your family is here and you need to spend time with them, as you should. Go hang out with family and just call me when you are ready because I have some great ideas for you and some songs that you need to practice later."

"Okay, no problem I will call you when I am done. Thanks for everything Terrence and for believing in me." She hugs and kisses him again and he walks away.

Terrence purposely wanted to avoid spending any time with her family because he knew James did not like him and he seemed to be able to see right through him. He could care less because the only thing Terrence cares about is making money.

Katrina changed clothes because no way did she want her family, especially her Dad to see her the way she was dressed any longer than necessary. She quickly changed into some dress pants and a nice blouse. They all greeted her back stage as well giving her hugs and many compliments for a wonderful show but James wanted to be the last to greet her so he could focus.

Sherry hugged her.

"Baby I am so proud of you and your voice is all that and then some." She whispered in her ear. "We know who to thank for that voice." She kissed her on the cheek.

The moment James hugged Katrina he could feel something very spiritually wrong but he has been feeling this from her for a while and Sherry as well but he was not going to spoil this day for his daughter.

"Hi sweetie. The show was good and your voice is beautiful I love you and always will. You know I am very proud of you no matter what." He hugged her again.

Katrina smoked some weed before her performance to relax, more before coming out to greet her family and hopefully no one could smell it on her. As she looked into her Dad's eyes she has to hold back the tears because she sees so much care and love in his eyes.

"Thank you Dad, even though you did not want me to live this life I know you love me." She stares at him and the tears fall and all she can do is hug him. "Thanks Dad for loving me so much."

Katrina talks and laughs with everyone and eventually Jocelyn has a moment with her.

"I am proud of you Katrina for all of your hard work and the show was fantastic."

"Thanks Jocelyn for your support. I know you are doing big things as well. Singing in clubs all over Charlotte and other places as well, girl you are doing it and your dedication is paying off. I wish you and Raymond nothing but the best."

Raymond is standing by Jocelyn's side and is all smiles as he hugs and kisses her.

"That's my baby." He kisses her again.

"Okay, that is enough of that. You two can do all of that kissing later." Sherry said and lightly punches Raymond on his arm.

John, Jacob and Crystal talk with Katrina for a while until they all leave together in limos and their own vehicles.

Chapter 41
Tashianna's Time

Tashianna loves the money she is making at her job but things at the office were not the same because Lewis has not been his usual playful self. She fully understands this, especially after hearing the details of Lewis catching his wife at the hotel having sex with another man, a black man at that and he may not be prejudice at all but this must mess with his head. Then Veronica mysteriously disappearing but Tashianna felt in her heart that Lewis had something to do with her disappearance. She would never mention it to him or anyone because of Doctor Eyes and his reputation.

Lewis legal firm finances are great now and he is rich but still very sad. One day Lewis was in his office crying and she heard him so she went in to talk and just listen to him but things went a lot further than she had anticipated. Lewis kissed her which she did not mind because he was so distraught and wanted to comfort him but they ended up on the sofa having sex which surprisingly, Lewis was good. Tashianna felt so bad because she really like Jimmy. They talked afterwards and Lewis repeatedly apologized and it never happened again. She would never tell Jimmy because she strongly believes that some things in life you do not tell, ever and this was one of them. She would never want Jimmy to find out because she knew he would leave her with a quickness. Lewis promised that he would not tell anyone as well, so he hugged her and continued with business as usual.

Jimmy and Tashianna have become very close after spending so much time together and going so many different places doing different things. Their conversations have been very detailed and personal which is always a risk in the process of getting to know someone but is the only real way this can be accomplished. Shawn has not been spending that much time at the shop in months so Jimmy has been basically running the business. It has prospered a lot and he desires to get involved in something else because he knows he does not want to work on cars all his life. He and Tashianna have been talking about starting some type of business together that they both would enjoy and would work for them. Tashianna enjoys doing legal work but she gets tired of being in the office so much and Jimmy enjoys working on cars but he is tired of the dust and want to do something else using his hands. So, they seriously discussed going into real estate and flipping houses. Buying property that need work and fixing them up and selling them which they both like this idea and talked about a fifty percent partnership in this venture. Tashianna has been saving her money and wanted her and Jimmy to purchase their first property and see how things go. She did not mind doing all the paper work but wanted to do some of the light construction work as well. Three weeks later they purchased their first property in Raleigh. A four-bedroom house that needed work. Even after the cost of the house and they figured in renovations, the property could still make them a fifty-thousand-dollar profit. Six weeks later renovations on the house was complete and a month later the house was sold, making them a profit of sixty-five thousand dollars which they split equally. You can tell a lot about someone when you deal with them on a financial level because money makes the true spirit of a person come out but things with them went great. It was at this time that Jimmy asked Tashianna to be his lady in a committed relationship. She smiled and said yes. They celebrated their commitment to business with each other with a four-day trip to Maui Hawaii. They stayed at the Grand Wailea

Waldorf Astoria Resort. Their hotel room suite was very nice and overlooked the ocean. The first day they walked on the beach and did some shopping and although they wanted each other sexually with no question they showered together and laid down on the bed and fell asleep holding hands. In the morning, you could feel the breeze coming in from the windows, hear the waves hitting the rocks and moans coming from the bedroom as Tashianna and Jimmy are making passionate love for the first time. Tashianna told Jimmy she loves him as tears rolled down her cheeks and she is staring into his eyes.

"Jimmy I don't get attached to people easily because I do not allow people to get that close to me but you have been able to touch my heart deeply in such a short time. I am not asking you to do the repeat after me thing but I hope that you feel the same way about me."

Every word she spoke resonated in Jimmy's heart and he admitted to himself that what they shared and how he feels about her is very special.

"Tashianna, I thank you for opening up your heart to me and I am sure it was not easy for you to do especially after the various things that you have been through. But just so you will know I am in love with you and I have been for a while or we would not be here."

The look he gave Tashianna and what she felt from that look said volumes and all she could do is snuggle closer to him.

"I am not ready to get up yet Jimmy will you hold me for a while, please."

"That's easy." He held her until they both fell asleep.

Hours later after they had eaten in one of the great restaurants in the hotel, they felt energetic and in the mood for some water sports

RONALD GRAY

209

so they went jet skiing, para sailing, and later they snorkeled in the incredible blue waters. The next two days were much of the same except, on the day before they left and the sun was close to setting they were swimming in a secluded part of the beach. Their playing and affection moved to having sex in shoulder deep water that hid their activities. Jimmy picked up Tashianna while in the water and sat her on his dick with her arms around his neck holding on as she rode him hard and fast. Only the crashing of the waves and wind drowned out Tashianna's cries of ecstasy when the orgasm hit her body making Jimmy almost fall but he managed to stay upright before his own passions took over and he exploded inside her. They both submerged themselves under the water and came up at the same time laughing and walked back to their hotel room, showered and slept good.

Chapter 42
Eliza's Greed

Crystal talked Jacob into going with her and two of her female friends to the movies which he did not want to because he was supposed to meet some buddies of his in the gym to do some sparring. Jacob has been training in the martial arts since he was ten and now at seventeen he was good in mixed martial arts and wanted to compete full time. He agreed to go because he was attracted to one of the girls going with them. He wanted to use this opportunity to talk with her even when Crystal told him to be a gentleman. He agreed and said sure and she gave him a mean look. All four of them went out to eat first before the movies and Jacob and Michele, the girl he was attracted to were able to talk and connected well. Michele was five feet four eighteen years old and attractive with a lean figure. She had curves and was a little wilder than Jacob but he liked it. They went to the movies after wards.

Eliza was in the theater as well and happened to be sitting right behind them with one of the guys that was harassing Jacob and Crystal in the mall some time ago. His name is Derek and he sold weed on a regular basis. Throughout the show, Eliza kept hearing Jacob and Michele talk and heard her call his full name several times while laughing and having fun. Crystal and her friend told them to be quiet. Eliza now knew who Jacob was because of the Richardson's name. Jacob is John's brother who chose Aurora over her, which she did not like but was about to have some fun. Eliza told Derek who Jacob was and told him to do something for her and she would have sex with him later which was a lie.

When the movie was over and everyone was walking out of the theater Derek walked up behind Crystal and smacked her hard on the butt and she quickly turned around.

"Are you crazy boy?"

Derek never saw Jacob move in front of him until it was too late and Jacob hit him three times real fast. Two jabs to the body and one to the jaw and he fell down bleeding. Security quickly escorted Derek out and Eliza apologized to them saying she did not know he was that type of guy and she invited them to a house party for later that night and they agreed to go.

It was eleven thirty that night. Jacob, Crystal and Michele rode together and arrived at the address Eliza gave them. It is a large house in a nice-looking neighborhood on the south side of Raleigh. Eliza saw them when they came in and greeted them with hugs like she has known them for years introducing them to others as they walked throughout the house. Music was playing loud and food was plentiful. You could smell marijuana and Jacob wanted to leave but Michele talked him into staying by kissing and hugging him hoping they would have sex later. Crystal and Michele managed to slip away from Jacob to go with some others to smoke some weed. Eliza used this opportunity to talk with Jacob. An hour later Jacob and Eliza were in a bedroom by themselves and she was laying on the bed in her bra and panties but Jacob was still dressed. As fine as she is and as badly as Jacob wanted her something inside of him told him to go find his sister.

"Look, I know this is really bad timing but I need to go check on my sister first and then I will be back."

Eliza looked at him like he is crazy.

"Your sister, are you crazy? You can't leave all of this."

He just kissed her and walked out.

Crystal and Michele were in a bedroom drinking and smoking weed with other people for a while and fell asleep. One of the guys that Crystal was smoking with put something in her drink that made her pass out. She woke up lying on a bed naked in an empty room and some guy were on top of her. She started screaming, kicking and hitting to get the guy off her but he was too strong and was able to penetrate her. She screamed so loud that Jacob heard it and tried to open the door but it was locked so he quickly kicked it in. The sight he saw enraged him like nothing in his life. His sister was being raped. He ran over and pulled the guy off her and hit him repeatedly kicking him hard as he tried to fight back. Jacob broke his ribs, arm and leg. Crystal was quickly getting dressed as Jacob was beating the guy then Michele, Eliza, and a few others walked in after hearing screams. Jacob was behind the guy and had him in a choke hold which was killing him but he did not realize this because of his rage and Michele and Eliza ran over to him.

"Jacob, stop you are going to kill him, please stop." Eliza said.

"Stop Jacob you are choking him to death." Michele said and hit him on the arm.

This got his attention and made Jacob snap out of his enraged state of mind and he let the guy go and kicked him away. His body rolled on the floor unconscious. It was only then that Jacob's actions bring him to reality.

"I killed him."

Michele slowly walked over to check the guy's pulse and he is breathing.

"He is not dead Jacob." She walked back over to comfort Crystal who was standing against the wall staring at the guy on the floor secretly wishing he was dead for what he just did to her. She knew wishing him dead was so wrong and Jacob would be in so much trouble. Jacob stood up and walked over to Crystal and hugged her.

Eliza set all this up but it did not go exactly like she planed because she wanted to have some freaky sex with Jacob. First to mess up his mind and get him sprung on her, then to dump him and use his hurt to get to John by distracting him so he would leave Aurora but he walked out of the room. No one has ever walked out on Eliza which bruised her ego a little but nothing some weed and great sex with someone else's man would not fix.

Crystal, Michele and Jacob walked out of the house and got in the car and drove away. Crystal and Michele were sitting in the back and Michele was holding her.

Jacob looked at Crystal's face in the rear-view mirror seeing her fear and unwillingness to talk. His heart went out to her and the image of what he saw will forever be burned in his head. He has a very protective nature but he feels on this day, he let her down and it was hurting him deeply.

"Crystal what happened? Please talk to me I am so worried, what happened? Did the guy attack you, did he rape you?"

"I don't want to talk about it Michele I am fine."

"I am taking you to the hospital Crystal." Jacob said holding back his own tears as he looked at her in the rear-view mirror.

"No!" Crystal shouted looking up at Jacob as he was driving. "No Jacob just take me home I will be fine, please take me home."

"No, you have to get checked out Crystal."

"No Jacob, I just want to go home. Please, please take me home, please Jacob."

All Jacob could see was such intense pain and hurt in his sister's eyes so he had no choice but to take her home after dropping Michele off first. He walked Michele to the door and she hugged and kissed him and went inside the house. Jacob wiped off his lips with his hand and spit on the ground because of his anger toward Michele, she smelled like weed. Jacob also blamed her because he felt if she remained by his sister's side like friends do, then this would not have happened. He got back in the car and Crystal was sitting up front now and when he drove away she laid her head on his shoulder for the entire ride home but never said a word.

After arriving home, Crystal hit Jacob lightly on the arm after they got out of the car.

"Jacob, I know you are hurting from what you saw and we both need help from God but you have to promise me Jacob that you will not tell a living soul and I mean it. This has to stay between us, so do not tell Mom, Dad or anyone please. Oh, and do not get weak on me and do the, I just had to confess it to somebody thing. Please keep my secret to the grave Jacob, please."

"Okay I will not tell and just for the record I am not weak but you really need to get checked out Crystal for your own health."

"I will get a physical later but for now, I am going in the house, take a shower, cry myself to sleep and wake up and pretend all this was just a horrible nightmare." She hugged him.

They walked in the house hoping not to wake James or Sherry. Jacob went to his room and fell on the bed with tears running down his face. Crystal spends thirty minutes in the shower, then put her night clothes on and got in bed. She put her face in the pillow and screamed, crying hysterically because she lost her virginity to a rapist.

"Oh God help me please." She cried until she fell asleep.

Chapter 43
New York

John and Aurora flew to New York and both are dressed very nicely. A limo took them to the Baccarat Hotel in midtown Manhattan and of course Aurora was turning heads as they walked but John enjoyed every minute of it. They checked into their suite and John quickly but gently pushed Aurora against the wall taking off her clothes and his. He started kissing her lips, neck, breasts, and worked his way down until she felt his warm mouth between her legs giving Aurora a quick orgasm. Then he slid inside her and ten minutes later it was over. Aurora was smiling because although it did not last long, the sex was so good and she loved his spontaneity. They played around in the shower for a while then got dressed and went shopping.

Raymond was in New York on business concerning one of his endorsement deals and Jocelyn was with him. A crowd of people were around them trying to get his autograph as he walked out of Madison Square Garden. John and Aurora were walking across the street carrying shopping bags when John saw his brother.

"Raymond Richardson." He yelled. "You are not all that." Smiling, because he loves his brother.

Raymond and Jocelyn looked across the street seeing John and Aurora. Raymond was all smiles. He thanked the crowd of people, grabbed Jocelyn's hand, ran across the street and hugged John and Aurora.

"It's great to see you John but you two are the last people I expected to see today. What are you and Aurora doing in New York?"

"I am surprised to see you as well my brother. We are just having fun. Aurora is taking me shopping." He smiled and kissed her then winked at Raymond.

Raymond put his arm around John's neck and they stepped away so the girls would not hear what he was about to say.

"Oh, so you got it like that now. She is taking you shopping not you taking her. Man, you must have put some work in my brother."

"We had very stimulating conversations which allowed us to connect in a special way." He looked at Raymond and they both laughed.

"Aurora, it's great to see you again and I hope you and John are having a good time in New York. Are you really taking him shopping?" Jocelyn said looking at her.

"Yes, it's true. I like John a lot and we have connected well."

"I am sure you two have my sister." They both laughed.

Raymond and John walked back over to the girls and they all decided to go out to eat together. Afterwards John and Aurora will continue shopping.

Katrina and Terrence are sitting down eating at the Pcr Sc restaurant in Manhattan taking a break from a hectic recording session. Katrina's fame and fortune has continued to increase significantly which she enjoys but she does miss the simple life at times, spending time with family. Her energy has been a little low and she's not feeling her best. Terrence noticed Katrina's distant behavior and was doing what he could not to tire her out because that would be messing with his money, however he was becoming irritated with the constant mood swings.

"Katrina, are you okay, you don't seem your usual self and you are not really eating your food. Are you sick?" He is thinking, *Please, don't be sick with these upcoming shows I have booked.*

"Maybe you need to go back to the hotel and get some rest baby and let me take care of you. I'll give you a nice massage and then I can tap that ass." He smiled at her.

Katrina frowned at him.

"Is that all you think about Terrence is sex, never mind don't answer that. I will be okay but I do miss spending time with my family. All you speak of is sex, what about love?"

"Yeah alright. Love is good but so many people talk that love stuff, get married and then divorced and fight in court, not over love but money. Love is great but overrated. You are left with a broke crushed heart and your mind is all messed up thinking about jumping off a damn bridge somewhere." He looks at her then lowers his head not wanting Katrina to see his deep long ago pain.

This is the very first time Katrina has seen this side of Terrence and wonders did all of this happen to him which would be the reason why he only seems to care about money and sex but no real emotional attachment.

"Terrence, did you fall in love with someone years ago, and she broke your heart? Please talk to me because I do care and you know it."

He looks at her wondering should he talk to her after keeping all this pain to himself for so long. No, but she almost had him.

"Everyone has a story to tell Katrina but life moves on pretty lady." He smiled and winked at her to change the subject and lighten the mood.

Katrina blew him a kiss then looked up and a huge smile comes across her face because she sees Raymond, Jocelyn, John and Aurora walk in the door. Without even thinking about it she quickly stands up.

"Richardson family." She yelled and quickly runs over to them hugging Raymond first then John, Jocelyn, and Aurora. "Wow, what a surprise I can't believe this, all of you here in New York and in here."

"Sis, it's great to see you with your busy schedule." Raymond said hugging her again.

"Look who is talking basketball star." Jocelyn said playfully hitting him in the chest.

"Katrina I miss you and you look good, a little tired but good." John said.

"You do look good Katrina. So, are you here by yourself?" Aurora said.

"No Terrence is here." She turns her head and points at him then waves at him to come over.

Terrence stood up and gave her a fake smile because dealing with her family is not a priority on his list but necessary. He walked over to them smiling.

Raymond greatly dislikes Terrence but tolerates him for his sister's sake. He shook his hand hard and Terrence squeezed back giving him the look that men do.

"What's up Raymond. Hi everyone." Terrence said smiling and waving.

Everyone spoke and they all sat down together to eat and talk. An hour later Terrence excused himself saying he had a meeting to attend and kissed Katrina and left which was all a lie but he wanted to get away from them.

"Katrina I am very happy for you and all of your success we all are and you know this but I don't like that guy and never have. Something about him is just bad, so please be careful and read all the paperwork well before signing it. If he ever gets it twisted and put his hands on you call me so I can…"

Raymond never finished his sentence because Jocelyn hit his arm giving him that look.

"Don't talk like that Raymond and do not get in trouble please."

John gave Jacelyn a look wondering whose side was she on.

"He did not say anything wrong, family is family."

"Everyone just relax please. I am fine. Terrence is not crazy and I can handle myself. Anyway, skip all of that because I am in the mood to go shopping. Aurora and Jocelyn what do you say?"

Both of them looked at each other smiling and said at the same time."

"Yes!" And laughed.

They talked for a while longer and left going from store to store buying clothes. After three hours of walking they were tired and called it quits hugging each other and went their separate ways.

Katrina and Terrence are staying at the Peninsula Hotel in midtown. When Katrina got back to her room she was glad that Terrence was not there because all she wanted to do was shower and sleep. A hot shower made her relax and feel better and she put a robe on and sat on the edge of the bed putting lotion on her legs. Suddenly she became dizzy and nauseous. Katrina quickly ran to the bathroom and threw up and sat on the floor crying and then got up brushed her teeth and laid down on the bed and fell asleep. Katrina woke up feeling bad but she had to know so she left the hotel and walked to a drug store that was close by and purchased a pregnancy test. She went back to her room and took the test. It was positive, she is pregnant. She laid back down crying and fell asleep.

Terrence walked in an hour later seeing Katrina on the bed with a robe on asleep. He was not happy because he was horny and wanted her. He laid on the bed and smacked her on the butt.

"Baby girl wake up, I am back." He kissed her on the lips and slid her robe open revealing that tight body which always sexually turned him on and made him rise. His hand gently caressed her breasts.

Katrina smacked his hand away and sat up looking at him frowning.

"Hi Terrence. Baby you know I do not turn you down but I am not feeling well and…" She quickly put her hand over her mouth and ran to the bathroom closing the door and threw up again.

This instantly changed Terrence's mood so he started smoking weed while lying on the bed. Katrina walked out holding her stomach looking at Terrence.

"Terrence, I do not feel well at all and I know what it's. Terrence, I am pregnant." Sitting on the bed next to him smiling.

He sat up and looked at her with a blank expression on his face.

"Pregnant, girl you can't be pregnant right now because it would interfere with your career." He is thinking, *Damn that baby crap, get rid of it and keep this money flowing.* "I don't want to sound mean but the timing is not good right now for you to be pregnant. And how do you know you are pregnant it could be that time of the month."

"You men are all alike. I know because I walked to the drug store and got a pregnancy test, its positive and it's in the bathroom trash if you want to see it. I know it's not great timing Terrence but be happy for us. You are going to be a Daddy." She moved closer putting her head on his shoulder while caressing his chest with her hand then looked up at him smiling.

His demeanor instantly changed and he got off the bed looking at her full of anger and resentment.

"No, damn all that baby Daddy crap. I have been down that road and the bitch lied to me and I bought a house and everything but found out later the baby was not even mine. After I spent all that money, over a million dollars for a house and furniture. Hell no, I don't want no baby today or tomorrow, so get rid of it." His look was so hard and heartless. "I will even go with you to the doctor for support so you can get it sucked out or whatever it is that is done these days. Bottom line is, just get rid of it and keep making this money so we all can live good. You will thank me later with no question. You are very young and can have a bunch of little babies later."

Katrina stared at Terrence with her mouth open in shock with all that he just said and the way he said it, totally heartless.

"I can't believe you Terrence I thought you cared about me. Fine, I can take care of myself and still have my baby I don't need you. To hell with you Terrence." Looking at him with just as much contempt.

He emotionally snapped thinking about his past and looking at her. He roughly grabbed Katrina by the arm pulling her across the bed and started taking his clothes off then holding her arms down.

"Oh, so now it's to hell with me. All the stuff I have done for your ungrateful ass. Everything that you got is because of me little girl, but it's to hell with me. Okay, but you are not having no baby, at least not this one, damn that. You are getting rid of this baby Katrina, even if I have to fuck it out of you." He forced himself on her and was very rough in everything he did.

"No Terrence, stop you are hurting me, get off me, stop." Swinging hard and hitting him in the face but it did no good.

This extremely rough sex went on for thirty minutes and Katrina never thought he would do something like this to her. Now she hated him but hated herself more because as badly as his treatment was she still had an orgasm. Seeing him smile when she was climaxing made her sick to the stomach all over again because Katrina is sure he thought she enjoyed it. She pulled the sheets up to her neck to cover up her nakedness then balled up in the fetal position and started crying.

"I can't believe you did this to me. You raped me Terrence, you raped me."

Fear gripped Terrence because he knows all a woman has to say is a man raped her and it's over. He got off the bed wrapping a sheet around his waist.

"What, girl don't say that because it's a lie. I did not rape you and don't ever say that again. You want me to go to prison for life for a lie."

Katrina sat up holding on to the sheets looking at him with hate beyond measure.

"It's not a lie Terrence you did rape me. Bottom line is if a woman says no and stop then its rape. How many times did I say no Terrence and told you to stop, screamed at you to stop? But you kept going thinking it was funny taking me, you sick perverted bastard. You raped me." Crying even harder.

Terrence does not know what to say or do now because he realizes he went too far and his life could be over.

"Okay, maybe the sex was too rough but don't sit there and tell me you did not like it because you were screaming your ass off when you climaxed because the dick was so good." Smiling at her.

Katrina is looking at him in shock and total disbelief.

"What! Are you crazy you sick freaky bastard? I hate you." She smacked him hard and then grabbed her stomach from intense pain and threw up on the bed but she also noticed blood on her leg. Katrina ran to the bathroom slamming the door.

An hour later she was still in the bathroom and Terrence called to have the sheets changed and was sitting in the chair smoking weed and thinking of how he was going to get out of this mess. Katrina cried the entire time in the bathroom because she knows what happened. Finally, she took a shower and walked out with a towel wrapped around her, seeing Terrence smoking weed like he did not have a care in the world. Any feelings and care she had for this man was gone, she felt nothing for him but contempt and hate. But what Terrence did not know was Katrina also purchased a small voice activated recorder when she went to the drug store and hid it under the bed. The entire conversation and horrible event was now on tape and she is glad that inner voice told her to get the recorder because at the right time she was going to use this to get out of her contract with Terrence and do her own thing. The recorder was on still. Katrina sat on the bed and looked at Terrence.

"Terrence, you hurt me when you raped me and I was bleeding a lot and I know I lost the baby which is murder to me. So now, not only are you a rapist but you are also a murderer. So there is no misunderstanding between us, don't ever touch me again and I want out of my contract with you and anything to do with your company. We are finished, I want nothing to do with you ever again, you rapist. Now get out of here and away from me before I call the police and tell them you raped me." Katrina was not going to do this but it was the only thing she could think of to say to scare him enough to leave.

If looks could kill Katrina would be dead right now the way Terrence was looking at her.

"No matter what you say I did not rape you Katrina and you are dealing with the wrong man if you think I am going to let some young hot ass girl destroy me or my business that has taken me years to build. You must be crazy young girl." He walked closer and got in her face. "I own your contract so I own you, deal with it." He quickly kissed her on the lips and she tried to smack him but he ducked to avoid being hit then he walked to the door then turned around looking at her smiling. "By the way, you got some good damn pussy." He walked out laughing.

Katrina threw a lamp at him but it crashed on the wall. She laid down on the bed crying and thinking about revenge.

Chapter 44
Family

It has been a while since everyone was home to have dinner together but this is the day and it felt great for James and Sherry to have all their children at the table again. Everyone was holding hands as James was saying the grace.

"Father I thank you for your wonderful blessings and mercy allowing all of us here now as a family to share this moment. Bless this food oh Lord that we are about to receive, purify it and make it nourishing for our bodies. Touch every soul at this table in health, spirit and body in Jesus name, amen."

Everyone say amen and start eating.

"There really are no words that I can say to fully express how I am feeling right now looking at all of my children sitting here and my lovely wife, your mother. Every day my prayers go up for my family asking for mercy and protection spiritually and physically. God is my life and joy but you all mean so much to me that my life would not be the same without you." James holds his glass of tea up in the air. "To God be the glory."

They all hold up their glasses as well.

"To God be the glory."

"Mom, we all love you no matter what and I am proud of you for your accomplishments in the weight loss. As long as you are happy and at peace. Yes, mom you look great." Jacob said smiling at her.

"She has always looked good to me and personally I hope she does not lose any more weight." James said looking at Sherry.

"Yes dear and I am glad that you have always found me attractive but I did this for me to make myself feel better. So, my two youngest children how are you doing? Looking at Crystal.

"I am fine Mom and you look great."

"Thank you baby. Jacob how are you doing and have you been looking out for Crystal as I asked you to?"

He looked over at Crystal and almost lost it after seeing the look in her eyes as if she was begging him to please say the right thing. He wanted to yell but kept his composure.

"Yes, Mom I have been looking after the spoiled girl."

Crystal exhaled very slowly so no one would notice, she felt like she was about to pass out.

"Good for you son. I raised you right." Smiling at him.

"Yes, Dad you did." Jacob said but is thinking; *if you and everyone here only knew.*

Raymond looked at Sherry carefully and noticed she has lost more weight than the last time he saw her and he does not like how her eyes look. He also knows Katrina and Terrence are not that close anymore but he does not know why but will find out. He feels badly for the double life he has been living. So in love with Jocelyn but having sex with his brother's business partner girlfriend. He was meeting Alexandria at hotels in every state he plays in and having buck wild sex doing any and everything and with Theresa as well.

Katrina looked at everyone talking and eating but none of them could possibly know just how glad she is sitting here with them. Her heart and soul has been so heavy and even though her career is a dream come true and she is a millionaire times over, she has no peace. She lost her virginity and her baby to a man that raped her and is a murderer. Oh God what have I done for fame?

They all continued to eat and talk for the next two hours. Sherry, Raymond, John and Katrina are outside talking, sharing what has really been going on with them and none could hold back the tears as they hear each other's story of pain and heartache. They promised to keep each other's secret then hugged one another and walked back in the house.

It's getting late but before everyone left James prayed over them all and he felt tremendous foul spirits among his family and prayed that God reveals to him what is going on with all of them. He knows how to pray and what to do. As he continues to pray, he cries out in his spirit. Lord God, give me strength to do your will.

To the outside eyes the Richardson family look so good and are truly blessed and doing great but if they only knew the family is being ripped apart.

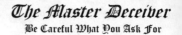
Chapter 45
Talking

It has been two months since Katrina and Terrence have seen each other and he will never know how hard it is for her to walk in his studio now. Knowing it was wrong and stupid, she wanted to tease him from a distance with the visual knowing he will never touch her again. She is wearing heels, very tight jeans and a low-cut top showing ample breast. Katrina saw her reflection in the glass doors as she was walking in the building, "damn she looks good". Pretty in the face, small in the waist, hips, sexy lips, pretty painted finger tips, big butt and gorgeous smile. As they say on the streets, she is a *FULL SEVEN.*

Terrence has been very busy and he has missed Katrina but did not want to harass her because he did not want her telling anyone that he raped her. She could not prove it but the allegation alone could ruin him personally and professionally. No one is here but him because he planned it this way and watching her walk in gives him an immediate erection. Damn young girl looks good in those jeans fat ass and hips and sexy looking breasts.

"Hi Katrina. You still look great." He caresses his erection so she can see it.

Katrina wants to be repulsed by him but for some reason she is not. He does look great and his body is always tight from working out. And the man's sex skills are incredible but she is on a mission.

"I don't have time for any of your games Terrence we need to talk and that is the only thing that I came here for, not your dick so keep it in your pants." Staring at him while standing arms distance in front of him. His cologne smells good but it always does and she easily feels his strong lust spirit which she misses. Stay focused Katrina she tells herself.

Terrence can see the desire in Katrina's eyes that she is trying so hard to hide. He grabs her by the hips pulling her forward pressing his body into hers and kisses her. She smacks him but he grabs her butt hard and kisses her again then starts sucking on her neck while feeling her hips.

Katrina slowly leans back and presses her body into him feeling her suppressed sexual desires coming to the surface as she grinds on his erection. This quickly brought the images of Terrence raping her and she slaps him and pushes his body off hers.

"Get the hell off me Terrence, you sick rapist. What, you are trying to seduce me so you can rape me again. You bastard."

He points his finger at her.

"I told you long ago young girl that I do not play games so you can stop the dick tease and give me what you came here for. You and that hot tight ass of yours and I mean that literally." He smiles.

The hate comes back and she wants to stab him to death if she could get away with it but Katrina has something else much better in mind. She reaches in her pocket and pulls out an envelope handing it to Terrence.

"Open it rapist. I should Instagram and Facebook you."

"I told you to stop calling me that." He snatches the envelope and opens it pulling out a piece of paper which is a legal document Katrina had it prepared by her attorney which states that Terrence relinquishes Katrina from her contract, gives her all the masters to her songs and pays her a balance of nine million dollars owed to her. He looked at Katrina and started laughing.

"You must be smoking something a whole lot stronger than weed if you think I am agreeing to this garbage. If you drop to your

Black Wall Street New Dream Publishing Presents... **The Master Deceiver**
Be Careful What You Ask For

knees now and get busy slobbering this knob, just maybe we can work something out, Young Girl." Smiling and then laughing.

Katrina is repulsed but she came prepared and she pulled out a small recorder, pressed play and put it on the table close to Terrence. He listened to what happened in the hotel room in New York which proves he did rape her, every word was on tape. He looked at her gritting his teeth then screamed out his frustration and threw the recorder against the wall shattering it in pieces.

"You fucking…"

Katrina quickly held up her hand in front of him.

"Stop, don't you call me that B word. Just sign the paper and write me my check or that recording and me will be on CNN and you will spend the rest of your days in prison getting done to you what you did to me. Oh, and don't even think about doing anything to me because if I so much as fall down a hill and scrape my knee, to life in prison for you baby, and its rape time."

Terrence walked slowly toward her and it took everything in him not to strangle her to death but she is right. Katrina had him in a corner and there is no way out but to do as she asks and he knows it. He signed the paper and wrote her the check for nine million dollars and hands them to her without a word spoken.

Katrina looks at the legal document and the check then puts both in her pants pocket.

"Have a horrible life Terrence Rapist Murderer Washington. I hope to never see you in life." While walking out of his office she smacks her butt and looks back at him.

"Yes! I am free!" She screamed when outside and kept walking.

Chapter 46

Too Much Pain

Lewis is a very successful attorney by anyone's standard. He moved to a high-rise office building renting out an entire floor for his office practice, he has three other attorney's practicing various fields of law working with him, two paralegals and Tashianna still works with him as well. However, Lewis has been living in a vacuum for some time and he has nightmares. He wakes up sweating, losing weight from not eating properly and migraines at least twice a week that makes him dizzy and gives him blurred vision. Every night when he lays down, Lewis sees the images of Veronica having sex with the black guy. He really does not know if the guy being black adds to his pain but the fact is, it happened. Does skin color really matter? It's the last thing he wants to remember but for some reason he can't seem to get the image of seeing this strong looking black man ramming his dick inside his wife and seeing the look on her face hearing her moans and screams. She was loving it. One night he had a horrible nightmare seeing Veronica walking towards him with her arms out holding a shovel. He woke up screaming and started repeatedly slapping the sides of his head with both hands and then threw up on his bed. Lewis needed peace or knew he would not last another week in his present condition. He asked James to come over to his house and told him everything and afterwards he broke down emotionally and cried like a baby screaming Veronica's name over and over. James knew this was a man whose spirit and soul was being tormented and only God could give him peace. Lewis agreed to turn himself in and James went with him.

Lewis was charged with first degree murder and he has a no bail status. With the money that Lewis has and his connections he hired a team of the best criminal attorneys to defend him. Mary, Lewis, Sherry, Jimmy and Tashianna were in court every day for Lewis' trial. The prosecution had Veronica's body dug up. An autopsy was done revealing a broken neck and he subpoenaed Wilson and Reginald Grimes as witnesses to what happened in the hotel room. Wilson had to testify to Lewis yelling repeatedly that he was going to kill his wife. Lewis fate was sealed and even with the emotional stress strategy that his legal team used to argue Lewis emotionally snapped after catching his wife in bed with another man, was not good enough to find him not guilty. The prosecution proved beyond a reasonable doubt that Lewis did preplan to kill his wife from the moment he left the hotel room carried out the plan. Lewis was found guilty and received the death penalty at his sentence hearing. Mary, Tashianna and Sherry broke down crying in court and Tashianna's guilt was tremendous because she knew Lewis would not be in this situation if she had never told him about Doctor Eyes. When James and Sherry arrived home after Lewis sentence hearing James went to his room and cried and all Sherry could do was hold him.

"Sherry, my friend is going to be put to death and there is nothing that I can do."

"I know James, I know baby." They both are crying and holding each other.

Lewis knew his life was over and he repeatedly cried out to God with everything in him, for God to forgive all his sins and come into his heart and deliver him from this life. That night was the best sleep Lewis had in such a very long time and the following morning for the first-time Lewis was not in pain. He had peace and joy in his heart. He thought long and hard about it after spending two weeks in prison and he concluded that he did not want to spend years in prison on death row waiting to be put to death. So, against the advice of his attorney's he chose to wave all his motions for appeals and agreed to be put to death in six months. In his heart, mind and spirit Lewis was ready to go. He did ask James to be there for his day of death as his pastor and true friend. James did not want to do it at all but Lewis begged him so he would not die alone. James agreed to be there for his friend, knowing it would be heart breaking. Mary begged him repeatedly to change his mind telling him that this is giving up and he does not know what God will do. In spite of all her pleading and begging, Lewis mind was made up because he is at peace and he was not going to change it. Mary told him that no way would she be there and watch her son be put to death because it would not only break her heart but probably give her a heart attack.

Six months later James was allowed in prison and prayed with Lewis and watched him be put to death by lethal injection. Lewis had a smile on his face and he never took his eyes off James the entire time. The very last words that Lewis spoke was, "thank you Jesus." Lewis was gone from this world and in pain no more. James cried the entire way home because his longtime friend was gone. James and his family was at the burial with James presiding. Tashianna fainted at the burial and Mary just broke down and dropped to her knees sobering uncontrollably. Her son was gone.

Chapter 47
Too Slow

Shawn spent less time in the shop these days because of his increased traveling due to his growing drug business. He did not live a flashy lifestyle like so many other people getting caught up in making money and he was making a lot of money at this point. Fact is, he was making millions of dollars but you could not tell because he was not a big spender and lived a conservative life. He put his money in various safe deposit boxes in banks across the country and it was always a minimum of five hundred thousand dollars in each box. He mailed Jimmy an envelope asking him to never open it unless something horrible happened to him. The envelope contained all the bank locations where his money is and how much. Alexandria's name was listed as a person to have access to the boxes. He and Alexandria were not seeing a lot of each other and when they did spend time together, they argued about them not spending enough time together. Shawn felt like she was seeing someone else which bothered him a lot because he does care for her a great deal and she is his good clean sexy girl. Although, when he would go out of town on business he would attend parties and meet someone and end up in a hotel room with her. He did feel bad about cheating on Alexandria so much. To him it was part of being big time now in the drug game, you do big things with big time people and keep it moving. Shawn had a private phone that Alexandria did not know about that had his special contacts in concerning his business and the many women that he dealt with. Jimmy ran the business full time and his own real estate business with Tashianna which was doing great.

Shawn and Alexandria decided to get away for a while and went to Paradise Island in the Bahamas. They stayed at the One & Only Ocean Club Hotel. It has been a while since they spent any real quality time together and away from everyone and anything related to business. What Alexandria did not know was this trip is business for Shawn because he is meeting a very important client from Columbia that will take him to a whole new level in the drug world. Shawn decided that since he was protected by Doctor Eyes and was untouchable that he may as well go all the way to the top in the business and become a major distributor and still remain low key.

Alexandria and Shawn are walking on the beach holding hands, laughing and having fun. She is looking fabulous in her black one-piece bathing suit showing the tight and sexy body she works out so hard to get and keep. Shawn had on sandals and beach shorts and the pouch that Doctor Eyes gave him was inside a hidden pocket in his shorts. He never left home without it. They were doing some snorkeling together and having sex under the water when a shark approached them. They both swam away as fast as they could but Alexandria was a faster swimmer than Shawn and the shark bit his hip. He screamed in pain. Others saw them and helped Shawn to the beach but blood was pouring from his wound and he is still screaming from the bite. Alexandria is right by his side holding his hand while the medics attend to his injury. Although his wound is bleeding a lot it's not as bad as it looks and the medics determined he would only need a few stitches at the local hospital to close up the wound. When the shark bit him it ripped his shorts and now the pouch that Doctor Eyes gave him was gone. Shawn did not notice this yet being so distracted by the pain. Alexandria was in the ambulance with Shawn and he was a lot calmer now so she was teasing him with jokes to keep him that way.

RONALD GRAY

"Shawn I know why that shark caught up with you and not me."

"I know you are going to say something smart, but why?"

"Baby, you were just a little too slow in trying to get away and you should have been looking at this hot body of mine. That would have motivated you to swim faster so you can take a bite of me instead of the shark taking a bite of you." She kissed him and laughed.

"Yeah, okay you got jokes." He smiled and was looking at Alexandria and thinking about her being right by his side in his time of great need making him realize even more of the awful choices he has been making in his life. None of the other women that he spent time with would be here now with him because they only cared about his money and status. "Alexandria thank you so much you know I love you."

"I love you too Shawn and don't get all mushy on me because you let the shark catch up with you and bite your hip. Seriously baby you need to change for us to remain together and the words are nice to hear but they are just words unless backed up by actions Shawn. Romance baby, romance." She smiled and kissed him.

"You are right and I will do better. That shark did get a good bite of my hip and tore my expensive beach shorts." He laughed and it was only now did he think about the pouch in his shorts. He quickly patted his shorts but it was gone. Shawn became frantic and started patting his shorts all over searching for it.

"My pouch, my pouch where is my pouch. Oh my God, it's gone. Noooo! I need my pouch."

Alexandria and the medics are looking at Shawn like he is losing his mind because they have no idea what he is talking about concerning a pouch. They are contributing this sudden outburst to the shark bite but he is becoming more frantic and the medics fear he will have a panic attack so they give Shawn a shot to relax him. Shawn is in the hospital now getting stitched up but the doctor had to give him another shot to calm him down. Now he is asleep and Alexandria is in the waiting room.

Word travels fast concerning any shark attack and the individual Shawn was supposed to meet is aware that it was him the shark attacked but business is business so Shawn is about to receive an interesting visitor. Two large well-dressed men in black business suits and a very attractive classy looking lady wearing a body hugging, white dress with heels walk in the waiting area. They recognized Alexandria from pictures taken of her without her knowledge. In this business, it pays to know who is close to the person that you are doing business with in case violence is necessary. The lady's name is Ariesa who is five-feet nine, great figure and truly gorgeous. She is Shawn's contact but he did not know. She walked over to Alexandria.

"Excuse me miss but how is Shawn doing?"

Alexandria looks up at this very stunning looking woman wondering who she is and why is she asking about her man. She stood up.

"Who are you and why are you asking about Shawn?"

Ariesa smiled and looked at Alexandria like she is beneath her but extends her hand.

"Forgive my manners but my name is Ariesa and my car company in Miami is interested in having our exclusive exotic car dealership business expanded to Raleigh, NC and have Shawn run the company. He has established such a great reputation concerning his present business. You are the lovely Alexandria."

Alexandria shakes her hand but she is not as naive as Shawn thinks she is and knows this woman is hiding something and she wonders could she be involved with him. She then looks over at the men dressed in suits that look like body guards.

"Yes, I am but how did you know?"

"Shawn talks about you but he did not do your beauty any justice. I would tease Shawn and tell him you better hold on tight to him before someone like me comes along and takes him." She gave a fake smile and laughed but she desired to smack Alexandria to the floor and step on her just for wasting her time in talking.

"That is sweet. I am sure Shawn will be out soon and we all can sit down and talk."

Shawn walked into the waiting room with a slight limp and sees Alexandria and this gorgeous lady standing next to her along with the two large well-dressed men and wonders could this be his contact and why is she talking to Alexandria who is walking towards him.

"Shawn, baby are you alright?" She hugged and kissed him.

"I am feeling pretty good considering a shark bit me so I am grateful to be alive." He is thinking, *I lost the pouch but it kept me alive because I should be dead maybe, it's still working.*

Ariesa walked towards Shawn and he can't take his eyes off her and Alexandria notices this.

"Shawn baby how are you doing darling? You know I need you so you can't go swimming with the sharks just yet. Business baby business." She laughed and then gave him a serious look.

Shawn got her message very clearly.

"I got bit but I'm not out, so enough about my shark bite. Let's go to lunch so we can sit down and discuss some business details."

"Oh that sounds good, let's go eat because I am hungry." Alexandria is no fool and where Shawn goes with this fake slut she is going.

Ariesa looked at Alexandria and lightly touched her on the arm. "Oh, I am sorry but unfortunately you cannot be at the meeting dear because we will be discussing some private company details that are confidential. I am sure you understand. I am sure that you want Shawn to have the best in life." Giving Alexandria that you will never be as good as me look.

Alexandria gives Shawn the look that he knows all too well but he ignores it.

"She understands and we can spend time together after the meeting." He limps over kissed and hugged Alexandria.

She pinches his side and whispers in his ear.

"I am so angry with you right now." She smiled and walked away so no one can see her tears because she is so hurt and was hoping this trip would bring them closer. Even after getting bit by a shark for which he could have been killed, Shawn still put business before his relationship. When Alexandria got back to the room she called Raymond on his private phone.

Shawn and Ariesa had lunch and talked business with the body guards sitting close by. Shawn was given a custom designed one hundred and eighty-thousand-dollar Range Rover as a gift for agreeing to do business with Ariesa. It would be at the airport when he and Alexandria arrived. Alexandria was so angry with Shawn that when he got back to the hotel room she told him the trip was over and she wanted to go back home. He tried persistently to change her mind but it was a waste of time, she was far too angry and hurt to listen to him. The following Sunday morning they were on a plane back to Raleigh and Alexandria did not say one word to him on the plane. The Range Rover was there and Shawn took Alexandria home first. She was still angry which is evident when she got out and slammed the door. Shawn got out to get her bags and was standing in front of Alexandria to talk but she waved her hand in front of him.

"No Shawn, don't talk because anything that you say will be just another broken promise, another lie. I don't know what to say to you anymore that I have not already said repeatedly. Obviously, you do not care enough about me and our relationship to put us first and show me that you really care so I am done talking to you. We are finished Shawn, goodbye." She walked away with bags in her hands and tears in her eyes.

All Shawn could do is watch her leave because what could he say at this point. Anyway, he figured she needed time to cool off and then they could talk. He got in the Range Rover and drove it to the shop to switch vehicles because he did not want to drive in the Rover right now. He arrived at the shop and pressed the remote so the garage door would open and drove in. He walked over to another car, smiling because he knows he is about to be extra-large in the game now.

Several police cars quickly drive up to the shop and police get out with their guns in hand yelling at Shawn to get on the ground. The police officer showed him a search warrant and they search the entire shop and all the vehicles in the shop until they find ten kilos of cocaine hidden in the Range Rover. One of the police officers walked over to Shawn.

"Sir, put your hands behind your back, you are under arrest for narcotic possession and trafficking."

Out of habit Shawn patted his pants pocket but he remembered the pouch is gone and that Doctor Eyes told him to always have the pouch with him no matter what, at all times, but now it's, too late.

"Damn." He lowers his head.

He is handcuffed and put in the police car and more police vehicles show up with canine dogs and search the shop again but this time the dogs find more drugs. Shawn was using the shop to hide his supply of drugs and money but Jimmy never knew it. The dogs found sixty kilos of cocaine, one-hundred pounds of marijuana and five-million dollars in cash. The shop had yellow tape put in front of it and all the doors were padlocked. The shop was now officially out of business. Shawn was booked and his bail was set at ten-million dollars which he could make easily but he needed Alexandria so he called her collect.

"Alex, baby I am glad you accepted the call, oh I love you so much. Look I am in trouble and I need your help. Of course you know I am in jail and my bail has been set at ten-million dollars. Come see me tonight and bring a bail bondsman with you and I can explain how to get me out."

"Oh, so now you need me. No Shawn, why don't you call one of your sluts that you have been dealing with and get them to help you. Do not call me again, goodbye Shawn." She slammed her cell phone down and cried because of so much hurt. She is going to help Shawn but needed him to suffer a while.

Two DEA agents came to visit Shawn the following morning telling him that he would spend the rest of his life in prison if he did not corporate with them. They wanted to know who his supplier was but Shawn told them he needed time to think. After another hour of talking he was taken back to his cell. Ariesa, who Shawn met in the Bahamas heard that he had been arrested and questioned by the DEA agents. Later that night all the lights went out in the cell area and five minutes later they came back on. Shawn was lying on the floor in a pool of blood. His throat had been cut and he was dead.

Shawn's funeral was a week later. The Richardson family, Alexandria, and Theresa were there but Raymond was not because he had a game. Alexandria was taking his death very hard and could not believe he was dead but it was the guilt that gripped her the hardest because she hung up on him. She thought over and over if she had just listened to Shawn and helped him get out he would be alive today. She also found out a lot about his drug activities and so much made sense now as to why he traveled so regularly and spent less time with her. James presided over his burial, speaking kind words to comfort people. Jimmy was devastated as well, because he had no idea what was going on and Shawn was his best friend. After the burial Alexandria talked to the family members for a while and then left. Jimmy and John was also questioned by the police because they believed the two also were involved in the drug business. The family name and good attorneys proved otherwise. The shop was gone for good and everything in it, fruits of a poison tree. Alexandria cried every day for two weeks with Theresa by her side until it all became too much for her and she felt like she was going to have a nervous breakdown. She moved away, after spending one last night with Theresa. The memories were just too much for her to deal with.

Chapter 48
Moving On

Weeks later Jimmy was still in emotional shock that his best friend is gone and was becoming depressed. John was dealing with Shawn's death better but it still bothered him a lot even though he would become angry at times because of the risk that Shawn put them in. He had no job now which means no income. Aurora would offer him money but he would always turn it down which she did not like but understood and respected him for it. One day James had a long conversation with John and Jimmy about John possibly joining Jimmy in his real estate business which is doing well. Jimmy smiled and thought it would be a great idea but he told John that currently he and Tashianna are partners in the business but John could still work with them. John loved the idea and he knew that his brother was making some serious money. James volunteered to loan them one million dollars for the business which they agreed. The sons thanked their Dad for the money and talking with them. John shared the good news with Aurora and she was excited for him. She saw a business potential so she wanted to match the million dollars that his Dad was loaning them. John looked at her in surprise.

"I know you told me that you come from money but that is family money just like my family. Well my Mom and Dad have money but not me. Anyway, you got it like that?"

"Yes, baby I do and we can build together, you and your handsome face." Her fingers caressed his face and she kissed him.

John is thinking, *if she only knew how I got this handsome face.*

Chapter 49
Together

Raymond's career was doing great and so was Jocelyn's but because of their busy schedules they were spending less time together. Raymond was finding comfort spending time with Theresa and they talked about Alexandria often even though she was gone. Raymond is not in love with Theresa and she is not in love with him but they have so much fun together. They never discuss anything even remotely related to business and always practice safe sex. This was working out well until one night in Houston in a hotel room after they had sex and showered. Lying in bed together naked, Theresa asked Raymond to leave Jocelyn alone and be only with her. Raymond looked at her and laughed then got up and started getting dressed.

"You are out of your mind and delusional. You and I are just fun, that is it, nothing more and I damn sure am not leaving my queen over you."

Theresa sat up in bed looking at him hard while trying to remain calm.

"Just fun, so that is it. I know we don't love each other but I thought at this point we were building something together." She started getting dressed as well but stopped when the anger was too much to hold in. She stepped closer to him. "You are a serious piece of work Raymond and such a hypocrite. You give your woman the title of a queen but you are a walking dog. Does your queen, know you are fucking me, does your queen, know I am sucking your dick and balls, does your queen, know you bury your face between my legs licking this pussy good and then you go home to your queen, and kiss her on the mouth with my juices on your lips? So, is this how a queen, gets treated, Raymond? Maybe I should tell the queen, about me and what I can do, she might want some of this good pussy as well, Raymond." Staring at him.

Raymond has never hit a woman in his life. He has never wanted to hit one so badly as he does right now. He remains calm and walked toward the door and reaches into his pocket pulling out a roll of money counting out five, one hundred dollar bills and threw them on the bed.

"Take this money and buy you a life. We are done." He walked out smiling but hears Theresa yelling that she is going to call Jocelyn.

Raymond was just leaving the airport in Charlotte headed home in his Bentley when his phone rings and it was Jocelyn. She was beyond upset and was yelling and calling him every foul name she could think of because Theresa did call her giving details about her and Raymond's activities. Raymond was trying to talk to Jocelyn but it was not working. He dropped his cell phone and bent down to pick it up and a truck was coming at him head-on. The truck hit his Bentley so hard it flipped over and caught on fire and Jocelyn heard and explosion and Raymond yelling, "No".

Jocelyn and all of Raymond's family are at the hospital visiting him. He has been in a coma for five days but he woke up today and besides some major lacerations on his face and neck, which will heal in time, he is okay, except for his hands. His hands got badly burned when the truck caught on fire and he would have died if some others coming to his rescue did not pull him out of the vehicle just before it exploded. The necklace given to him by Doctor Eyes came off his neck during the wreck and was destroyed in the explosion. Raymond suffered third degree burns to both his hands. Over a period of time and various surgeries, skin grafts and therapy, his hands will get better. Doctors have told his family that he will never have the use of his hands as he once did and he will never play pro basketball again. Raymond was so happy to be alive and see his family again but it was hard for him to even look at Jocelyn and he is surprised that she is even here. The doctors came in and checked on Raymond and informed him that he suffered third degree burns to his hands and will never play pro ball again. He asked to be alone and his family went back out to the visiting area. He cried knowing all that he has worked so hard for is over but Raymond thought about the irony of his current situation. The very thing that he went to Doctor Eyes to get help for, is the very thing that he lost, his hands.

Days and weeks went by and Raymond's friends and family have been very supportive. Jocelyn has been trying hard to support him emotionally as well, but it's hard to stop someone else from bleeding when you are bleeding to. She does visit him in the hospital when she can but she is busy with her singing career and traveling more. Jocelyn still loves Raymond but she cannot bring herself to tell him because her heart is still hurting so much from what he did. Theresa was so descriptive when telling her about their sexual activities and this hurt her heart to the core. At times, she wanted to hug Raymond and other times she wanted to smack one of his burned hands. This very thought let her know just how hurt she is. Jocelyn is beyond thankful to have her singing career now to keep her mind and body busy because she and Raymond could not possibly be together at this point.

Since Raymond's career is over he was released from his contract and endorsement deals. Now he has no money coming in but he is not broke because he saved his money even though he has not been playing that long. Raymond has ten million dollars in his bank account. The weeks and months have been very difficult for Raymond emotionally and he has become more depressed. He does some running and swimming at times and lifting weights with his trainer to keep his body in good physical condition. However every time he looks at his badly burned hands it depresses him. Jocelyn has been very busy and has a gig in New York now and this is a perfect time to go because she needed some space from Raymond.

Just being away and in New York is making Jocelyn feel better but she also desires to remain in shape while here so she contacted a very popular professional fitness trainer. His name is Manny Rothmiller currently and he is currently working in Laurel, MD. He has an excellent reputation for getting anyone in shape and has a wonderful attitude in the process. He trains and develops a team of certified professional trainers, coaches, nutrition consultants, nutritionist, group fitness instructors, corrective exercise specialists and other health and fitness companies. She contacted him mentioning to pay for a week of his time, travel, and lodging. Manny agrees to fly in and work with her at the fitness center in the Sheraton Hotel where she is staying while in New York. A week of intense but fun training with Manny and she felt great and it was well worth it. She hands him his check, hugged him and he walked away towards his room. She watched him walk away and is thinking, *he is fine and he better be glad he is married or I might have to try him.* She smiled and went to her room.

Jocelyn is feeling great now because she is doing her thing by being in a studio in New York working on a song titled, *AM I READY.* It was sent to her and written by Ronald Gray but is being produced by famed movie actor, producer, director and writer Sid Burston out of Vegas. Sid has been in the entertainment business for over thirty years. They have been working with the song for a few hours today and she loved it. It has an old and new school flavor. This guy walks in the studio while she is singing and she locks eyes with him as he is staring at her while talking to Sid.

"Wow, I have heard this girl's music of course but hearing her in person is something and damn she is fine Sid."

Sid lightly taps him on the chest.

"Yeah she's fine but stay focused Brandon and get in there and sing your part."

"No problem my brother." He walks in the recording room and extends his hand to her. "Hi, I am Brandon and it's a pleasure to meet you." Smiling and staring at her.

She shakes his hand and immediately felt something. He is not just fine with a great body but his eyes and overall demeanor is so sexy.

"Hi Brandon, it's good to meet you. We are about to do this duet together, well I hope you can sing because I really like this song and have been working hard on it with Sid."

"You be the judge if I can sing." He put his headset on looked at her and smiled.

You would think they had been singing together for years, the way things flowed and the chemistry between them was intense. But the entire time Jocelyn is singing the song; *AM I READY* she is dealing with her own deep emotions thinking about Raymond and fighting back her tears. She is thinking, *Lord that man hurt me so bad but I have so much love in my heart to give. Am I ready, am I truly ready to give my heart and love again to him or any man, Lord am I ready?* If they only knew while singing this very powerful song, Jocelyn wants to fall on the floor and cry a thousand tears. After many interruptions from Sid, the song will be sung just right, they finished singing. The other people in the studio started clapping. The two walked out to the sound board room where Sid and the others are.

"So, Sid because you are a perfectionist do you like the way the song flows?" Jocelyn said.

"Love it, love it and you two sing well together. Now go get something to eat while we put on the finishing touches."

"We can do that and the song is great. Sid, so when is the song coming out because the world needs to hear it, because the message is so real?" Brandon said.

Sid looks at Brandon, Jocelyn and others in the room because they are looking at him with anticipation and he looks back at Brandon.

"Soon! Now go eat. Okay everybody, let's get back to work and touch up this song."

Brandon and Jocelyn look at each other and smile then walked out and found a nice place to sit down and eat, talking for hours.

"It has been great singing and talking with you today and I am enjoying your company. I have to ask; do you have a boyfriend?"

Jocelyn was enjoying his company a lot as well, but she knew this question was coming and did not know how to answer. She did not know if there was any chance to reconcile with Raymond or if she even wanted to.

"I will not lie to you. I have been in a serious relationship for a while but I got very hurt and now I do not know about us."

"Thank you for being direct and honest which is not easy to come by these days, people lie so much about the simplest things."

"Very true. Anyway, I am here on business and to relax and have fun. How about we go to a club and get our dance on. You can dance a little bit, right?" She smiled at him.

"I will let you be the judge, which is better, my singing or dancing?"

"Okay, you are on. I am going back to my hotel room at the Sheraton and lay down for a while since it's still early and if you do not mind you can meet me in the lobby at ten o'clock and we can go to the, *Browns Sugar* night club that I have been hearing so much about in Harlem."

"Perfect, and it's a date and I will see you at ten tonight."

"Looking forward to it but it's not a date."

"Whatever you say Jocelyn." He kissed her on the cheek and walked away.

She watched him walk away and shook her head.

"Lord keep me."

At ten thirty that night Jocelyn and Brandon were walking in the club. Brandon had on Salvatore Ferragamo shoes, dress slacks and a short sleeve Egyptian cotton dress shirt. Jocelyn had on heels, skirt and a top that is almost see-through. They found an empty table, sat down for a while and ordered glasses of wine and talked.

"I know you hear this all of the time but you are very nice looking, sexy fine." Brandon said smiling.

Jocelyn could not help but smile.

"Okay, I am not just fine but sexy fine, as you put it."

"Oh yeah, sexy fine."

"Okay, well since I am sexy fine, come with me to the dance floor so I can see what you got."

She walked toward the floor and Brandon is behind her.

"Sexy walk."

Jocelyn turned her head and looked back at him smiling and kept walking. Just like in the studio their chemistry on the dance floor is great and they move very well together, like years of dancing as one.

Jocelyn was having fun dancing and flirting with Brandon. She knows she should not be dancing with him like this especially all the grinding she has been doing on him but she was having fun. They go back to their table, order drinks and talk for a while and then went back to the dance floor. Brandon is from the streets and a gentleman so when leaving the club, he escorted Jocelyn back to her hotel room and they stopped at her room door.

"Brandon I thank you for this night because I have not had this much fun in a long time and yes you are a great dancer."

"The pleasure was mine and you move very well yourself. Actually, we move good together." He stared at her and slowly leaned forward, never taking his eyes off hers and they kissed.

Jocelyn felt his kiss deeply, too deep and wanted more so she put her arms around his neck and leaned into him desiring to feel his body. They continued kissing and the passion increased. Brandon's hands was up her skirt and on her butt caressing it ever so slowly then he whispered in her ear.

"I want you Jocelyn."

"Don't do this to me. You know I want you too." She kissed him back with more passion, then pushed away from him to open the room door and they walked in.

Jocelyn and Brandon did not take their clothes off but laid down on the bed and started kissing and grinding on each other as if in heat until Jocelyn could not take it anymore and sat up and started crying.

"I am sorry but I can't do this please forgive me. I thought that I could but I just can't. Brandon, I did not bring you here to tease you like some school girl but my body can't do what my heart won't let it do."

"Jocelyn, relax. I understand what you are dealing with and I respect you." He stood up. "I need to go and get a pack of ice before I leave." Looking down between his legs seeing the print of his erection.

Jocelyn looks between his legs and is thinking, *Lord have mercy, keep me* and she laughs.

"Forgive me Brandon, I have a big favor to ask you but I'll understand if you say no."

"What is the favor?"

"Would you spend the night with me. No sex, but I really don't want to be by myself tonight."

"Sleep with you. You are trying to kill me but okay. But first I need to go get me some zip lock bags and a lot of ice." He smiled at her.

Jocelyn laughed and hugged him tightly.

"You don't need all that and thank you so much for being understanding and a gentleman."

"Nice guy, okay so does this mean you have changed your mind and I get some hot booty?" He was not serious but he wanted to make her laugh again.

"No." She smiled then gave him a quick kiss.

Jocelyn turned out the lights in the room kicked off her shoes and laid down on the bed. Brandon removed his shoes and laid down with her and whispers in her ear.

"I hope we can at least be friends."

She kissed him and closed her eyes.

Jocelyn did a lot of thinking on the plane ride back to Charlotte and she already missed Brandon. Her heart and spirit misses Raymond so much more and this bothers her because she must admit to herself that she not only still loves him but also is in love with this man who crushed her heart like no other. She wanted to go home and rest but she had to go see Raymond first to check on him. Jocelyn was ringing his door bell repeatedly but Raymond did not answer so she let herself in with her own key. She had forgotten she still had it until now. She walked in the living room and Raymond was sitting on the sofa holding a gun to his head with his two burned hands. He looked up and saw Jocelyn and pressed the gun tighter against his head.

"No Raymond." Jocelyn screams. She ran over and smacked the gun from his hands and it went off and Jocelyn jumps, looks at Raymond and smacks him. "Are you crazy Raymond? Have you lost your mind? So, you want to kill yourself now, you want to take the coward's way out. I can't believe you." She stared at him and then screams. "Ahhhhhhhhh." Then emotionally snaps allowing so much anger and hurt come to the surface and started hitting and smacking Raymond repeatedly.

Raymond is trying to block the blows with his hands but get hit anyway and it hurts his hands.

"Stop hitting me." He yells. "You are hurting my hands."

This makes Jocelyn stop immediately and stare at him while slowly kneeling and falling to the floor crying.

"Oh God, Raymond I am sorry, so sorry for hurting your hands. I can't believe you would do this to yourself, your family and to me."

"I am done Jocelyn." He starts crying. "I have nothing left and have lost everything. Career gone, contract gone and you, gone. I have nothing left."

She stood up and walked over standing directly in front of him.

RONALD GRAY

"What! You are so selfish. It's not all about you Raymond. Okay, so you got hurt and can't play ball anymore and lost millions but you have so much left in you to give and you have people that genuinely love you. You are not exactly on welfare. That is not enough for you so you want to sit here and feel sorry for yourself and do the coward thing." She looks up then raises her hands in the air shaking them and screams out of total frustration. "What is wrong with you, God you are so selfish." Pointing her finger at him. "People like you never realize how good you have it until it's gone. You hurt my heart and soul so badly because of your selfishness, because of a piece of ass Raymond. I have been so good to you and loyal but you messed it up. You will never truly know just how much I, still care, how much I still love you. You idiot."

Raymond looks at Jocelyn with shock.

"How can you still love me Jocelyn for all of the pain that I know I have caused you? I understand that you have to leave me and move on with your own life."

She looks at him and places her hands on the sides of his face with tears coming down her eyes.

"God help me, but I am not leaving you Raymond because I love you and want you, oh Jesus." She cries even harder and wrapped her arms around his neck. "I want us, together."

"Oh Jocelyn, I love you baby, I love you so much." He pulled her closer into him and they hold each other crying.

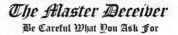

Chapter 50
Redemption

Raymond did not want to call because of shame and pride but after putting a gun to his head he knew getting immediate help was very important, so he called his Dad and asked him to come over. Jocelyn was at Raymond's sitting in the den with him when James arrived. He gave them both hugs and smiled at Jocelyn because he was glad to see her knowing she and Raymond have been dealing with a lot. He also knew that she truly loved his son. They sat down and James prayed first, then Raymond began to talk and once he started he could not stop even to the part of putting a gun to his head and Jocelyn walking in just in time to save his life and soul. He did not tell his Dad about Doctor Eyes. Jocelyn cooked and they sat down and ate enjoying her cooking and they continued talking. James prayed some more and then he told Raymond that despite all he has done or not done God is giving him another chance and that he needs to change his life in order to receive the best from God and to wait on him. After James leaves, Raymond and Jocelyn talk for a while and agreed to take things slow and one day at time but Jocelyn made it clear to Raymond to leave his past in the past if he wants her in his life. She kissed him and said she had to go and practice on some songs. After she left Raymond called Sherry just to hear his Mom voice and to say that he loved her. Raymond kneeled and prayed asking God to forgive him for all his sins and come into his heart. He was rubbing his neck while praying thinking about how glad he is that the necklace is gone and was burned in the explosion. Now he must do right and wait on God.

Chapter 51
Wait on Him

Crystal, Katrina and Sherry are spending more time together and enjoying every minute. They are out shopping today in Crabtree Valley Mall spending too much money and talking about what has been going on in their lives. When Katrina and Sherry were talking Crystal was thinking, *I have been through something that only I, Jacob and God knows about and how much it still emotionally hurts me. How do you ever get over being sexually assaulted and losing your virginity at the same time and be normal again? Well in my mind you don't you suppress the horror deeply in your soul and learn how to deal with it day by waking day and enjoy life to the best of your ability. Except for an act of God healing your mind, heart, body and soul you become the walking wounded. But thank God for his mercy and my family.*

"Mom you do look great and I am proud of you for working so hard to lose the weight that you have been complaining about for years. Since it's just us girls here Mom how does Dad really feel about you losing all that weight. As far back as I can remember Dad has always had the hots for you, hugging and kissing on you constantly loving your size." Crystal said smiling at her

"I know that's right Mom. Dad's got it bad for you and always has. You know what they say, more cushion for the pushing baby." Katrina was smiling and laughing knowing her mom would say something smart.

"You two are just nasty and should be ashamed of yourself for talking dirty about your Dad. Anyway, nosey girls your Dad makes smart comments at times about me getting too skinny and for me to stay healthy so he can have something to hold on. He will get over it and besides, he's sprung." Looking at her girls and laughing but hiding the extreme guilt and emotional pain that she has currently. She gives a fake smile again but is thinking; *God if they only knew my horrible secret of having a weak moment and having sex one time with my trainer from the gym and the price I have paid from that one moment of weak selfish pleasure. I found out later that I was pregnant and knew it was his so I had an abortion. The worst of it is after feeling weak so often I had a physical yesterday and tested positive for HIV. Oh God, what have I done and what am I going to do?* She smiled hard to suppress the building tears.

"Mom, you should be ashamed talking dirty. You know I am not old enough to hear such language." Crystal said and looked at Sherry and Katrina and they all laugh. But she does notice that her Mom has lost too much weight but would not say anything to hurt her feelings.

Katrina is looking at her Mom when they are walking and noticed she has lost too much weight. She heard her throwing up a few days ago when she was home. She has not been feeling the best either, her stomach and throat have been hurting a lot lately. She believes this is the result of pushing herself too hard.

Sherry and Katrina stopped taking the liquid Doctor Eyes gave them because they decided now that they have what they want, taking the nasty tasting liquid is not needed or Doctor Eyes for that matter. They continue talking and shopping and end up in the food court to get something to eat then sit down at a table.

"Crystal, how has life been treating you baby sister? Are you seeing someone and do you have a boyfriend who is trying to, hold your hand?" Katrina said looking at her smiling.

"That is a good question Crystal. Do you have a boyfriend these days and don't lie to your Mother?"

Crystal gives them a fake smile but the very thought of a guy even touching her at this point is repulsive. Looking around she sees the last person she wants to see, Eliza. She is sitting at a table with some low life looking guy smiling, hugging, and kissing on him to seduce him no doubt so she can get what she wants. Crystal remembers that fake smile of hers well. Eliza looks up and sees Crystal and they lock eyes. Crystal emotionally goes into suppressed beast mode and grips the table where she's sitting and is about to walk over to Eliza's table when she sees Jacob, John and Aurora walking in the food court. They are close to Eliza's table.

John has his hand on the small of Aurora's back but his fingers are touching the top of her butt and Aurora is loving his light touch and the attention. Jacob sees John's hand, he is looking at Aurora but is trying not to be obvious and is thinking, *This girl is so fine and got body for days. The things I would like to do to her, Lord have mercy. Forgive me Lord.*

"John stop being nasty and take your hand off Aurora's butt, be a gentleman, my brother." Smiling at him

"Mind your own business. Why are you looking at my lady's butt, brother?" He laughed and winked at John.

"So, John. I am your lady now?"

He stopped walking and so does Aurora and Jacob.

"You already know the answer to that. Yes, you are." Looking at her with a serious expression.

"Good, very good. Now relax and get that mean looking expression off your face." She hugged and kissed him and they both laugh.

They started walking and Jacob sees Eliza sitting at the table with some guy and all his anger for her instantly comes back.

"Eliza." Jacob angrily says and he quickly walks towards her table with John and Aurora next to him. Crystal sees Jacob walking towards Eliza's table and the anger on his face, so she stands up to walk over there as well but gets dizzy.

Eliza sees Jacob, John, and Aurora approaching her table and the anger on Jacob's face realizing its fight or flight time so she quickly hits the guy she is with on the arm.

"That is the guy I have been telling you about that spit on me because I would not talk to his young ass." Eliza knew telling that lie to him would come in handy one day and today is that day.

Jacob, John and Aurora are standing in front of Eliza's table.

"I need to talk to you, sorry slut." Jacob said.

The guy with Eliza quickly stood up and swung on Jacob but he was not fast enough because John saw his move coming and hit him so hard in the jaw you heard it crack and he hit the floor unconscious. Eliza grabbed her hot coffee and threw it at John's face and got up and ran away. John is holding his hands to his face screaming loud because the coffee was very hot and was burning his face.

Katrina, Sherry, and Crystal saw John and heard him screaming and Katrina ran towards them but she became very weak and fell to the floor shaking.

"Oh my God, Katrina." Sherry screamed then stood up and threw up blood and hit the floor unconscious.

Chapter 52
James

Jimmy has been very concerned about Tashianna ever since she fainted at Lewis burial because she took his death so hard and has not been the same. She has not been her usual smart mouth self and has been very affectionate and close to him as well but not in a sexual way. So, they have been spending a lot of time together and today they are having lunch with James at the house.

"Tashianna it's good to see you again and I know you are still deeply hurting but I have been praying for you so just take it slow because time heals all things with prayer."

"Thank you, Mr. Richardson I, appreciate all of your kindness and prayers."

"Amen Dad. Dad where is Mom and the rest of the family?"

"That is a good question son."

James cell phone rings and it's from a friend of his at the police station. He answers it and seconds later he drops the phone and falls to his knees crying.

"Noooo!" He screams.

EPILOGUE

You have worked so hard to accomplish your goals. Made various sacrifices, persistent, consistent, long hours and so much more. You hear on a regular basis the following: if you really want it bad enough you can get it and don't allow anything or anyone get in your way. Beware of the dream stealers, including family. When you desire success as badly as you need air to breath then, and only then, will you achieve it. All these things and more are part of the society that we live in. But what you do not hear said enough is, what price are you willing to pay for your achievements and do you even know what that price is? How many people did you hurt or destroy in the process of getting what you want?

WHAT PRICE WILL YOU PAY AND HAVE YOU PAID IT
OR IS IT COMING...?

The Master Deceiver 2
Be Careful What You Ask For

The trilogy that started it all

A message of love and power

I do not preach or embrace hate and I never will. Why? When you have hate in your mind, heart and soul you are already dead but just breathing. With this said the truth is the truth. The act of oppression for any person or group of people is done out of fear. Fear because they cannot be used or controlled so let's destroy them and in doing so we can make a lot of money. How? By using what they have, take what they have and control what they have. Thus, we become even richer. Then we teach the oppressed to forgive and commit no acts of violence, all the while the oppressor has and still is using violence to control and become rich. The back bone and core of wealth in this country has been obtained through violence and bloodshed. Acts of terrorism! So, before you point the finger at anyone else for taking a stand for equality for all people, please look at yourself. How much blood is on your hands? Look into your own heart and then down at your feet. What do you see? Steps of love or steps of blood?

CPSIA information can be obtained
at www.ICGtesting.com
Printed in the USA
LVOW10s2352240418
574789LV00009B/200/P